Frankenstein

or The Modern Prometheus

MARY SHELLEY

Annotated and Modernized
Sentence Structure

ADAPTED BY: William J. McMahon

EDITED BY: Douglas Grudzina

DESIGN: Larry Knox

COVER PHOTOGRAPHY: Larry Knox

PRODUCTION: Wendy Smith

ISBN: 978-1-58049-553-0

Frankenstein

or The Modern Prometheus

MARY SHELLEY

CONTENTS

AN ANNOTATED ADAPTATION

2

Contents Continued

To the Reader

MOST PEOPLE in the publishing and education industries agree that there are some books that everyone should read. While there might be a good deal of disagreement on exactly which books should be included on that must-read list, almost everyone agrees that some books are just so important that no one should be able to leave school without having read them.

The problem with many of these books, however, is that they were written in a time and place when the standards of written and spoken English were very different from twenty-first century American English—so different, in fact, that the language alone can block a full understanding of the plot, characterization, imagery, tone, or whatever it is that makes the work worth reading in the first place. By the same token, if you have to invest too much time simply decoding the text (the lowest level of reading comprehension), there's a good chance that you'll simply give up. Your English teacher probably sees this happen nearly every day.

One "solution" to this problem has been for publishers to offer "adapted" and "condensed" versions of these important works. The problem with these adaptations is that they are usually too condensed, oversimplified to the point that there is little left but the plot events. All of the rich texture of narrative voice, foreshadowing, irony, sophisticated characterization, and theme are cut, along with the archaic diction and syntax.

Another popular "solution" has been to bring film versions of great literature into the classroom. While there are some excellent reasons to conduct a "book-to-film" comparison, it is a disservice to everyone involved to assert that watching the movie and reading the book are similar experiences at all.

Recognizing the need for a text that is accessible to the average reader, yet rich enough to maintain the original's literary quality, we developed the *Prestwick House Spotlight Edition*. Each Spotlight Edition is a complete and thoughtful adaptation that allows you to examine the structure, themes, character development, and richness of great literature without having to fight with the archaic language that makes much great literature such a challenge.

To further enhance your reading experience, we've added the sidebar commentary and guided reading questions to the margins. These are your aids—road signs as it were—to guide you through the text, to note the foreshadowing, and to follow the development of a character or the gradual revelation of plot facts.

You may choose to read this Spotlight Edition *instead* of the original. Or you may choose to use this Spotlight Edition as a resource *while reading* the original, referring to the adaptation to help clarify a particularly difficult passage.

Use the sidebar commentary and guided reading questions as tools to help you navigate the unadapted original. Reading groups might find the sidebar comments and questions helpful in their discussion of either the Spotlight adaptation or the original. The offered writing opportunities invite even deeper thought.

Similarly, the research opportunities are not intended to be major papers or projects (unless your teacher wants them to be). The primary purpose of the research opportunities is simply to encourage you to examine the social, historical, and philosophical environments in which the text was written or on which the text was based. All of the research questions can be answered by consulting one or two magazine articles or by clicking on one or two links of a basic web search.

There is some apparent repetition of guided reading questions and writing and/or research opportunities in the book to illustrate that reading is often a recursive process in which you will re-encounter the same concept or question again and again, each time adjusting original impressions and theories to reflect new information, additional character growth, plot development, and so on. Each time an idea or question reappears, you should expand your understanding of the issue under consideration.

Most of all, enjoy the book. Get to know (to like, dislike, love or hate) the characters. Live as accurately and completely as possible in the setting. Delve into the history and culture. Let your foray into great literature truly be an excursion into a new world where you will learn as much about yourself as you will about the people you meet there.

Frankenstein

or The Modern Prometheus

MARY SHELLEY

In Greek mythology, Promotheus was the Titan charged with giving abilities to the animals of the earth. By the time he got to the human race, he had nothing left to give, so he stole fire from the gods and gave this to humankind. This fire symbolizes Humanity's supposed supremacy over Nature. It has also come to symbolize human intellect, science, and technology. During the Industrial Revolution, it also represented the newly-unleashed power that drove the factories of England. It is important to remember, however, that—in the original myth—fire belonged to the gods and Promotheus was severely punished for giving this enormous power to humanity.

Mary Shelley began **Frankenstein** the summer of 1816, when England was in the midst of the Industrial Revolution. The steam engine had been refined to the point that it could be commonly employed for a number of tasks. It required coal to generate its steam, but it also powered the pumps that made coal mining more efficient. The effects of rampant coal mining, and the smog produced by the burning of coal, rapidly turned what had been a beautiful, green country into an environmental nightmare. Economically, a new class of poor was developing, those who were driven from the country into poor-paying factory jobs in the cities. Skilled craftsmen found their goods no longer in demand, replaced by cheaper factory-made goods. Because of the negative changes associated with the harnessing of steam power and the use *of machines, many people protested sceintific and technological advancement. The Romantic writers were especially appalled at the destruction of Natural Beauty and the social and economic oppression of the lower classes.*

For writers like Mary Shelley, the novel was a brand new literary form. It was important for them to make the story appear true, and presenting at least part of the novel in the form of letters was one way to maintain this appearance of truth. This desire to seem true is also why Ms. Shelley does not fully identify the year.

Frankenstein
or The Modern Prometheus

MARY SHELLEY

LETTER I

To Mrs. Saville, England
St. Petersburg, Dec. 11th, 17-

You will be overjoyed to hear that my adventure has started without disaster, even though you were so terrified. I arrived here yesterday, and I immediately wrote this letter to assure you—my dear sister—that I am all right, and confident of the success of my quest.

I am already far north of London, and as I walk in the streets of Saint Petersburg, Russia, I feel a cold northern breeze on my cheeks, which strengthens my courage and fills me with delight. Do you understand this feeling? This breeze, which has come from my destination, gives me a taste of that icy climate. Inspired by this "wind of promise," my daydreams become more eager and vivid. I try in vain to convince myself that the North Pole is the capital of frost and desolation. Instead, I imagine it to be the region of beauty and delight. There, Margaret, the sun is forever visible, skimming around the horizon and spreading a never-ending splendor. There—for if you don't mind, I will trust the navigators who have tried this journey before me—there snow and frost are banished. And, sailing over a calm sea, we find ourselves at a more wondrous or beautiful place than any that has ever been discovered on the entire planet. Its landscape

✔ A novel that uses letters as the means of telling its story is called an epistolary novel. An epistle is a long letter.

✔ The quality of a work of fiction's appearing true is called verisimilitude.

❓ What superstitions about the North Pole does Walton seem to believe?

may be unequalled, just as the stars and planets in the far off regions of the Universe probably are. Who knows what's possible in a country of eternal light? I may discover there the wondrous power that attracts the compass needle, and may discover the secrets of a thousand astronomical observations that require only what I'll discover on this voyage to clarify forever what now seems impossible to understand. I will satisfy my burning curiosity, seeing a part of the world no one has ever before visited, and may set foot on a land on which the foot of man has never trod before. These are my motivations, and they are strong enough to conquer all fear of danger or death and to spur me to begin this difficult voyage with the joy a child feels when he sails off in a little boat, with his friends, on an expedition of discovery up his hometown river. But even if all my theories are false, you still cannot debate the enormous benefit which I shall offer to all mankind forever, by discovering a passage near the Pole to those countries in Asia that currently take many months to reach; or by discovering the secret of the compass magnet, which—if it can be discovered at all—can be only by a journey such as mine.

These thoughts have driven away the anxiety with which I began my letter, and I feel my heart glow with an enthusiasm that raises my spirits, for nothing helps to calm the mind as much as a steady purpose—a point on which the soul may fix its intellectual eye. I have dreamed of going on this expedition since I was a boy. I have read with passion the accounts of the many voyages that have been made in an attempt to arrive at the North Pacific Ocean through the seas that surround the North Pole. You may remember that a history of all the explorers' voyages was all that our good Uncle Thomas ever had in his library. My education was neglected, yet I loved to read. These books were my study day and night, and my familiarity with them increased the intense sorrow that I felt when I learned that my father's dying command had forbidden my uncle to allow me to embark in a seafaring life.

These visions faded when I read, for the first time, those poets whose work excited my spirit and elevated

❷ *What two traits does Captain Walton identify as his main motivators for his enterprise?*

❷ *So what is Captain Walton's quest?*

my mind. I also became a poet and, for one year, lived in a paradise of my own creation; I fantasized that I also might one day be as famous as Homer or Shakespeare. You know too well how badly I failed and how disappointed I was. But just at that time, I inherited my cousin's fortune, and again I began to think of becoming an explorer.

Six years have passed since I made the decision to go forward with this idea. I can, even now, remember the hour I made that resolution. I began by strengthening my body. I accompanied the whale-fishers on several expeditions to the North Sea. I voluntarily endured cold, famine, thirst, and lack of sleep. I often worked harder than the common sailors during the day and devoted my nights to studying mathematics, medicine, and the areas of science most relevant to naval adventure. Twice I actually was hired as a sailor on a Greenland whaler, and acquitted myself to admiration. I must admit I was proud when my captain offered me the second in command of the vessel and sincerely asked me to remain—so valuable did he consider my services. And now, dear Margaret, do I not *deserve* to accomplish some great purpose? I may have spent my life in ease and luxury, but I desire glory far more than wealth. Oh, how I wish to hear some encouraging voice! I am firm in courage and resolution, but my hopes fluctuate, and I am often depressed. I am about to embark on a long and difficult voyage, the ordeals of which will demand all of my strength. I am required not only to raise the spirits of others, but also to sustain my own when theirs are failing.

Note Walton's strong desire for a friend—a social and intellectual equal—someone who can fully understand him. This will be a significant issue throughout the book.

This is the best period for traveling in Russia. The sleighs fly quickly over the snow. The motion is pleasant, and—in my opinion—far more agreeable than that of an English stagecoach. The cold is not excessive, if you are wrapped in furs—as I usually am—for there is a big difference between walking the deck and sitting motionless for hours and simply letting the blood freeze in your veins. I have no ambition to lose my life on the post-road between St. Petersburg and Archangel. I shall depart for the latter town in a fortnight or three weeks, and my intention is to hire a ship there, which can easily be done by paying the insurance for the owner, and to hire as many sailors as I need among those who are used to the whale-fishing. I do not intend to sail until the month of June.

I can hear you asking when I will return. Dear sister, how can I answer that question? If I succeed, it will be many, many months—perhaps years—before we see each other again. If I fail, you will see me again soon, or possibly never. Farewell, my dear, excellent Margaret. May Heaven shower down blessings on you, and save me, that I may again and again show my gratitude for all your love and kindness.

Your affectionate brother,
R. Walton

Frankenstein

or The Modern Prometheus

MARY SHELLEY

LETTER 2

To Mrs. Saville, England
Archangel, March 28, 17-

How slowly the time passes here, surrounded as I am by frost and snow! But I have taken the next step in my adventure. I have rented a ship and begun to hire my sailors. Those whom I have already employed appear to be both dependable and brave.

But I have one need I have been unable to fulfill, and I feel the lack all too painfully: I have no *friend,* Margaret. When I am glowing with success, there will be no one to share my joy. If I am beset by disappointment, no one will comfort me. I can write in my diary, and to you, it is true. But those are poor substitutes for having someone to talk to. I desire the company of a man who could sympathize with me, whose eyes would reply to mine. You may think me romantic, my dear sister, but I bitterly feel the absence of a friend. I have no one near me, gentle yet courageous, someone educated and intelligent, whose tastes are like my own, to approve or amend my plans. How would such a friend improve the character of your poor brother! I am too hasty in my actions and too impatient of difficulties. But it is an even bigger disadvantage to me that I am self-educated. For the first fourteen years of my life, I did nothing but play and read nothing but our Uncle

❷ *What "criteria" does Walton want in his "friend"? What role does he see friendship playing in his quest?*

Thomas' books of voyages. At that age, I began to read the celebrated poets of our own country; but I realized far too late in life how advantageous it is to be fluent in a language other than your own. Now that I am twenty-eight, I am, in reality, more illiterate than many schoolboys of fifteen. It is true that my fantasies become more and more elaborate—in need of focus and discipline—and I greatly need a friend who would not become too impatient with my romantic dreams, yet care enough to try to tie me to reality. Well, these are useless complaints. I shall certainly find no friend on the wide ocean, nor even here in Archangel, among merchants and seamen. Yet even these rough and rugged men seem to have some of the same needs and feelings as I do. My lieutenant, for instance, is a man of wonderful courage and enterprise. He longs for fame, or at least advancement in his profession. He is an Englishman, and, despite lack of advantage or education, is nevertheless an admirable human being. I first became acquainted with him on board a whale vessel; finding that he was unemployed in this city, I easily hired him to assist in my enterprise. The master is an even-tempered man and is respected in the ship for his likeability and fairness. This quality, added to his well-known integrity and dauntless courage, made me want to hire him. Your influence during my upbringing has so affected my character that I can't help but dislike the normal crudeness, vulgarity, and violence of a typical ship's officers and crew. I have never believed it to be necessary, and when I heard of a mariner equally noted for his kindliness of heart and the respect and obedience paid to him by his crew, I felt myself very fortunate in being able to secure his services. I heard of him first in rather a romantic manner, from a lady who owes her happiness to him.

This, briefly, is his story. Some years ago he loved a young Russian lady of moderate means, and since he had won a considerable sum in prize-money, the girl's father consented to the match. The man saw his fiancé once before the wedding, but she cried and threw herself at his feet. She begged him not to force her to go through with the marriage, confessing at the same time that she loved someone else, but he was poor, and her father would never consent to the marriage. My generous friend

The contrast between "romantic" love of equals and the idea of a marriage for social or financial convenience is another familiar literary convention. As a Romantic, Mary Shelley would, of course, side with the notion of "true love."

reassured the young woman, and—finding out the name of her lover—instantly released her from the engagement. He had already bought a farm with his money, on which he had intended to spend the rest of his life, but he gave the farm to his rival, along with what was left of his prize money. He even tried to convince the young woman's father to consent to her marriage with her lover. But the old man absolutely refused, thinking himself bound in honor to my friend, who, when he found the father unmoved, left his country, never returning until he heard that the young woman was married according to her own desires.

"What a noble fellow!" you will exclaim. He is, indeed, but he is also wholly uneducated. He almost never speaks, and exhibits a kind of ignorant carelessness, which, while it renders his conduct the more astonishing, makes him much less interesting than one would hope.

But don't think that because I complain a little or because I can fantasize about rewards for my work that may never materialize, that I am wavering in my resolve to go forward. My decision is made, and my voyage is only now delayed until the weather permits my departure. The winter has been dreadfully severe, but the spring is promising, and may even arrive early, so that perhaps I may sail sooner than I expected. I shall do nothing rashly. You know me enough to have confidence in my judgment whenever I am responsible for the safety of others.

I cannot describe to you how excited I am when I think about this venture. It is impossible to give you any idea of the trembling sensation—half-pleasurable and half-fearful—with which I am preparing to depart. I am going to unexplored regions, to "the land of mist and snow," but I shall kill no albatross. Therefore do not worry about my safety or about my coming back to you as worn and woeful as the "Ancient Mariner." You will smile at my reference, but I'll tell you a secret: I have often attributed my attachment to—my passionate enthusiasm for—the dangerous mysteries of the ocean to that poem by Coleridge. There is something at work in my soul which I do not understand. I am practical, hardworking, and able to persevere—but besides this, there is a love for the marvelous, a belief

The three later Romantics (Lord Byron, Percy Shelley, and John Keats) knew each other, read each other's works and alluded to each other frequently. They also greatly admired the work of the early Romantics, especially Samuel Taylor Coleridge's The Rime of the Ancient Mariner *in which a sailor kills an albatross— an omen of good luck for sailors—and recieves a series of supernatural punishments for his crime. This line and the reference to the albatross are allusions to this poem.*

in the marvelous, intertwined in all my projects, which makes me take the more difficult roads in life, even to the wild sea and unvisited regions I am about to explore.

But to return to more important matters, shall I meet you again, after having sailed vast seas, and returned by the most southern cape of Africa or America? I dare not expect such success, yet I cannot bear to consider the possibility of failure. Continue for the present to write to me at every opportunity: I may receive your letters at the times when I need them most to raise my spirits. I love you very tenderly. Remember me with affection, should you never hear from me again.

Your affectionate brother,
Robert Walton

Frankenstein

or The Modern Prometheus

❧

MARY SHELLEY

LETTER 3

To Mrs. Saville, England
July 7th, 17-

My Dear Sister,

I write a few lines in haste to say that I am safe—and well advanced on my voyage. This letter will reach England by a ship now on its homeward voyage from Archangel; more fortunate than I, who might not see my native land for many years. I am, however, in good spirits. My men are brave and apparently dedicated. The floating sheets of ice that continually pass us—indicating the dangers ahead—do not appear to dismay them. We have already reached a very high latitude. But it is the height of summer, and although not so warm as in England, the southern gales, blowing us speedily toward our destination, breathe a certain amount of welcome warmth that I had not expected.

No cataclysmic event has occurred for me to report to you in this letter. One or two stiff gales and the springing of a leak are accidents which experienced navigators hardly even remember to record. If nothing worse happens to us during this voyage, I shall be grateful.

Goodbye, my dear Margaret. Be assured that for my own sake, as well as yours, I will not be reckless. I will be cool, persevering, and prudent.

✔ *Captain Walton exhibits the trait of* hubris *here, an overbearing pride that makes one claim equality with a god. Notice how Walton says he "deserves" to succeed and that a benevolent Nature will help him.*

But success SHALL crown my efforts. Why not? I've come this far, tracing a secure way over the pathless seas, with only the stars in the sky as witnesses to my triumph. Why shouldn't I continue over the untamed yet obedient ocean? What can stop the determined heart and resolved will of man?

My heart is full as I write. But I must finish. Heaven bless my beloved sister!

R.W.

Frankenstein
or The Modern Prometheus

❧

MARY SHELLEY

LETTER 4

To Mrs. Saville, England
August 5th, 17-

Something so strange has happened to us that I cannot resist recording it, although it is very probable that you will see me before this letter reaches you.

Last Monday (July 31st) we were nearly surrounded by ice, which closed the ship in on all sides, scarcely leaving her the sea-room in which she floated. Our situation was somewhat dangerous, especially as we were surrounded by a very thick fog. And so we stayed put, hoping that some change would take place in the weather.

About two o'clock the mist cleared away, and we saw—stretched out in every direction—vast and irregular ice flows, which seemed to have no end. Some of my comrades groaned, and I too began to feel nervous about our situation, when a strange sight suddenly attracted our attention and distracted our concern from our own situation. We saw a low carriage, fixed on a sleigh and drawn by dogs, moving toward the north, at the distance of half a mile. A...*being*...that had the shape of a man, but was apparently gigantic, sat in the sleigh and guided the dogs. We watched the rapid progress of the traveler with our telescopes until he was lost among the distant glaciers. This appearance absolutely amazed us. We had believed that we were hundreds of miles from any land, but this

❷ *Who or what do you think they are seeing ride by?*

apparition indicated that we were closer to land than we had thought. Shut in, however, by ice, it was impossible to follow his track, which we had observed very closely. About two hours after this occurrence, we heard the sea beneath our ship. Before night, the ice broke and freed our ship. We, however, stayed put until the morning, afraid of ice bergs. I took advantage of this time to rest for a few hours.

In the morning, however, as soon as it was light, I went up on deck and found all the sailors busy on one side of the vessel, apparently talking to someone in the sea. It was, in fact, a sleigh, like the one we had seen the day before, which had drifted toward us in the night on a large chunk of ice. Only one dog remained alive, but there was a human being in the carriage. My sailors were persuading him to board our vessel. He was not—as the *other* traveler seemed to be—a savage inhabitant of some undiscovered island, but a European. When I appeared on deck, the master said, "Here is our captain, and he will not allow you to die on the open sea."

On seeing me, the stranger spoke to me in English, but with a foreign accent. "Before I come on board your vessel," he said, "will you be so kind as to tell me where you are bound?"

You can imagine my astonishment on hearing such a question from a man on the brink of death, one to whom my vessel meant a rescue he couldn't exchange for all the money in the world. I replied, however, that we were on a voyage of exploration toward the North Pole.

He appeared satisfied and agreed to come on board. Good God! Margaret, if you had seen the man who then surrendered for his safety, you would have been shocked. His limbs were nearly frozen, and his body dreadfully emaciated by fatigue and suffering. I never saw a man in so wretched a condition. We tried to carry him into the cabin, but as soon as he left the fresh air he fainted, so we brought him back to the deck and revived him by rubbing him with brandy and forcing him to swallow some. As soon as he showed signs of life we wrapped him up in blankets and placed him near the chimney of the kitchen stove. He slowly recovered and ate a little soup, which restored him wonderfully.

❷ *Who must this traveler be?*

Two days passed before he was able to speak, and I often feared that his suffering had affected his perception. When he had in some measure recovered, I brought him to my own cabin and looked after him as much as my duty would permit. I never saw a more interesting creature. His eyes frequently have an expression of wildness—and even madness—but there are moments when, if anyone performs an act of kindness toward him or does the smallest thing for him, his whole face lights up, as it were, with a kindness and sweetness the likes of which I have never seen before. But he is generally melancholy and despairing, and sometimes he gnashes his teeth, as if crushed by the weight of woes that oppress him.

When my guest had recovered a little, I had great trouble keeping him separated from the men, who wished to ask him a thousand questions. But I would not allow him to be tormented by their idle curiosity while it was so obvious that he needed complete rest. Once, however, the lieutenant asked why he had come so far upon the ice in so strange a vehicle.

With an expression of deepest gloom, he replied, "To seek someone who has run away from me."

"And did the man whom you pursued travel the same way?"

"Yes."

"Then I believe we have seen him, for the day before we picked you up, we saw some dogs drawing a sleigh, with a man in it, across the ice."

This aroused the stranger's attention, and he asked several questions concerning the route which the demon—as he called the giant—had followed. Soon after, when he was alone with me, he said, "I have, doubtless, excited your curiosity, as well as that of these good people. But you are too considerate to ask questions."

"Certainly. It would indeed be very rude and cruel of me to bother you with my curiosity."

"And yet you rescued me from a strange and dangerous situation. You have so kindly restored me to life."

Soon after this, he asked whether I thought the breaking up of the ice had destroyed the other sleigh. I replied that I had no way of knowing, for the ice had not broken until near midnight, and the traveler might have arrived at a safe place before that time. But I couldn't be sure. From this time the decaying frame of the stranger seemed to glow with new life. He was suddenly eager to be up on deck to watch for the sleigh that had appeared before. But I have persuaded him to remain in the cabin, for he is far too weak to endure the rawness of the icy air. I have promised that someone would watch for him and tell him immediately if any new object should appear in sight.

So this is my journal of everything related to this strange occurrence up to the present day. The stranger has gradually improved in health but is very silent and appears uneasy when anyone but me enters his cabin. Still, he is so polite and gentle that the sailors are all interested in him, although they have had very little contact with him. For my own part, I have begun to love him as a brother, and his constant and deep grief fills me with sympathy and compassion. He must have been a noble creature in his better days. Even now—although he is a wreck—he is still appealing and friendly. I said in one of my letters, my dear Margaret, that I would find no friend on the wide ocean; yet I have found a man who—before his spirit had been broken by misery—I would have been happy to have possessed as the brother of my heart.

I shall, from time to time, continue my journal about this stranger, should I have any new stories to tell.

Recap:

What characters and themes or motifs have been introduced? What events have begun to build suspense?

August 13th, 17-

My affection for my guest grows every day. He simultaneously stirs my admiration and my pity. How can I see so decent a man destroyed by misery without feeling the most poignant grief? He is so gentle, yet so wise. His mind is so cultivated, and—when he speaks—his words are artfully chosen, yet flow quickly and eloquently. He is now much recovered from his illness and is continually on the deck, apparently watching for the sleigh that preceded his own. Yet, although unhappy, he is never so distracted by his own misery that he fails to let others confide in him.

He always listens to my thoughts, which I have confided to him truthfully. He listened attentively to all of my arguments in favor of my eventual success and to every tiny detail of the steps I had taken to secure my success. The sincere sympathy he showed made it easy for me to speak my heart, to confide my dreams and ambitions and to say, with all the fervor that warmed me, how gladly I would sacrifice my fortune, my existence—my every hope—to the success of my enterprise. One man's life or death was but a small price to pay for the knowledge I wanted, for my triumph over the elements. As I spoke, a dark gloom spread over his face. At first, I realized he was trying to suppress his emotion. He placed his hands before his eyes, and my voice quivered and failed me as I saw tears trickle fast from between his fingers. A heavy groan burst from his heaving breast. I paused, and he finally spoke, in a breaking voice, "Unhappy man! Do you share my madness? Have you drunk from the cup of your imagined power? Hear me. Let me tell you my tale, and you will throw the cup from your lips!"

✔ Note the extent of Walton's commitment to his cause.

✔ Note the metaphor of ambition being like a cup of wine. Too much makes one drunk and heedless.

Such words, you may imagine, made me curious, but the spasm of grief that had seized the stranger overcame his weakness, it took many hours of rest and comforting words to restore his composure. Having conquered his fear, he regretted his outburst, and encouraged me to talk about myself again. He asked me the history of my earlier years. The tale was quickly told, but it awakened various trains of reflection. I spoke of how much I wanted a friend, of my need for a greater closeness with a fellow mind than I'd ever known, and expressed my conviction that a man could boast of little happiness without this blessing. "I agree with you," he replied, "we are imperfect creatures, incomplete unless someone wiser, better, and dearer than ourselves—for that's what a friend ought to be—does not lend his aid to bolster our weak and faulty natures. I once had a friend—the most noble of human creatures—and I well know the value of friendship. You have hope, and the world before you, and have no cause for despair. But I—I have lost everything and cannot begin life anew."

As he said this, his expression betrayed a calm, settled grief that touched me to the heart. But he was silent and presently retired to his cabin.

Even broken in spirit as he is, no one can feel more deeply than he does the beauties of nature. The starry sky, the sea, and every sight afforded by these wonderful regions seem still to have the power of lifting his spirits. Such a man lives a double life—he may be miserable and disappointed, yet within himself he has the strength to be like a guardian angel to others in need.

Will you smile at my enthusiasm for this fascinating wanderer? You would not if you saw him. You have been tutored and refined by books and protected from the world, and you are, therefore, somewhat fastidious, but this makes you more able to appreciate the extraordinary merits of this wonderful man. Sometimes I have tried to understand what distinguishes him from any other person I ever knew. I believe it to be intuition, a quick but never-failing power of judgment, a perceptive intellect, unequalled for clearness and precision, and an expressive ability and voice that sounds as soothing as music.

August 19, 17-

Yesterday the stranger said to me, "You might easily see, Captain Walton, that I have suffered great misfortunes such as no man before has ever suffered. I had decided that the memory of these evils would die with me, but you have changed my mind. You seek knowledge and wisdom, as I once did, and I deeply hope that it will not become a serpent to sting you, as it did me. I do not know whether my story will be useful to you, but when I see you pursuing the same course, exposing yourself to the same dangers that made me what I am, I think you may learn from my tale, whether or not you are successful in your quest. Prepare yourself to hear about events that are usually considered supernatural. If we were in a tamer location, I would accept your skepticism, even your ridicule. But many things will appear possible here that would normally make those who don't understand the full wonders of nature as well as you and I do laugh. Nor can I doubt but that my tale conveys—within itself—evidence of its own truth."

You may easily imagine that I was grateful for his offer, yet I had no desire for him to renew his grief by a recital of

Here the stranger begins to exhibit hubris and some of the traits of the tragic hero.

The challenge that Mary Shelley answered with this book was to write a "ghost story."

his misfortunes. I was eager to hear his story, partly from curiosity and partly from a strong desire to help him if I was able. I expressed these feelings in my answer.

"I thank you for your sympathy," he replied, "but it is useless. My fate is nearly fulfilled. I wait for one more event, and then I shall rest in peace.

"I understand your feeling," he continued, before I could interrupt him, "but you are mistaken, my friend, if you will allow me to call you that. Nothing can alter my destiny. Listen to my history, and you will see how irrevocably my fate is determined."

He said he would begin his tale the next day. I thanked him warmly. I have resolved every night, when I am not completely occupied by my duties, to record, as nearly as possible in his own words, what he tells me during the day. If I should be too busy, I will at least make notes. This manuscript will surely entertain you, but to me—knowing him and hearing it from his own lips—with what interest and sympathy shall I read it in some day when I am old! Even now, as I begin, his resonant voice swells in my ears. His gleaming eyes settle on me with all their melancholy sweetness. I see his thin hand raised, while the lines of his face are lit by his soul.

So strange and harrowing is his story—so frightful the storm that embraced the gallant vessel on its course and wrecked it—thus!

Note the metaphor. Walton is comparing the ruined Frankenstein to a wrecked sea vessle.

Research Opportunity:

Look up and list some of the major characteristics of the Romantic hero and the Tragic Hero.

I am by birth a Genevese, and my family is one of the most distinguished of that republic. My ancestors had been counselors and advocates for many years, and my father had filled several public positions with honor and reputation.

VICTOR FRANKENSTEIN
FRANKENSTEIN, CHAPTER 1

Frankenstein
or The Modern Prometheus

❧

MARY SHELLEY

CHAPTER 1

I am by birth a Genevese, and my family is one of the most distinguished of that republic. My ancestors had been counselors and advocates for many years, and my father had filled several public positions with honor and reputation. He was highly respected for his integrity and untiring attention to public service. His youth was spent immersed in the affairs of his country. Several circumstances had prevented his marrying early, and it was not until he was much older that he became a husband and the father of a family.

Since the circumstances of his marriage show the type of man he was, I must tell you them. One of his closest friends was a formerly wealthy merchant who had fallen into poverty through numerous misfortunes. This man named Beaufort—proud and unbending—could not bear to live in poverty and oblivion where he had once been distinguished by rank and status. Having paid his debts, therefore, in the most honorable manner, he retreated with his daughter to the town of Lucerne, where he lived in unknown wretchedness. My father truly loved Beaufort as a friend and was grieved by his retreat in these unfortunate circumstances. He bitterly deplored the false pride which led his friend to behave in a manner so unworthy of their friendship. He lost no time in seeking Beaufort out, with the hope of persuading him to

✔ Do not lose track of the levels of narration. Victor Frankenstein is telling the story to Captain Walton who is writing it in a letter to his sister.

❷ What is Victor's native nationality?

✔ Notice how Beaufort is proud and honorable. He may not have money, but he does have breeding and rank.

The River Reuss is one of the largest rivers in Switzerland. It flows through Lake Lucerne.

make a fresh start with my father's credit and assistance. Beaufort had worked very hard to remain hidden, and it was ten months before my father discovered where he was living. Overjoyed at this discovery, he hastened to the house, which was located in a dangerous street near the Reuss. But when he entered, misery and despair alone welcomed him. Beaufort had saved only a very small sum of money from the wreck of his fortunes, but it was sufficient to allow him to survive for some months, and in the meantime he hoped to find a respectable position in a merchant's store. The period between was, consequently, wasted. His grief only became deeper and more galling when he had enough time to think, and at length it took such a hold of his mind that—within three months—he lay on his sickbed, incapacitated.

His daughter took care of him with the greatest tenderness, but she saw with despair that their money was running out and that there was no other prospect of support. But Caroline Beaufort possessed an uncommon mind, and her courage rose to support her in her adversity. She found handwork weaving straw. By this and various other means, she managed to earn a pittance—scarcely enough to support herself and her father.

Notice how Mary Shelley employs many fairy-tale like elements in the story of Victor's parents' marriage. Note also that—although Caroline Beaufort was poor at the time of her marriage to the wealthy Frankenstein—she is from a "good family."

Several months passed in this way. Her father grew worse. Her time was almost entirely occupied caring for him. Her money dwindled, and ten months later her father died in her arms, leaving her an orphan and a beggar. This last blow overcame her, and she knelt by Beaufort's coffin weeping bitterly, when my father entered the chamber. He came like a protecting spirit to the poor girl, who committed herself to his care. After the funeral, he brought her to Geneva and placed her in the home of a relative. Two years later, Caroline became his wife.

There was a considerable difference between the ages of my parents, but this circumstance seemed to bring them closer. My father was the type of man who could not love without respect. Perhaps in his youth he had been hurt by some romantic betrayal and therefore set a greater value on integrity. There was gratitude and worship in his attachment to my mother, transcending the mere fondness of an older man for a younger woman, for it was inspired by reverence for her virtues and a desire to compensate her for the sorrows she had endured. His behavior toward her was kind and graceful in every way. Everything was made to yield to her wishes and her convenience. He strove to shelter her—the way a gardener shelters an exotic flower—from every rough wind and to surround her with everything that could please her. Her health, and even the calmness of her faithful spirit, had been shaken by what she had gone through. During the two years before their marriage my father gradually retired from his public functions, and immediately after their union they sought the pleasant climate of Italy. The change of scene and the wonderful trip fully restored her weakened body.

From Italy they visited Germany and France. I, their eldest child, was born at Naples, and as an infant, accompanied them in their journeys. I remained for several years their only child. Much as they loved each other, their affection for me knew no limits. My mother's caresses and my father's smiles on seeing me are my first memories. I was their plaything and their idol, and something better—their child, the innocent and helpless creature bestowed on them by Heaven, for whom they were responsible and whose future rested in their hands. With this deep understanding of what they owed toward the being to which they had given life, added to the tender spirit they shared, I learned patience, charity, and self-control. This education seemed simple, enjoyable, and natural to me. For a long time I was their only care. My mother had much wanted a daughter, but I continued to be their only child. When I was about five years old, while making an excursion beyond the frontiers of Italy, they spent a week on the shores of Lake Como. Their kindness often made them enter the cottages of the poor. This, to my mother, was more than a duty; it was a necessity, a passion—remembering the poverty that she had suffered, and how she had been relieved. During one of their walks, a poor cottage seemed particularly miserable to them. The number of half-clothed children gathered outside revealed the worst poverty. One day—when my father had gone by himself to Milan—my mother and I visited this cottage. She found a peasant and his wife,

Remember how Victor describes his birth, his parents' reception of him, and his earliest memories. This will prove to be ironic later on.

Explain the principle of Noblesse Oblige. How does Caroline's generosity surpass this value?

❓ *What was the stereotypical European standard of beauty as represented in such stories as Cinderella and Sleeping Beauty?*

✓ *Note how the simile also establishes that the child's beauty is in her fairness contrasted with the darkness of her Italian guardians.*

✓ *Notice how this child also, while poor, is actually of noble birth.*

✓ Schiavi ognor frementi *is Latin for "slaves forever in a rage," and represents an historical inaccuracy on Mary Shelley's part. The issue here is that the young girl's guardian was lost fighting for northern Italy's freedom from Austrian rule—which actually took place only a few years before* Frankenstein *was written. Still, Mary Shelley wants to emphasize the independence-loving, revolutionary zeal of the child's guardian. The* schiavi ognor frementi *were a party of revolutionaries centered in Milan. Many of them were convicted of sedition and imprisoned.*

hard-working, bent down by care and labor, distributing a scanty meal to five hungry children. Among these was one child that attracted my mother more than the rest. She appeared of a different stock. The four others were dark-eyed, hardy little vagrants. This child was thin and very fair. Her hair was the brightest living gold, and despite the poverty of her clothing, seemed to set a crown of distinction on her head. Her brow was clear and ample, her blue eyes cloudless, and her lips and the shape of her face showed her to be so sensitive and sweet that she appeared to be a separate species, an angel in all respects. The peasant woman, perceiving that my mother looked with wonder and admiration at this lovely girl, eagerly told her story.

She was not her child, but the daughter of a Milanese nobleman. Her mother was German and had died in childbirth. The infant had been placed with these good people to nurse, as they were better off then. They had not been long married, and their eldest child was recently born. Their guardian was one of those Italians raised with memory of the ancient glory of Italy—one among the schiavi ognor frementi, dedicated to securing the liberty of his country. He became the victim of its weakness. Whether he had died or still lingered in the dungeons of Austria the family did not know. His property was confiscated, and his child became an orphan and a beggar. She continued with her foster parents and bloomed in their poor home, fairer than a garden rose among dark-leaved brambles. When my father returned from Milan, he found me playing in the hall of our villa with a child fairer than a cherub—a creature who seemed to glow and whose form and motions were lighter than the mist over the hills. The vision was soon explained. With his permission, my mother convinced the peasants to allow them to adopt the child. The peasants were fond of the sweet orphan. Her presence was like a blessing to them, but it would be unfair to her to keep her in poverty and want when she had the opportunity of such powerful protection. They consulted their village priest, and the result was that Elizabeth Lavenza came to live with us—my more than sister—the beautiful and adored companion of all my occupations and my pleasures.

Everyone loved Elizabeth. On the evening before she came to my home, my mother had said playfully, "I have a pretty present for my Victor—tomorrow he shall have it." And when, the next day, she presented Elizabeth to me as her promised gift, I—with childish seriousness—took her literally and looked at Elizabeth as mine—mine to protect, love, and cherish. All praises bestowed on her I received as praise to me as well. We thought of one another as cousins. Nothing could express the way I felt about her—my more than sister—since she belonged to me forever.

✔ *Having a revolutionary spirit and fighting for freedom were strong values of the Romantic writers.*

✔ *The Romantic notion of "true love" included what we today would call a "soul mate," two people who had perfect affinity for one another. (Consider Robert Walton's desire for a "friend.") Because of this, the later Romantic writers often found themselves involved in scandals not very different from today's popular performers. Just before the trip to Europe during which Mary Shelley started* Frankenstein, *the Shelleys' traveling comanion, Lord Byron, had ended an incestuous affair with his half-sister whom he claimed to be the only woman he truly loved. This closeness of brother/sister/soulmate is mirrored in Victor and Elizabeth's relationship.*

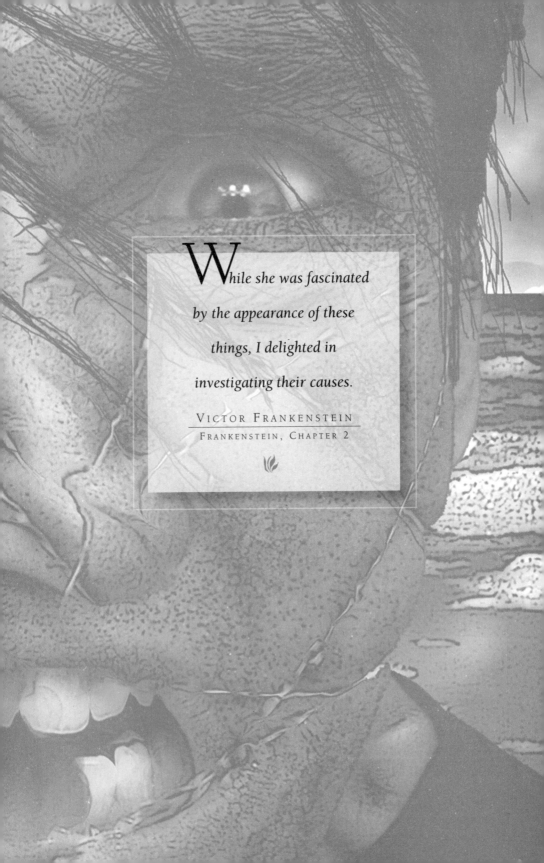

While she was fascinated by the appearance of these things, I delighted in investigating their causes.

VICTOR FRANKENSTEIN
FRANKENSTEIN, CHAPTER 2

Frankenstein
or The Modern Prometheus

MARY SHELLEY

CHAPTER 2

We were brought up together. There was not quite a year difference in our ages. Needless to say, we never argued or fought. Harmony was the soul of our companionship, and the differences between us drew us nearer together. Elizabeth was calmer and more disciplined. I was more restless and more deeply smitten with the thirst for knowledge. She studied the work of the poets, as well as the majestic and wondrous scenes that surrounded our Swiss home. The sublime shapes of the mountains, the changes of the seasons, tempest and calm, the silence of winter, and the life and turbulence of our Alpine summers all provided her with endless diversion. While she was fascinated by the appearance of these things, I delighted in investigating their causes. The world was, to me, a secret I wanted to know. Curiosity, earnest research to learn the hidden laws of Nature, and delight as they revealed themselves to me, are among the earliest sensations I can remember.

On the birth of a second son, seven years younger than I, my parents gave up travel and settled in their native country. We possessed a house in Geneva, and a summer home in Belrive, on the eastern shore of the lake, a bit more than a league out the city. We lived mostly in the summer house, and my parents lived in considerable seclusion. It was my habit to avoid a crowd and instead

✔ *To the Romantics, Nature—especially the wild and rugged beauty of Nature—was almost a goddess. Being in Nature could cure one's illness—both physical and mental. Being in Nature could restore the heart and mind of a criminal. Notice this motif as Mary Shelley returns to it and develops it throughout the book.*

❷ *Do you think the Romantics would favor scientific inquiry? Why or why not? What does this suggest about Mary Shelley's treatment of Victor Frankenstein?*

✔ *A league is a distance ranging anywhere from 2.4 to 4.6 miles.*

The Romantics were also fascinated by medieval romance, the stories of chivalry and knights.

A "masquerade" is what we might today call a tableau. The performers dress in costume and then assume a pose that depicts a famous painting or scene from history or literature. The tradition still exists today in the use of live persons, and sometimes animals, to create a Christmas Nativity scene.

The epic poem: Cantar de Roncesvalles, *which is possibly a Spanish version of the Old French* Chanson de Roland (Song of Roland), *tells the story of a knight in Charlemagne's army who dies while nobly fighting the Saracens (Muslim knights) in Spain.*

have a small circle of friends. I was, therefore, indifferent to my classmates in general. But I became close friends with one of them. Henry Clerval was the son of a merchant in Geneva. He was a particularly talented and imaginative boy. He loved adventure, hardship, and even danger for its own sake. Books of chivalry and romance absorbed him. He composed heroic songs and began to write tales of enchantment and knightly adventure. He tried to make us act out plays and to enter into masquerades, in which the characters were drawn from the heroes of Roncesvalles, of the Round Table of King Arthur, and the chivalrous soldiers who shed their blood in the Crusades, trying to redeem the Holy Sepulcher from the hands of the infidels.

No human being could have passed a happier childhood than I. My parents were possessed by the very spirit of kindness and indulgence. We never looked at them as tyrants to rule over us according to their whims, but as the source of all the many delights that we enjoyed. When I visited other families I was able to understand how especially fortunate I was, and my gratitude increased my love for them.

My temper was sometimes violent, and my behavior passionate, but this was not due to my being spoiled or immature, but to an eager desire to learn—and not just to learn everything indiscriminately. I confess that neither foreign languages, nor history or civics interested me. It was the secrets of heaven and earth that I desired to learn. Sometimes I found myself wondering about the physical nature of things—the structure of leaves and flowers, the chemical and biological processes of life; but then there were times when I was equally curious about the *inner spirit* of Nature and the mysterious soul of man. Still my inquiries were always directed to the scientific secrets of the world.

Meanwhile Clerval occupied himself with the *moral* relations of things. The history of the world, the virtues of heroes, and the actions of men were his subjects. His hope and dream was to be one day worthy of standing in the company of those heroes. The saintly soul of Elizabeth shone like a candle in our peaceful home. Her sympathy was ours. Her smile, her soft voice, the sweet glance of her heavenly eyes ever there to bless us. She was the embodiment of love and devotion. I might have become sullen in my study, through my impulsive nature, if she hadn't been there to calm me. And Clerval—could anything alter the noble spirit of Clerval? Yet he might not have been so perfectly humane, so thoughtful in his generosity, so full of kindness and tenderness amidst his passion for adventurous exploit, had she not shown him the true beauty of kindness and generosity and made compassion the ultimate aim of his soaring ambition.

I take immense pleasure in my memories of my childhood, before any misfortune had polluted my mind and changed its youthful optimism and idealism into gloomy and narrow introspection. Besides, in recalling my early days, I also record those events that led—by unconscious steps—to the misery of my later life. When I trace the birth of my ruling passion, I find that it arises, like a mountain river, from inferior and almost forgotten sources, becoming the flood which has swept away all my hopes and joys. Scientific theory is the genius that has regulated my fate. I really hope, therefore, in telling this story, to make clear those facts that led to my inclination for that discipline. When I was thirteen years old, we all went on a vacation to the baths near Thonon. One day rainy weather confined us to the inn. I happened to find a volume of the works of Cornelius Agrippa. I opened it carelessly. The theory which he attempts to demonstrate and the wonderful facts which he relates soon charged me with enthusiasm. A new light dawned on my mind, and—bounding with joy—I showed my discovery to my father. My father looked carelessly at the title page of my book and said, "Ah! Cornelius Agrippa! My dear Victor, do not waste your time upon this. It is sad trash."

If, instead of this remark, my father had taken the pains to explain to me that the principles of Agrippa were entirely outdated, and that a real and practical modern science had been introduced that possessed much greater powers than the ancient, which had been based on superstition and legend, then I would certainly have thrown Agrippa aside and returned to my former studies with enthusiasm. It is even possible that my imagination would never have been captured by the fatal impulse

In 1792, Mary Shelley's mother, Mary Wollstonecraft Godwin, wrote a pamphlet entitled "A Vindication of the Rights of Women." It is ironic that this early feminist's daughter would portray her primary female character as merely a source of domestic harmony.

According to the Oxford English Dictionary, genius *is the singular form of the more-familiar* genii. *Used here, it means a sort of guardian or guiding spirit.*

Heinrich Cornelius Agrippa von Nettesheim (1486—1535) was a magician and occult writer, a mystic, and an alchemist. He may also be considered an early feminist. His most famous work, Three Books of Occult Philosophy, *is a book about magic and is still a cult-classic for occultists today. Hence, Victor's first dabblings into the life sciences is actually the study of magic.*

that led to my ruin. But the cursory glance my father had taken of my volume by no means assured me that he was familiar with its contents, and I continued to read with great interest. When I returned home, the first thing I did was to get the complete works of this author, and afterwards of Paracelsus and Albertus Magnus. I read and studied the wild fantasies of these writers with delight. They appeared to me treasures known to few beside myself. I have described myself as always having been endowed with a fervent longing to probe the secrets of nature. In spite of the intense labor and wonderful discoveries of modern scientists, I always came from my studies discontented and unsatisfied. Sir Isaac Newton is said to have sworn that he felt like a child picking up shells beside the great and unexplored ocean of truth. Those of his successors in each branch of science with whom I was acquainted appeared even to my boyish understanding as mere novices searching for the same answers I was.

The layman could look at the elements of the natural world around him and understand their practical uses. The most learned scientist knew little more. He had partially unveiled the face of nature, but its true character—was still a wonder and a mystery. He might dissect, anatomize, and give names, but a final answer—or even the beginning steps toward one—was utterly unknown to him. I understood the obstacles between human beings and ultimate knowledge of the secrets of nature, and rashly and ignorantly I had despaired of ever learning those truths.

But here were books, and here were men who had penetrated deeper and knew more. I took their word as gospel truth, and I became their disciple. It may seem strange in this day and age, but while I followed the routine of education in the schools of Geneva I was—to a great degree—self-taught with regard to my favorite studies. My father was not scientific, and I was left to struggle with a child's blindness, added to a student's thirst for knowledge. Under the guidance of my new frame of mind, I entered with great diligence into the search of the philosopher's stone and the elixir of life; but the latter soon had my undivided attention. Wealth

---

Paracelsus, born Auroleus Phillipus Theostratus Bombastus von Hohenheim (1493—1541), was a famous alchemist, physician, astrologer, and general occultist. Unlike Cornelius Agrippa, however, whose science was almost exclusively magical in nature, Paracelsus contributed to sceintific knowledge and is sometimes called the "father" of toxicology.

What modern science is Victor describing?

Note both the allusion and the pun. The allusion is, of course, to the Gospels, which are regarded by many as the truth. The pun is that a disciple is anyone who follows a certain subject or discipline, but is also the title given to the original followers of Jesus in the New Testament Gospels.

was an inferior pursuit, but what glory would I earn if I could banish disease from the human body and make man invulnerable to anything but a violent death! Nor were these my only visions. The raising of ghosts or devils was a concept embraced by my favorite authors, one that I eagerly wished to test. If my incantations always failed, I believed the failure was my own rather than my instructors'. And so, for a time, I was occupied by out-of-date systems, incompetently mingling a thousand contradictory theories and floundering desperately in a stew of miscellaneous knowledge, guided by a vivid imagination and childish reasoning, till an accident again changed my thinking. When I was about fifteen years old we were on vacation at our house near Belrive, when we witnessed a most violent and terrible thunderstorm. It advanced from behind the mountains of Jura, and the thunder burst suddenly and frightfully from the heavens. I watched its progress with curiosity and delight. As I stood at the door, suddenly I saw a stream of fire flame up from an old and beautiful oak that stood about twenty yards from our house. As soon as the dazzling light vanished, the oak disappeared, and nothing remained but a blasted stump. When we visited it the next morning, we found the tree shattered in a strange manner. It was not splintered by the shock, but entirely reduced to thin ribbons of wood. I never saw anything so utterly destroyed.

Before this I was not completely unfamiliar with the more obvious laws of electricity. On this occasion, a man who was a true scientist was with us. Excited by this catastrophe, he explained a theory that he had formed on the subject of electricity and galvanism, which was at once new and astonishing to me. Everything he said completely contradicted the ideas of Cornelius Agrippa, Albertus Magnus, and Paracelsus, the lords of my imagination. The overthrow of these men's theories discouraged me from pursuing further study in the field. It seemed to me as if nothing would or could ever be known. Everything that had completely taken up my attention for such a long time suddenly grew despicable. By one of those whims which we are perhaps most subject to in early youth, I at once gave up my former occupations, put

---

The primary goal of alchemy was to find the means to change base metals like iron and lead into precious metals like silver and gold. The Philosopher's Stone was the legendary substance that would make this change possible. Thus, every alchemist sought this Philosopher's Stone. The power of transmutation, however, was the least of the "stone's" alleged power. It was believed to be able to also cure diseases, make a person invisible, enable him to fly, and even make him immortal.

What is the nature of Victor's scientific inquiry at this point? Why is he meeting with continued failure in his "experiments"?

The Jura Mountains are a series of parallel mountain ranges that run along the French–Swiss border between the Rivers Rhône and Rhine.

The use of two negatives to create a mild positive is an example of litotes.

✔ Galvinism has to do with the ceation of an electrical current. During the time Frankenstein *was being written, scientists were experimenting with "animation" by running electical currents through inanimate objects, and the severed legs of frogs, etc. to see if the electricity would bring the object to life.*

❓ What do you suppose is being foreshadowed here?

aside science and everything related to it as a deformed and abortive subject, and showed great contempt for a subject which, I felt, could never even *step* within the threshold of real knowledge. In this mood of mind I took up mathematics and all of the subject related to that. I believed that math was built on a more solid foundation, and, therefore, worthy of my consideration.

How strangely are our souls constructed, and what flimsy ties bind us to success or failure. When I look back, it seems to me as if this almost miraculous change of heart was the suggestion of my guardian angel—the last effort of this protective spirit to prevent the storm that was even then beginning and growing ready to envelop me. Her victory was announced by an unusual calm after I had abandoned my ancient and torturous studies. And thus I learned to equate evil with their pursuit, happiness with their disregard.

Virtue fought hard, but in vain. Destiny was too potent, and her absolute laws had decreed my utter and terrible destruction.

> ### Writing Opportunity:
> *Write an essay in which you discuss the role of destiny or fate in the downfall of the tragic hero.*

Frankenstein
or The Modern Prometheus

❦

MARY SHELLEY

CHAPTER 3

When I was seventeen, my parents decided that I should become a student at the University of Ingolstadt. Until that time I had attended the schools of Geneva, but my father thought it necessary for the completion of my education that I should be exposed to countries and cultures other than my own. My departure was, therefore, fixed at an early date. Before that day could arrive, however, the first misfortune of my life occurred—an omen, as it were, of my future misery.

Elizabeth had caught the scarlet fever. Her illness was severe, and she was in great danger. During her illness, my mother was urged not to attend to her. She did, at first, listen to this advice, but when she heard that the life of her favorite was in danger, she could no longer control her anxiety. She sat at Elizabeth's sickbed. Her unceasing care and attention eventually won out over the severity of the illness. Elizabeth was saved, but at the cost of her caretaker. On the third day, my mother got sick. Her fever was accompanied by the most alarming symptoms, and the looks of her doctors and nurses indicated the worst. On her deathbed, the strength and kindness of this best of women did not desert her. She joined the hands of Elizabeth and myself. "My children," she said, "my greatest hope of future happiness hinged on the prospect of your marriage. It will now be your father's consola-

The town of Ingolstadt is located in the German state of Bavaria on the Danube and Schutter rivers about 45 miles north of Munich.

Before the discovery of penicillin and the development of other anti-biotics, scarlet fever could lead to complications—some of them deadly—that included pneumonia, hepatitus, and kidney damage.

tion. Elizabeth, my love, you must now be mother to my younger children. Alas! I regret that I am taken from you, and, happy and beloved as I have been, it is hard to leave you. But these are not appropriate thoughts. I will try to resign myself cheerfully to death and will hope to meet you in another world."

She died calmly. Her face expressed love even in death. I need not describe the feelings of those who experience the loss of their closest and dearest loved ones to that most irreparable evil, the void that we know as death, and the despair that is evident on their faces. It is so long before the mind can accept that one so close, so much a part of our life, can be gone forever—that the brightness of a beloved eye has been extinguished and the sound of a voice so familiar and dear to the ear can be hushed—never more to be heard. These are the thoughts of those first days, but then the passage of time proves the reality of the loss. Then the actual bitterness of grief begins. Yet who among us has not seen the rude hand of Death seize a loved one? And why should I describe a sorrow that everyone alive has felt, and must feel? The time finally comes when grief turns into self-indulgence, and it is time once again to allow happiness into one's heart. My mother was dead, but we still had duties to fulfill. We had to go on with our lives and learn to consider ourselves fortunate for the time we were given with her.

Research Opportunity:

Look up the various theories related to stages of grief, processing loss, etc.

The original concept of a liberal education originated in the idea that a gentleman (one who would not have to work in order to make a living) should still be well-educated. The "liberal arts" that such a gentleman would study are called liberal (from Latin [Continued on next page]

My departure for Ingolstadt—which had been delayed by the death, funeral, and mounring period—was rescheduled. I had persuaded my father to allow me to remain home several weeks. It seemed sacrilege to me—so soon after a period of mourning—to rush into the thick of life. Sorrow was a new experience to me, yet I felt it no less keenly. I was unwilling to take leave of my remaining family, and above all, I wanted to console my sweet Elizabeth to some degree.

She indeed hid her grief and tried to comfort the rest of us. She looked steadily on life and assumed its duties with courage and zeal. She devoted herself to those whom she had been taught to call her uncle and cousins. Never was she so enchanting as at this time, when she recalled the sunshine of her smiles and spent them upon us. She forgot even her own regret in her efforts to make us forget.

The day of my departure finally arrived. Clerval spent the last evening with us. He had tried to persuade his father to allow him to go with me and become my fellow student, but his pleas were useless. His father was a narrow-minded merchant and saw laziness and failure in the aspirations of his son. Henry felt a sharp disappointment in being denied a liberal education. He said little, but when he did speak, I saw his determination not to be trapped in a life devoted to mere commerce.

We sat up late. We could not tear ourselves away from each other, nor persuade ourselves to say the word "Farewell!" Finally we did say it, and we went to bed under the pretence of needing rest. But when dawn broke, I descended to the carriage which was to take me away, they were all there—my father again to bless me, Clerval to press my hand once more, my Elizabeth to renew her pleas to write often.

I threw myself into the coach and indulged in the most melancholy reflections. I—who had always been surrounded by loved ones, constantly trying to please one another—I was now alone. In the university, I would need to form my own friends and be my own protector. My former life had been remarkably sheltered, and this had given me inherent distrust of new acquaintances. I loved my brothers, Elizabeth, and Clerval. These were "old familiar faces," but I believed myself totally unsuited for the company of strangers. Such were my thoughts as I began my journey; but as I proceeded, my spirits and hopes rose. I deeply desired an education. When at home, I had often thought it hard to spend my youth cooped up in one place, and I longed to claim my place in the wider world. Now I had my wish, and it would, indeed, have been foolish to regret it.

I had time to think these thoughts and many others during my journey to Ingolstadt, which was long and tiring. At last, the high white steeple of the town met my

liber, *meaning "free"), because they serve the purpose of training the free man. They were intended to provide general knowledge and intellectual skills rather than the specialized knowledge or skill needed to pursue a particular occupation or profession.*

There were seven Liberal Arts in all, divided into the Trivium *("the three roads") and the* Quadrivium *("the four roads").*

The Trivium *consisted of:* Grammar—*the rules of language.* Rhetoric—*the skillful application of those rules.* Logic—*the appropriate structures of thought and language in order to communicate ideas or achieve a desired effect.*

The Quadrivium *consisted of:* Arithmetic—*the study of numbers and their properties.* Geometry—*the study of numbers in space.* Music, Harmonics, or Tuning Theory—*the study of numbers in time.* Astronomy or Cosmology—*the study of numbers in space and time.*

While Clerval desires, like Victor, to pursue ideas, his father sees no need for him to have anything more than the practical training he will need to be a merchant.

eyes. I left the carriage and was taken to my lonely apartment to spend the evening as I pleased.

The next morning I delivered the letters my professors gave me as a way of introducing myself and paid a visit to some of the principal professors. Chance—or rather the evil influence, the Angel of Destruction, which held complete influence over me from the moment I left my father's home—led me first to M. Krempe, professor of science. He was a vulgar man, but well-versed in the secrets of his field. He asked me several questions concerning my progress in the different branches of science pertaining to physics. I replied carelessly, and partly in contempt, mentioned the names of my alchemists as the principal authors I had studied. The professor stared. "Have you," he said, "wasted your time studying such nonsense?"

I replied that I had.

"Every minute," continued M. Krempe warmly, "every instant that you have wasted on those books is utterly and entirely lost. You have burdened your memory with outmoded systems and useless names. Good God! In what desert land have you lived, where no one was kind enough to inform you that these fantasies you so readily accepted as fact are a thousand years old and as musty as they are ancient? I little expected, in this enlightened and scientific age, to find a disciple of Albertus Magnus and Paracelsus. My dear sir, you must begin your studies entirely anew."

The "science" of reading a person's character (honesty, kindness, bitterness) in his or her face was called "physiognomy." In its simplest form, it was used in fairy tales and children's stories to show that good people were beautiful and wicked people were ugly (Cinderella and her stepsisters). Notice how the Romantic Mary Shelley portrays all of the scientists as physically ugly.

So saying, he stepped aside and wrote down a list of several books on physics which he suggested I read, and dismissed me after mentioning that in the beginning of the following week he would begin a course of lectures upon basic physics, and that M. Waldman, a fellow professor, would lecture on chemistry on the alternate days.

As I returned home, I realized that I was not overly disappointed by the professor's low opinion of Magnus and the others since I had begun to dislike and distrust them long ago. But neither was I any more interested in returning to the study of science. M. Krempe was a little squat man with a gruff voice and an ugly face. The teacher, therefore, did nothing to attract me toward his subject. I may have gone into too much detail describing this youthful disillusionment of mine. As a child I had not been content with the results promised by the modern professors of natural science. With a confusion of ideas that can only be explained by my inexperience and lack of a qualified teacher, I had actually back-tracked the steps of knowledge and traded the advances of modern science for the dreams of forgotten alchemists. Besides, I had contempt for the uses of modern physics. It was very different when the masters of the science sought immortality and power. Such aspiration—although futile—were grand, but now the scene was changed. The only ambition of modern science seemed to be the elimination of all the fantasies that had first drawn me to it. I was forced to exchange splendid visions for common realities.

Such were my thoughts during my first two or three days in Ingolstadt, which I chiefly spent becoming acquainted with the town and its principal residents. But as the week began, I thought of the lecture M. Krempe would be giving. And although I could not consent to go and hear that little conceited fellow deliver sentences out of a pulpit, I remembered what he had said about M. Waldman, whom I had not yet seen.

Partly out of curiosity and partly out of boredom, I went into the lecture hall. M. Waldman entered shortly after. This professor was very unlike his colleague. He appeared about fifty years of age, but with a kindly expression. A few gray hairs covered his temples, but those at the back of his head were nearly black. He was short but stood straight as an arrow, and his voice was as musical as any I'd heard. He began his lecture by reviewing the history of chemistry and the various advancements that had been made, pronouncing with excitement the names of the distinguished scientists responsible for them. He then took a brief view of the present state of the science and explained many of its elementary terms. He concluded with an overview of modern chemistry, and I shall never forget his words.

"The ancient teachers of this science," he said, "promised the impossible and delivered nothing. The modern masters promise very little. They know that base metals cannot be turned into gold and that the elixir of life is a fairy tale. But these scientists—whose hands seem only made to dabble in dirt, and their eyes to pore

⊘ Today we associate the ancient "science" of alchemy with attempts to change base metals like lead and iron into precious metals like silver and gold, but alchemy was actually the great-grandfather of modern chemistry.

❷ How does Victor's complaint express the Romantic view of science?

❷ What is the significance of this metaphor comparing a scientist to a preacher?

over the microscope or laboratory vessel—have indeed performed miracles. They delve into the far corners of nature and show how she works in her hiding places. They soar into the heavens; they have discovered how the blood circulates, and the nature of the air we breathe. They have acquired new and almost unlimited powers. They can command the thunders of Heaven, mimic the earthquake, and even mock the invisible world with its own shadows."

Research Opportunity:

Look up the status of science in Mary Shelley's day, the first half of the nineteenth-century. What was known and commonly believed in the sciences of chemistry, biology, and physics?

Such were the professor's words—or perhaps I should say the words of fate—which were enough to destroy me. As he went on, I felt as if my soul was possessed. One by one the various keys were touched which formed the core of my being, as chords form a piece of music. Soon my mind was filled with one thought, one idea, one purpose. So much has been done, but I, Victor Frankenstein, would achieve far more, following in the steps of those before me, I would pioneer a new way, explore unknown powers, and reveal to the world the deepest mysteries of creation.

I never slept that night. My mind was in a state of revolt and turmoil. I hoped that I would soon calm down, but I had no power to calm myself. Gradually, after the dawn, sleep came. I awoke, and my previous night's thoughts were like a dream. There only remained a resolution to return to my previous studies and to devote myself to a science for which I believed myself to possess a natural talent. On the same day I paid M. Waldman a visit. His manner in private was even more polite and friendly than in public, for there was a certain dignity in his appearance during his lecture that in his own house was replaced by courtesy and kindness. I gave him pretty nearly the same account of my earlier studies as I had given to his fellow professor. He heard with attention my history and smiled at the names of Cornelius Agrippa and Paracelsus, but without the contempt that M. Krempe had exhibited. He

✔ Explain this simile.

✔ This is the first time we hear Victor's full name. Many first-time readers are surprised to learn that Frankenstein is the creator's name, not the creature's.

✔ This boastful pride with which a human somehow aspires to a more-than-human or godlike accomplishment is called hubris.

said, "These were men to whose untiring zeal modern scientists were indebted for most of the basis of their knowledge. Their legacy to us was the task of naming and categorizing the facts that they had first discovered. The labors of men of genius—however misguided—hardly ever fail in ultimately turning to the solid advantage of mankind." I listened to his statement, which was delivered without any presumption or affectation, and replied that his lecture had removed my prejudices against modern chemists. I expressed myself carefully, with the respect due from a youth to his instructor, trying hard not to appear too overly enthusiastic, and thus betray my lack of experience. I requested his advice concerning what books I should read.

❷ *Beware of the first-person narrator. Is Mary Shelley saying this or is Victor? How closely do you think it reflects what Mary Shelley actually believes?*

"I am happy to have gained a student," he said, "and if your effort equals your ability, I have no doubt of your success. Chemistry is that branch of science in which the greatest discoveries have been and are yet to be made. That is why I have made it my specialty. And yet I have not neglected the other branches of science. A man would be a very sorry chemist if he focused on that alone. If your wish is to become a true man of science and not merely a petty experimentalist, I would advise you to study every branch of science, including mathematics." He then took me into his laboratory and explained to me the uses of his various machines, instructing me as to what I ought to buy for myself and promising me the use of his own equipment once I had advanced far enough in the science not to damage it. He also gave me the list of books which I had requested, and I took my leave.

Thus ended a memorable day for me, a day that decided my future destiny.

> **Writing Opportunity:**
>
> *Study the list of attributes of the Tragic and Romantic Heroes you researched at the beginning of this book (you may do more research if necessary) and write an essay in which you begin to discuss Victor as either a Tragic Hero or a Romantic Hero.*

❷ *Notice the tension here between a human decision (Free Will) and the role of Fate or Destiny. The roles of Free Will and Destiny in human actions and their consequences are important issues in discussing the Tragic Hero.*

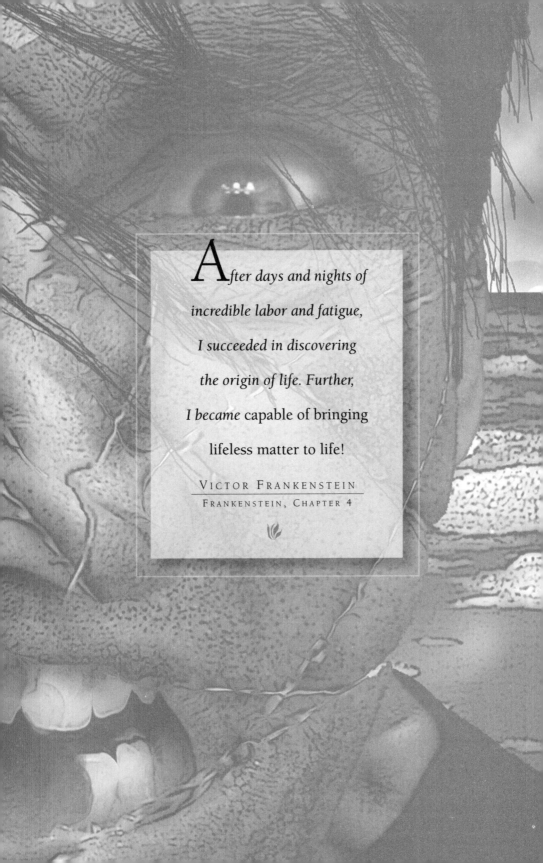

After days and nights of incredible labor and fatigue, I succeeded in discovering the origin of life. Further, I became capable of bringing lifeless matter to life!

VICTOR FRANKENSTEIN
FRANKENSTEIN, CHAPTER 4

Frankenstein

or The Modern Prometheus

❧

MARY SHELLEY

CHAPTER 4

From that day, science—and particularly chemistry, in the broadest sense of the term—became nearly my sole occupation. I eagerly read those works, so full of genius and insight, which modern inquirers had written on these subjects. I attended the lectures and made it a point to meet the men of science of the university. I even found in M. Krempe a great deal of sound sense and real information. His knowledge was combined—it is true—with a repulsive face and manners, but it was valuable nonetheless. In M. Waldman, I found a true friend. His gentleness was never tinged by narrow-mindedness, and his instructions were given with an air of frankness and good nature, without a trace of tediousness. In a thousand ways he smoothed the path of knowledge for me and made the most obscure questions clear and understandable. My effort was at first fluctuating and uncertain. It gained strength as I proceeded and soon became so dedicated and eager that the stars often disappeared in the light of morning while I was still working in my laboratory.

As hard as I worked, it followed that my progress was rapid. My devotion astonished my fellow students, and my skill astonished the professors. Professor Krempe often asked me—with a sly smile—how Cornelius Agrippa went on, while M. Waldman expressed true and heartfelt

❓ *Do you agree with this?*

❓ *Where do you see Victor's story going?*

✅ *Again, an exaggerated human characteristic—like Victor's "almost abnormal enthusiasm" is a trait of the Tragic Hero.*

❓ *How would the Romantics, especially Byron and the Shelleys, feel about this non-superstitious upbringing?*

delight in my progress. For the next two years I paid no visit to Geneva. I was instead occupied—heart and soul—in the pursuit of my research and studies. Only those who have experienced the allure of science can understand. In other studies, you go as far as others have gone before you, and there is nothing more to know. But in a scientific pursuit there is continual food for discovery and wonder. A fairly intelligent mind that closely pursues one study must eventually fully master that study. I pursued each object of study so single-mindedly, and progressed so rapidly that at the end of two years I had brought about the improvement of some chemical instruments, which brought me great esteem and admiration at the University. At this point, since I was as knowledgeable in physics as any of the professors at Ingolstadt, there seemed no reason to continue there. I thought of returning to my friends and my native town, when an incident happened that caused me to stay.

One subject that particularly absorbed me was physiology, the study of the various life functions of the human body, or indeed those of any living creature. *How,* I often asked myself, *did life begin?* It was a bold question, and one that has always been a mystery. Yet how often are we upon the brink of a great discovery but for the barriers of cowardice or carelessness? I reflected on this and determined from that point on to apply myself exclusively to those branches of science that relate to physiology. Without my almost abnormal enthusiasm, my application to this study would have been tedious and nearly unbearable.

To examine the causes of life, we must first examine death. I became acquainted with the science of anatomy—the study of the structure of living things—but this was not enough. I also needed to observe the natural decay of the human body. In my education my father had taken the greatest precautions that my mind *not* be exposed to any supernatural horrors. I have no memory of trembling at a tale of superstition or even the fear of ghosts. Darkness had no effect on my imagination, and a churchyard was to me merely the receptacle of bodies deprived of life. Now I needed to examine the cause and process of this decay. I needed to spend days and nights in burial vaults and morgues. My attention was fixed on spectacles that violated the normal delicacy of the human feelings. I saw how the human form became degraded and wasted. I watched the physical decay of death replace the blooming cheek of life. I paused, examining and analyzing all possible causes, as embodied in those changes from life to death, and death to life, until a sudden light dawned on me. It was a light so brilliant and wondrous— yet so simple—that I was surprised that so many men of genius had pursued the same science, yet I would be the ONE who would ultimately discover it.

Remember, I am not recording the vision of a madman. As surely as the sun shines in the heavens, the story I relate is true. Some miracle might have produced it, yet the stages of the discovery were distinct and probable. After days and nights of incredible labor and fatigue, I succeeded in discovering the origin of life. Further, I became *capable of bringing lifeless matter to life!*

My astonishment soon gave place to delight and rapture. After so much time spent in painful labor, to finally achieve my goals was the most gratifying fulfillment of my labor. But this discovery was so great and overwhelming that I forgot all the steps that had led to it, and saw only the result. That which the wisest men had studied and pursued since the creation of the world was now within *my* grasp. Not that, like magic, everything was revealed to me at once. Instead, the knowledge I had gained would lead me in the right direction for further study. I was like the Arabian who had been buried with the dead and found a passage to life, aided only by one glimmering and seemingly ineffective light. I can tell by your eagerness and the look in your eyes, my friend, that you want me to tell you the secret. That cannot be. Listen patiently until the end of my story, and you will understand why. I will not lead you on—as I myself was led—to your destruction and misery. Learn from me—if not from what I say, at least by my example—the danger of knowledge and how much happier that man is who believes his native town to be the entire world, than he who aspires to become greater than human nature will allow.

❷ *What is the significance of this metaphor?*

✔ *This is an an allusion to "The Fourth Voyage of Sinbad" in* The Arabian Nights *(also known as* The Thousand and One Nights). *An earlier French translation of this book of Arabian legends had recently been "rediscovered" by the Europeans, and the culture of the Middle East became wildly popular in the early nineteenth century. In the story alluded to here, Sinbad the sailor is given a beautiful wife as a present by a friendly king. He later discovers that it is this country's custom to bury the living spouse with the dead spouse. Sinbad's wife dies, and Sinbad is buried with her in a cave. He sees a small spot of light by which he is eventually able to escape from the cave.*

❷ *Do you agree or diasgree with the sentiment? Why?*

> *Think:*
>
> *If Victor "creates" a human, is he really creating?*

When I found such an astonishing power placed in my hands, I hesitated a long time thinking about how I would use it. Even though I possessed the ability to bestow life, to prepare a body to receive it remained an unbelievably difficult task—with its intricate arrangement of tissue, muscles, and veins. I debated at first whether I should attempt the creation of a human, or even a simpler organism, but I was too awed by my first success to have any doubt about my ability to give life to an animal as complete and wonderful as Man. The tools, instruments, and other materials available to me in my laboratory and that M. Waldman was willing to let me use were inadequate to such a huge task, but I nevertheless had no doubt of my ultimate success. I prepared myself for many setbacks. My efforts might be constantly frustrated, and the final project might be imperfect. Yet, when I considered the advances which every day take place in science and mechanics, I believed my present attempts would at least lay the foundations of future success. Nor could I allow myself to believe that the task was impossible simply because it would be huge and difficult. It was with these feelings that I began the creation of a human being. As the smallness of the parts presented a challenge to my speed, I resolved—contrary to my first intention—to make the being of a gigantic stature, that is to say, about eight feet in height, and proportionately large. After having made this decision and having spent some months in successfully collecting and arranging my materials, I began.

No one can understand the variety of feelings that carried me forward—like a hurricane—in the first flush of success. Life and death were suddenly boundaries to be broken through, pouring a flood of light into our dark world. A new species would bless me as its creator and source. Many happy and excellent creatures would owe their being to me. No father could claim the gratitude of his children so completely as I should deserve theirs. If I could bestow animation upon lifeless matter—regardless of how impossible it seemed at that moment—I might in

Notice how Victor perceives of himself as almost a god to this new species. This is another example of hubris.

time renew life where death had apparently devoted the body to decay.

These thoughts raised my spirits while I pursued my work with unfailing zeal. Long hours in the darkness of my laboratory and library had made my complexion grow pale, and my body thin and emaciated. Sometimes, on the very brink of a breakthrough, I failed. Yet still I clung to the hope that the next day or the next hour might bring success. I kept my deepest ambition secret, and the moon gazed on my midnight labors, while I relentlessly pursued Nature to her hiding places. Who can imagine the horrors of my secret toil as I experimented in graveyards or tortured living animals to animate lifeless ones? The memory of these horrible deeds makes me tremble, but I was unable to resist the frantic impulse which urged me forward. I seemed to have lost all soul or sensation except for this one pursuit. I collected bones from graveyards and disturbed—with godless fingers—the tremendous secrets of the human body. In a single chamber—more like a small cell—at the top of the house, and separated from all the other apartments by a hallway and staircase, I kept my workshop of filthy creation. My eyes nearly hung from their sockets in attending to the details of my work. The dissecting room and the gallows furnished many of my materials. Torn between an instinctive disgust at my occupation and an increasing eagerness, I brought my work near to a conclusion.

✓ Note the use of personification here.

The summer months passed while I was occupied—heart and soul—in this one pursuit. It was a most beautiful season. Never did the fields offer a more plentiful harvest or the vines yield a more luxurious vintage. But my eyes were blind to the charms of nature. I also found myself neglecting friends who were so many miles away, and whom I had not seen for such a long time. I knew my silence upset them, and I could hear my father saying, "I know that while you are pleased with yourself you will think of us with affection, and we shall hear regularly from you. I also know that when we don't hear from you, it will mean that you are displeased both with yourself and with your work."

❓ In terms of Romantic values, what is happening to Victor here?

I knew well that my father would disapprove of what I was doing, but nevertheless my loathsome project had

❓ Why would Victor's father disapprove?

taken an irresistible hold of my imagination. I wished, as it were, to procrastinate all that related to my feelings of affection until the great object, which swallowed up every habit of my nature, should be completed.

I believed my father would be unjust if he attributed my neglect to vice or bad behavior, but he was certainly justified in thinking I was not altogether free from blame. A human being should ideally be able to preserve a calm and peaceful mind, not allowing passion or fleeting desire to disturb that tranquility. I do not think that the pursuit of knowledge is an exception to this rule. If the study to which you apply yourself has a tendency to undermine your well being, then that study is certainly unhealthy and inappropriate. If no man ever allowed his ambition to interfere with his peace of mind, then Greece would not have been enslaved by the Turks, Caesar would have spared his country, America would have been discovered more gradually, and the empires of Mexico and Peru would not have been destroyed.

But I am moralizing just as I come to the most interesting part of my tale, and the look on your face reminds me to proceed. My father did not reprimand me in his letters and only mentioned science by making more a point of asking about my work than before. Winter, spring, and summer passed away during my labors; but I took no notice of the seasons, so deeply was I engrossed in my occupation. The leaves of that year had withered before my work drew near to a close, and now every day showed me more plainly how well I had succeeded. But my enthusiasm was held in check by my anxiety, and I might just as well have been a mineworker, rather than a man working in his chosen field. Every night I suffered from a slow fever, and I became painfully nervous. The fall of a leaf startled me, and I shunned other people as if I had been guilty of a crime. Sometimes I grew alarmed at the wreck I had become. The energy of my purpose alone sustained me. My work would soon end, and I believed that rest and recuperation would then drive away the beginnings of any disease I might be developing. I promised myself both of these when my creation was complete.

Lord Byron, with whom the Shelleys were travelling when Mary Shelley began this book, would die of malaria on April 19, 1824 while he was in Greece preparing to help the Greeks in their fight for liberation from the Ottomans.

Here, again, is more evidence of hubris—Victor is comparing himself to Caesar, Columbus, and the Spanish Conquistadors. Remember, though, that this is Victor speaking. Mary Shelley's tone suggests that the "accomplishments" of these "great" men were not necessarily good.

This intense suffering and heightened sensory awareness are traits of both the Tragic and Romantic heroes.

Research Opportunity:

Look up the most recent advancements in the following fields: cloning (especially human cloning); genetic engineering; mapping the human genome; in-vitro fertilization and infertility techniques; nano-bio-technology.

Debate/Discussion Panel:

Choose one of the topics above and begin to develop a pro or con argument regarding the moral, religious, and/or philosophical considerations of research in that field, or regarding the overall benefits versus risk of research in that field.

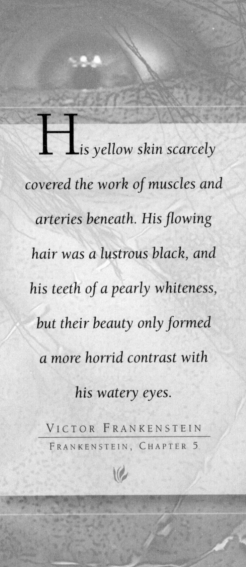

His yellow skin scarcely covered the work of muscles and arteries beneath. His flowing hair was a lustrous black, and his teeth of a pearly whiteness, but their beauty only formed a more horrid contrast with his watery eyes.

VICTOR FRANKENSTEIN
FRANKENSTEIN, CHAPTER 5

Frankenstein
or The Modern Prometheus
❦
MARY SHELLEY

CHAPTER 5

It was on a dreary night of November that I looked at my accomplishment. With an agonizing anxiety, I collected the instruments of life that would perhaps infuse a spark of existence into the lifeless thing that lay at my feet. It was already one in the morning. The rain pattered dismally against the panes, and my candle was nearly burnt out, when, by the glimmer of the half-extinguished light, I saw the dull, yellow eye of the creature open. It breathed hard, and a convulsive motion shook its limbs.

How can I describe my emotions at this catastrophe, or describe the wretch I had tried to form with such infinite pains and care? His limbs were in proportion, and I had selected his features as beautiful. Beautiful! Great God! His yellow skin scarcely covered the work of muscles and arteries beneath. His flowing hair was a lustrous black, and his teeth of a pearly whiteness, but their beauty only formed a more horrid contrast with his watery eyes, almost the same color as the dun-white sockets in which they were set, his shriveled complexion and straight, black lips.

The different accidents of life are not as unpredictable and changeable as the feelings of human nature. I had worked hard for nearly two years, for the sole purpose of infusing life into an inanimate body. For this I had deprived myself of rest and health. I had desired it with

The gothic setting: the rain, darkness, etc. was something of an innovation in Mary Shelley's time, but has been used so frequently that it has become a cliché.

What do you suppose accounts for this sudden change in Victor's mood and attitude?

Here is the Tragic Hero's realization that he has attempted something he possibly should not have.

❷ *What do you suppose is the significance of this dream?*

✔ *Dante Alighieri was an Italian Renaissance poet. His most famous work,* The Divine Comedy, *tells the story of a man's descent into Hell* (The Inferno), *ascent through Purgatory* (The Purgatorio), *and journey through Heaven* (The Paradiso). *In* The Inferno, *the narrator witnesses horrendous torments and hideous beings. What Victor is saying is that the creature was even uglier than Dante could have imagined for his hellish work.*

✔ *Here is where Victor admits that it is the fact of life that makes the creature so extremely ugly.*

a passion that far exceeded moderation. But now that I had finished, the beauty of the dream vanished, and horror and disgust filled my heart. Unable to even *look* at the being I had created, I rushed out of the room and continued a long time pacing in my bedroom, unable to sleep. At length exhaustion overcame my horror, and I threw myself on the bed in my clothes, desperate for a few moments of forgetfulness. But it was useless. I did sleep, but I was disturbed by the wild dreams. I thought I saw Elizabeth, in the bloom of health, walking in the streets of Ingolstadt. Delighted and surprised, I embraced her, but as I kissed her, her lips felt cold and 'dead. Her features appeared to change, and I thought that I held the corpse of my dead mother in my arms. A shroud enveloped her form, and I saw the grave-worms crawling in the folds of the fabric. I woke from my sleep in a cold sweat, my teeth chattered, and my body shook. Then, by the dim and yellow moonlight coming through the window shutters, I saw the wretch—the miserable monster whom I had created. He held up the curtain of the bed, and his eyes—if they can be called eyes—were fixed on me. His jaws opened, and he muttered some inarticulate sounds, while a grin wrinkled his cheeks. He might have spoken, but I couldn't understand. One hand was stretched out, as if to detain me, but I escaped and rushed downstairs. I hid in the courtyard, where I remained during the rest of the night, pacing nervously, listening closely and fearing each sound as if it were the demoniacal corpse to which I had so miserably given life.

Oh! No mortal could endure the horror of that face. A mummy brought to life could not be as hideous as that wretch. I had looked at him many times while he was unfinished. He was ugly then, but when those muscles and joints were rendered capable of motion, it became something even Dante could not have conceived.

I passed the night miserably. Sometimes my pulse beat so fast and hard that I felt the throb of every artery. At others, I nearly sank to the ground in weakness. Mingled with this horror, I felt the bitterness of disappointment. The dream that had sustained me for so long was now a hell to me. And the change had been so rapid, the overthrow so complete!

A dismal, wet morning dawned, revealed to my sleepless and aching eyes the church of Ingolstadt, its white steeple and clock. It was six in the morning. The porter opened the gates of the court, which had that night been my shelter, and I darted into the streets, moving quickly, trying to avoid the wretch I feared might be around every corner. I did not dare return to my apartment, but felt compelled to hurry on, although drenched by the rain that poured from a black and comfortless sky.

I continued walking for some time, trying to ease the load that weighed upon my mind, completely unaware of where I was or what I was doing. My heart fluttered in the sickness of fear, and I hurried on with irregular steps, not daring to look about me:

> Like one who, on a lonely road,
> Doth walk in fear and dread,
> And, having once turned round, walks on,
> And turns no more his head;
> Because he knows a frightful fiend
> Doth close behind him tread.
> [Coleridge's "Ancient Mariner"]

Continuing like this, I finally came to the inn at which the various stagecoaches and carriages usually stopped. Here I paused—not knowing why—and stood for several minutes with my eyes fixed on a coach that was coming toward me from the other end of the street. As it drew nearer, I saw that it was the Swiss coach. It stopped just where I was standing, and when the door was opened, I saw Henry Clerval, who saw me and instantly sprang out. "My dear Frankenstein," he exclaimed, "how glad I am to see you! How lucky that you should be here just as I'm arriving!"

It delighted me to see Clerval, since his presence brought memories of my father, Elizabeth, and all those dear scenes of home. I grasped his hand, and in a moment forgot the horror of the night before. I suddenly felt a calm and serene joy for the first time in many months. I heartily welcomed him, and we walked toward my college. Clerval continued talking for some time about our mutual friends and his own good fortune in being allowed to come to Ingolstadt. "You can only imagine," he said,

❷ *What is ironic about the fact that the first thing Victor sees when he arrives in Ingolstadt and on the morning after bringing the creature to life is the church spire?*

✔ The Vicar of Wakefield *is a
novel by Oliver Goldsmith
first published in 1766.
It begins in a state of
calm in the parish of Dr.
Primrose, the Vicar, but
disasters strike quickly and
frequently. The moral of the
tale is Primrose's strength
of character in times of
great difficulty. The Dutch
Schoolmaster alluded
to here is a pompous,
arrogant man who claims
that since he has been
"successful" without a
classical education, no one
must need one.*

"how difficult it was to persuade my father that everything worth knowing was not limited to the noble art of bookkeeping. Indeed, I believe he was still skeptical, since he was constantly quoting the Dutch schoolmaster in *The Vicar of Wakefield:* 'I have ten thousand florins a year without Greek, I eat heartily without Greek.' But his love for me is greater than his hatred of learning, and so he has allowed me to journey to the land of knowledge."

"I am delighted to see you, but tell me how my family is."

"Very well, and very happy, but a little upset that they hear from you so seldom. By the way, I mean to lecture you a little myself, for their sakes. But, my dear Frankenstein," he continued, stopping short and gazing full in my face, "I see how very ill you appear, so thin and pale. You look as if you hadn't slept for several nights."

"You have guessed right. I have lately been so deeply immersed in one experiment that I have not been getting enough rest, as you see. But I hope, I sincerely hope, that all that is now at an end and that I am finally free."

I trembled excessively, unable to think or even *allude* to what had happened the night before. I walked quickly, and we soon arrived at my college. It occurred to me, with a shiver, that the creature might still be in my apartment, alive and walking about. I dreaded the thought of seeing this monster, but I feared the possibility of Henry's seeing him even more. Urging him to remain a few minutes at the bottom of the stairs, I darted up toward my own room. My hand was already on the doorknob before I collected myself. I then paused, and a cold shivering came over me. I threw the door open, as children do when they expect to see a ghost waiting for them on the other side, but nothing appeared. I stepped fearfully in. The apartment was empty, and my bedroom was free of its hideous guest. I could hardly believe my good fortune, but when I was certain my enemy had indeed fled, I clapped my hands for joy and ran down to Clerval.

We entered my room, and the servant brought breakfast, but I was unable to contain myself. It was not only joy that possessed me. I felt my flesh tingle with an excess sensitivity, and my pulse beat rapidly. Unable to stay for a single instant in the same place, I jumped over

✔ *Notice how he immediately
calls his creature his
"enemy."*

the chairs, clapped my hands, and laughed aloud. Clerval at first thought I was simply overjoyed by his arrival, but when he studied me more closely, he saw an inexplicable wildness in my eyes, and my loud, unrestrained, heartless laughter frightened him.

"My dear Victor," he cried, "what, for God's sake, is the matter? Do not laugh that way. How ill you are! What is the cause of all this?"

"Do not ask me," I cried, covering my eyes with my hands, for I thought I saw the dreaded beast glide into the room. "HE can tell. Oh, save me! Save me!" I imagined that the monster had grabbed me. I struggled furiously and fell down in a fit.

Poor Clerval! What must he have felt? A meeting, which he had looked forward to, so strangely turned to sorrow. But I was unaware of his grief, for I was unconscious and did not recover my senses for a long, long time.

This was the beginning of a nervous fever that kept me in bed for several months. During all that time, Henry was my only nurse. I afterwards learned that, knowing my father's advanced age and weakness, and how much my sickness would worry Elizabeth, he spared them by concealing the extent of my illness. Because he was certain that I would eventually recover, he knew his deceit was the kindest thing he could do for them.

But I was really very ill, and surely nothing but the ceaseless and constant attention of my friend could have restored me to health. In my delirium, I continually saw the form of the monster lurking in front of me, and I raved about him without ceasing. My words must have surprised Henry. At first he thought they were a fantasy born of my disturbed imagination, but the way I kept returning to the same subject persuaded him that my disorder was indeed caused by some strange and terrible event.

Very slowly—and with alarmingly frequent relapses—I recovered. By the time I was able to take pleasure in seeing things, I saw that the fallen leaves had disappeared and that the young buds were emerging from the trees outside my window. It was a divine spring, which greatly helped my recovery. Joy and affection revived in

✔ *Again the exaggergerated sensitivity and reaction of the Tragic and Romantic Heroes.*

Note again how Mary Shelley emphasizes the healing power of Nature.

Here Victor identifies his tragic flaw, his hamartia.

As Elizabeth is Victor's adopted sister, it is not clear why Mary Shelley has her characters refer to her as his "cousin" unless shelley is using the term "cousin" to indicate any relative.

my heart. My gloom disappeared, and in a short time I became as cheerful as I had been even before I was possessed by my fatal ambition.

"My dear Clerval," I exclaimed, "how kind—how very, very good you are to me. This whole winter, instead of being in school, as you promised yourself, you have been in my sickroom. How can I ever repay you? I feel so guilty that I was the cause of your disappointment, but you will forgive me."

"You will repay me entirely if you do not upset yourself, but get well as fast as you can. And since you appear to be in such a good mood, may I may speak to you about something?"

I trembled. One subject! What could it be? Did he mean the Subject I was terrified to even think about? "Calm yourself," said Clerval, noticing the color drained from my face, "I will not mention it if it upsets you, but your father and cousin would be happy and relieved to get a letter from you. They have no idea how ill you have been, and your long silence has worried them."

"Is that all, my dear Henry? How could you not know that my first thoughts would be of those dear, dear friends whom I love and who so deserve my love?"

"In that case, you will be glad to see a letter that has been lying here several days for you. It is from your cousin, Elizabeth, I believe."

Frankenstein
or The Modern Prometheus

MARY SHELLEY

CHAPTER 6

Clerval then put the following letter into my hands. It was from my own Elizabeth:

"My dearest Cousin,

"You have been ill—*very* ill—and even the constant letters of dear, kind Henry are not enough to reassure me. You are forbidden to write—to hold a pen; yet we need just one word directly from you, dear Victor, to calm our anxiety. For a long time, I have hoped that each day's post would bring a letter, and I have been able to persuade your father not to come to Ingolstadt. I have rescued him from the inconvenience—and perhaps the danger—of so long a journey, yet you can't imagine how often I have wanted to make the trip myself! I imagine some greedy old nurse as your caretaker, neither guessing your wishes before you even know them, nor filling them with the care and love that I would. Yet that is over now: Clerval writes that you are getting better. I eagerly hope that you will confirm this news soon in your own handwriting.

"Get well—and return to us. You will find a happy, cheerful home and friends who love you. Your father is in excellent health, and he wants nothing more than to see you, and be assured that you are well. Then not a care will ever cloud his kind face. How pleased you would be to

⊘ *The Foreign Service that Ernest hopes to enter is probably the Swiss Guards. These were Swiss military units who fought for various European powers from the 15th century until the 19th century. They were called up from the separate cantons, or regions of Switzerland (Geneva is a canton and that is why Victor identified himself as "Genevese" and not "Swiss") and placed at the disposal of various foreign powers. Today, they serve only the Roman Catholic Pope and the Vatican City.*

❓ *This information about Justine is necessary plot exposition, as Justine will soon play an important role in the story. How could Mary Shelley have handled this exposition more skillfully?*

⊘ *Switzerland was a loose federation of republics (cantons) in a time when most European nations were still monarchies or constitutional monarchies that limited the monarch's power. The United States had recently formed a republican democracy, and the French Revolution had formed the First Republic. This atmosphere [Continued on next page]*

see how our Ernest has grown! He is now sixteen and full of activity and spirit. He wants to be a true Swiss and to enter into foreign service, but we cannot part with him, at least until his elder brother returns to us. My uncle is not pleased with the idea of a military career in a distant country, but Ernest never had your ability. He looks upon study as tedious, and his time is spent in the open air, climbing the hills or rowing on the lake. I fear that he will become lazy unless we yield the point and permit him to enter the profession he has selected.

"Nothing much has changed since you left. The children have all grown—that is true—but the blue lake and snow-clad mountains never change. I think it is our placid, unchanging home that keeps our hearts content. My little chores take up my time and amuse me, and I am rewarded for my efforts by the happy, kind faces around me.

"Since you left us, only one change has taken place in our little household. Do you remember when Justine Moritz entered our family? Probably you do not, so I will remind you of the story. Madame Moritz, her mother, was a widow with four children, of whom Justine was the third. This girl had always been the favorite of her father, but perversely, her mother disliked her. After the death of M. Moritz, the mother mistreated her. My aunt saw this, and when Justine was twelve years old, persuaded the mother to allow her to live at our house. The republican institutions of our country have produced simpler and happier manners than the nations that surround it. Hence there is less class distinction, and the lower ranks are more refined and moral than the poor of other nations. I believe this is because these peasants are more kindly and respectfully treated, so they learn how to be kind and respectful in return. A servant in Geneva does not mean the same thing as a servant in France and England. Justine, thus received in our family, learned the duties of a servant, which, in our fortunate country, does not include the idea of ignorance and a sacrifice of the dignity of a human being.

"Justine, you may remember, was a great favorite of yours. You once remarked that if you were in a bad mood, one glance from Justine could cheer you, for the same reason that Ariosto gives concerning the beauty of Angelica—she looked so frank-hearted and happy. My aunt became very attached to her, and decided to give her a better education than she had at first intended. This benefit was fully repaid, as Justine was the most grateful little creature in the world. She never made any great outward show of gratitude, but you could see in her eyes that she adored her protector. While her behavior was high-spirited and in many respects careless, she nevertheless paid close attention to my aunt's every move. She thought her the model of all excellence and tried to imitate her choice of words and manners, so that even now she often reminds me of her.

"When my dearest aunt died, every one was too distracted by their own grief to notice poor Justine, who had been a perfect nurse through the entire illness. Poor Justine was very ill, but still worse trials awaited her.

"One by one, her brothers and sister died, and her mother was left childless, except for Justine. The conscience of the woman was troubled. She began to believe that the deaths of her favorite children came as a judgment from Heaven to punish her for her favoritism. She was a Roman Catholic; and I believe her confessor confirmed this idea. Accordingly, a few months after your departure for Ingolstadt, Justine's repentant mother called her home. Poor girl! She wept when she left our house. The death of my aunt had changed her greatly, and grief had softened and calmed her manners. Returning to her mother's house did nothing to restore her liveliness. The mother was very inconsistent in her repentance. She sometimes begged Justine to forgive her unkindness, but more often accused her of causing the deaths of her brothers and sister. This endless fretting eventually threw Madame Moritz into ill health, which at first increased her irritability. But she is now at peace forever. She died on the first approach of cold weather, at the beginning of this last winter. Justine has just returned to us, and I assure you she is as dear to me as ever. She is very clever and gentle, and extremely pretty. As I mentioned before, her manner and her expression continually remind me of my dear aunt.

"I must say also a few words to you, my dear cousin,

of revolution, the toppling of monarchies, and the establishment of rights for all citizens were all ideals strongly supported by the Romantics. This is why Mary Shelley has Elizabeth criticize how other nations treat their poor and the types of people these poor become because of this treatment.

✔ This is an allusion to Orlando Furioso, an Italian Renaissance poem by Ludovico Ariosto in which the beauty of Angelica saves one lover's life while driving another mad.

✔ England was a Protestant country. Most of the English Romantics claimed to be atheists, so they would have considered Catholicism to be mere superstition.

of little darling William. I wish you could see him. He is very tall for his age, with sweet, laughing blue eyes, dark eyelashes, and curling hair. When he smiles, two little dimples appear on each cheek, which are rosy with health. He has already had one or two little WIVES, but Louisa Biron is his favorite, a pretty little girl of five years of age.

"Now, dear Victor, I'm sure you long for a little gossip about the good people of Geneva. The pretty Miss Mansfield has already received the congratulatory visits on her approaching marriage with a young Englishman, John Melbourne, Esq. Her ugly sister, Manon, married M. Duvillard, the rich banker, last autumn. Your best friend from school, Louis Manoir, has suffered several misfortunes since Clerval left Geneva. But he has already recovered his spirits, and is reported to be on the point of marrying a lively pretty Frenchwoman, Madame Tavernier. She is a widow, and much older than Manoir, but she is very much admired, and a favorite with everybody.

"Writing this letter has certainly improved my spirits, dear cousin, but my anxiety returns as I close. Please write, dear Victor. One line—one word will be a blessing to us. Ten thousand thanks to Henry for his kindness, his affection, and his many letters. We are sincerely grateful. Goodbye, my cousin; take care of yourself, and, I urge you, write!

Elizabeth Lavenza.
Geneva, March 18, 17—.

"Dear, dear Elizabeth!" I exclaimed, when I had read her letter. "I will write immediately and relieve them from the anxiety they must feel." I wrote, and the effort greatly tired me. Still, my recovery had begun, and continued regularly. In another two weeks, I was able to leave my room.

As soon I was able, I introduced Clerval to the major professors of the university. But this was traumatic for me, opening the wounds that my mind had sustained. Ever since that fatal night—the end of my labors, and the beginning of my misfortunes—I had a violent hatred even to the word "science." Even after I was in every other way recovered, the sight of a chemical instrument would renew all my anxiety. Henry saw this, and had taken all of my equipment away. He had also rearranged my apartment, for he saw that I now disliked the room that had been my laboratory. But all this effort was useless when I visited the professors. M. Waldman inflicted torture when he praised—with kindness and warmth—the astonishing progress I had made in the sciences. He soon noticed my discomfort, but thought I was being modest. He changed the subject from my improvement to the science itself, in an effort to draw me out. What could I do? He meant to please me, and yet he tormented me. I felt as if he had been the one who had given me—one by one—those instruments that would ultimately bring me to a slow and cruel death. His words made me squirm, but I didn't dare show the pain I felt. Clerval, who was always quick to recognize others' feelings, pretended not to understand and changed the subject. The conversation took a more general turn. I thanked my friend from my heart, but I did not speak. I could see his surprise at my new aversion to science, but he never pried. Although my affection and respect for him was boundless, I could never tell him about my awful discovery and my even more awful creation. The details would have frightened him beyond all imagining.

M. Krempe, however, was anything but subtle, and in my condition, his harsh and blunt declarations caused me even more pain than the kind praise of M. Waldman.

"Damn the fellow!" he cried. "Why, I assure you, he has outdistanced us all. Yes, stare if you please, but it is nevertheless true. A youngster who, but a few years ago, believed in Cornelius Agrippa as firmly as in the Gospel, has now set himself at the head of the university; and if he is not soon pulled down, we shall all be obsolete. Yes, yes," he continued, observing the suffering on my face, "Frankenstein is modest—an excellent quality in a young man. Young men should be self-effacing, you know, Clerval. I was myself when young, but that wears out in a very short time."

M. Krempe had now begun praising himself, which fortunately changed the subject.

Clerval had never shared my interest in natural science,

and his literary pursuits differed wholly from my own. He came to the University to master the Eastern languages—a necessary step in the plan of life he laid out for himself. Determined to distinguish himself, he looked toward the East, as offering the greatest opportunities. The Persian, Arabic, and Sanscrit languages interested him, and I was easily convinced to pursue the same studies. I'd always disliked being unoccupied, and now that I needed distraction and hated my former studies, I felt great relief in being the fellow-pupil of my friend. I found both instruction and consolation in studying Eastern literature. I did not, like him, try to become fluent in the languages. For me, they were only a temporary amusement. I studied the language only to be able to understand the literature. I found the stories of the Arabian Nights to be exactly what my troubled mind needed. Their melancholy was soothing, and their joy elevating—more so than the authors of any other country I have studied. When you read their writings, life appears to exist in a warm sun and a garden of roses, in the smiles and frowns of a fair enemy, and the fire that consumes your own heart. How different they were from the manly and heroic poetry of Greece and Rome!

Summer passed, and my return to Geneva was set for the end of autumn. It was, however, delayed by several accidents and the winter snows arrived. The roads were impassable, and my journey was delayed until the next spring. I was deeply disappointed for I longed to see my native town and my beloved friends. I had also been delaying my return, however, because I was unwilling to leave Clerval in an unfamiliar place, but he quickly met some friendly acquaintances, and the city and University became less foreign to him. The winter was happy, and although the spring was uncommonly late, when it came it was also uncommonly beautiful.

The month of May had already begun, and I expected the letter daily that was to set the date of my departure, when Henry proposed a walking tour in the countryside surrounding Ingolstadt, so that I might bid it a personal farewell. I happily accepted the invitation. I was fond of exercise, and Clerval had always been my favorite

Remember that The Arabian Nights *was a newly rediscovered book and the culture of the Middle East was very popular among European intellectuals and aristocrats of the time.*

companion for hiking through the scenery of my native country.

We spent two weeks in these travels. My health and spirits were restored. They gained additional strength from the fresh air I breathed, the journey itself, and the conversation of my friend. Years of study had secluded me and made me anti-social, but Clerval drew out the better part of myself. He again taught me to love nature, and the cheerful faces of children.

Again, the healing effects of Nature.

He was such an excellent friend! His love for me was sincere, and he tried to elevate my mind to his own level. My spirit had been cramped and narrowed by my selfish pursuits, until his gentleness and affection warmed and opened my senses. I became the same happy creature I had been, loved and beloved by all, someone who had no sorrow or care. He returned me to the time when happy, inanimate nature had the power of granting me the most delightful sensations. A quiet sky and lush, green fields filled me with ecstasy. The present season was indeed divine. The flowers of spring bloomed in the hedges, while those of summer were already in bud. I was undisturbed by thoughts which during the preceding year had nearly strangled me.

Remember how Robert Walton had lamented having no friend, no equal. Here Victor praises his friend Henry Clerval. This theme of friendship will be very important throughout this story.

Henry rejoiced in my happiness, and was sympathetic, trying hard to amuse me, while expressing his own feelings. The resources of his mind on this occasion were truly astonishing. His conversation was imaginative, and very often—just like the Persian and Arabic writers—he invented tales of wonderful fancy and passion. At other times he repeated my favorite poems, or ingeniously debated with me. We returned to our college on a Sunday afternoon. The peasants were dancing, and every one we met appeared happy. My own spirits were high, and I bounded along with feelings of unrestrained joy.

Predict:

Given what you know about the Prometheus myth, the Tragic Hero, and the Romantic Hero, where do you think this story is headed?

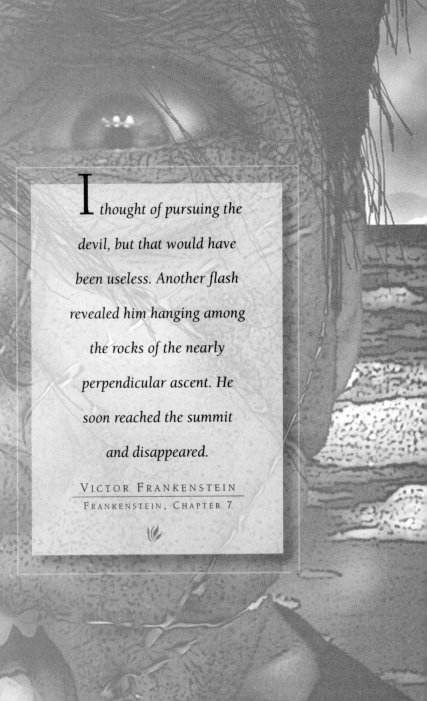

I thought of pursuing the devil, but that would have been useless. Another flash revealed him hanging among the rocks of the nearly perpendicular ascent. He soon reached the summit and disappeared.

VICTOR FRANKENSTEIN
FRANKENSTEIN, CHAPTER 7

Frankenstein

or The Modern Prometheus

MARY SHELLEY

CHAPTER 7

On my return, I found the following letter from my father:—

"My dear Victor,

"You have probably waited impatiently for a letter to confirm the date of your return to us; and I was at first tempted to write only a few lines, merely mentioning the day on which I would expect you. But that would be a cruel kindness, and I dare not do it. How surprised would you be, my son, when you looked forward to a joyful welcome, to see, on the contrary, tears and misery? And how can I tell you about our misfortune? Even though you've been gone for so long, surely your heart is not hard to our joys and sorrows. I wish to prepare you for the woeful news, but I know it is impossible. Even now your eye skims over the page to seek the words that will tell you the horrible tidings.

"William is dead! That sweet child, whose smiles delighted and warmed my heart, so gentle, yet so happy!

"Victor, he has been murdered!

"I will not attempt to console you; but will simply relate the circumstances of the transaction.

"Last Thursday (May 7th), I, my niece, and your two brothers, went to walk in Plainpalais. The evening was

Structurally, Mary Shelley has allowed Victor a brief period of happiness after the torment of his creation and before the shock of this announcement.

warm and serene, and we prolonged our walk farther than usual. It was already dusk before we thought of returning; and then we discovered that William and Ernest, who had gone on before, were not to be found. We consequently rested on a seat until they should return. Presently Ernest came, and asked if we had seen his brother; they had been playing, and William had run away to hide himself. He vainly searched for him, and afterwards waited for a long time, but William did not return.

"This account rather alarmed us, and we continued to search for him until night fell, when Elizabeth conjectured that he might have returned to the house. He was not there. We returned again, with torches; for I could not rest, when I thought that my sweet boy had lost himself, and was exposed to all the damp and cold of night; Elizabeth also suffered extreme anguish. About five in the morning I discovered my lovely boy, whom the night before I had seen blooming and active in health, stretched on the grass livid and motionless; the print of the murder's finger was on his neck.

"He was conveyed home, and the anguish that was visible on my face betrayed the secret to Elizabeth. She was very earnest to see the corpse. At first I attempted to prevent her but she persisted, and entering the room where it lay, hastily examined the neck of the victim, and clasping her hands exclaimed, 'O God! I have murdered my darling child!'

"She fainted, and was restored with extreme difficulty. When she was conscious, it was only to weep and sigh. She told me, that that same evening William had teased her to let him wear a very valuable miniature that she possessed of your mother. This picture is gone, and was doubtless the temptation that urged the murderer to the deed. We have no trace of him at present, although our efforts to find him are unremitting; but they will not restore my beloved William!

"Come, dearest Victor; you alone can console Elizabeth. She weeps continually, and accuses herself unjustly as the cause of his death; her words pierce my heart. We are all unhappy; but isn't that one more reason for you, my son, to return and be our comforter? Your dear mother! Alas, Victor! I now say, thank God she did not live to witness the cruel, miserable death of her youngest darling!

"Come home, Victor—not with thoughts of vengeance against the killer—but with feelings of peace and gentleness, that will heal our wounded minds. Enter our house of mourning with kindness and affection for those who love you, rather than hatred for your enemies.

"Your affectionate and afflicted father,
"Alphonse Frankenstein.
"Geneva, May 12th, 17—."

Clerval, who had watched my face as I read this letter, was surprised to see the despair that replaced the joy I at first expressed on receiving the letter. I threw it on the table, and covered my face with my hands.

"My dear Frankenstein," he exclaimed, seeing me weep, "are you always to be unhappy? My dear friend, what has happened?"

I motioned him to read the letter, while I paced the room in extreme agitation. Tears also gushed from the his eyes, as he read.

"I can offer you no consolation, my friend," he said. "Your disaster is beyond repair. What are you going to do?"

"I must go instantly to Geneva. Come with me to order the horses."

During our walk, Clerval offered a few words of consolation. He could only express his heartfelt sympathy. "Poor William!" he said. "Dear lovely child, he now sleeps with his angel mother! Anyone who had ever seen that beautiful, joyous child must weep over his untimely loss! To die so miserably; to feel the murderer's grasp! How much more a murderer that could destroy radiant innocence! Poor little fellow! Our one consolation is that, while his friends mourn and weep, he is at rest. His sufferings are at an end forever. The earth covers his gentle form, and he knows no pain. We must reserve our pity for his miserable survivors."

Clerval spoke as we hurried through the streets. His words stuck with me, and I remembered them later when I was alone. But as soon as the horses arrived, I hurried into a two-wheeled carriage, and bade my friend farewell.

My journey was very melancholy. At first I wished

✪ *Look up the literary terms* pathos *and* bathos. *Which do you think is functioning here?*

This is a brief quotation from the Third Canto of Byron's famous Childe Harold's Pilgrimage, *which Byron was writing during this period. Harold, was probably the first example of the Romantic or Byronic Hero—the turbulent, emotional young man who shuns humanity and wanders through life weighed down by a sense of guilt for mysterious sins of his past.*

to hurry on, for I longed to console my loved ones, but when I drew near my native town, I slowed down. I could hardly bear all the feelings that crowded into my mind. I passed through places familiar to my youth, but which I had not seen for nearly six years. How changed everything was! One sudden and devastating change had taken place, but a thousand quiet, little changes were just as significant. Fear overcame me. I dared not go forward, dreading a thousand nameless evils that made me tremble, although I was unable to define them. I stayed two days at Lausanne, in this painful state of mind. I watched the lake where the water was calm. The snowy mountains, the "palaces of Nature" were not changed. Slowly, the calm and heavenly scene restored me, and I continued my journey toward Geneva.

The road ran by the side of the lake, which became narrower as I approached my native town. I saw more clearly the black sides of Jura, and the bright summit of Mont Blanc. I wept like a child. "Dear mountains! My own beautiful lake! How do you welcome your wanderer? Your summits are clear; the sky and lake are blue and calm. Is this to predict peace, or to mock my unhappiness?"

I'm afraid, my friend, that I may be becoming boring by dwelling on these early events, but they were days of relative happiness, and I think of them with pleasure. My country, my beloved country! Who but a native can understand the delight I took in again beholding your streams, your mountains, and, more than all, your lovely lake!

Yet, as I drew nearer to home, grief and fear again overcame me. Night also closed around me, and—when I could hardly see the dark mountains—I felt even more gloom. It all seemed a vast and dim scene of evil. I saw myself destined to become the most lonely and unhappy human being alive.

Alas! I prophesied truly, and failed only in one single detail: that all the misery I imagined and dreaded was not even a tiny bit of the anguish I would actually suffer.

It was completely dark when I arrived in Geneva. The gates of the town were already shut; and I was obliged to spend the night at Secheron, a nearby village. The sky

Notice how Victor's sorrow has become such that even he perceives Nature as possibly mocking him instead of being his healer and nurturer.

Remember that Victor is talking to Captain Walton and that Captain Walton is writing a letter to his sister.

The walled city whose gates were shut at night and reopened in the morning was a holdover from ancient times.

was calm, and—as I could not sleep anyway—I decided to visit the spot where poor William had been murdered. I could not travel through the town so I crossed the lake in a boat to arrive at Plainpalais, another city on Lake Geneva. During this short voyage, I saw the lightning playing on the summit of Mont Blanc in the most beautiful figures. The storm appeared to approach rapidly, and, after I landed, I climbed a low hill, to watch it. It approached. The heavens were clouded, and I soon felt large drops of rain. Then, quickly the storm increased in violence.

I rose from my seat, and walked on, although the darkness and storm increased every minute, and the thunder burst with terrific crashes over my head. It was echoed from Saleve, the Juras, and the Alps of Savoy. Vivid flashes of lightning dazzled my eyes, illuminating the lake, making it appear like a vast sheet of fire. Then for an instant everything went dark, until my eyes could recover from the blinding lightning. The storm—as is often the case in Switzerland—appeared simultaneously in various parts of the heavens. The most violent storm hung exactly north of the town, over the part of the lake between the promontory of Belrive and the village of Copet. Another storm enlightened Jura with faint flashes; and another darkened and sometimes disclosed the Mole, a peaked mountain to the east of the lake.

While I watched the tempest—so beautiful yet terrifying—I kept walking quickly. This noble war in the sky excited me. I clapped my hands, and shouted out loud, "William, dear angel! This is your funeral—this your dirge!"

As I said these words, in the gloom ahead of me, I dimly saw a figure creep from behind a clump of trees. I stood and stared, frozen in my spot by terror and fury. I could not be mistaken. A flash of lightning showed the object, and revealed its shape plainly to me—its gigantic stature, and its hideously inhuman deformity instantly told me that it was the *wretch*, the filthy *demon*, to whom I had given life. Why was he there? Could he be (I shuddered at the conception) the murderer of my brother? No sooner did that idea cross my imagination, than I became

---

? *What are some things this imagery of the lightning might signify?*

✔ *Saleve and the Juras are mountains in the Alps range. Savoy was an independent principality that was later absorbed into France.*

✔ *This is possibly the first of many allusions to John Milton's* Paradise Lost *in which Hell is depicted as a lake of liquid fire that gives off heat but no light.*

? *Why is Mary Shelley making such a point of pinpointing where Victor is geographically?*

✔ *A dirge is a funeral march.*

✔ *Note the strong coincidence that Victor should see his creature for the first time since he abandoned it so close to his home. Even modern-day popular literature relies a great deal on coincidence.*

convinced that it was true. My teeth chattered, and I was forced to lean against a tree for support. The figure passed me quickly, and I lost it in the gloom.

Nothing human could have destroyed the fair child. HE was the murderer! I could not doubt it. The mere thought of it was its own proof. I thought of pursuing the devil, but it would have been useless. Another flash revealed him hanging among the rocks of the nearly perpendicular ascent of Mont Saleve, a hill that bounds Plainpalais on the south. He soon reached the summit and disappeared.

I remained motionless. The thunder stopped, but the rain continued, and the scene was cloaked in utter darkness. I replayed in my mind everything I had tried so hard to forget—the whole train of my progress toward the creation, the monster's appearance at my bedside and its departure. Nearly two years had passed since that night on which he first received life—and was this his first crime?

Alas! I had turned loose into the world a degenerate brute, who enjoyed slaughter and torture. Had he not murdered my brother?

No one can understand the anguish I suffered that night, which I spent—cold and wet—in the open air. But I was completely unaware of the weather. My imagination burned with scenes of evil and despair. I thought about the being that I had cast among mankind, and had given the Will and Power to commit acts of horror, such as the cruel, cruel murder of my brother. He was my own vampire, my own spirit let loose from the grave, forced to destroy all that was dear to me.

Day dawned; and I walked toward the town. The gates were open, and I hurried to my father's house. My first thought was to reveal what I knew of the murderer, and demand that the authorities pursue the creature immediately. But I paused when I thought about the story that I had to tell. A Being that I myself had formed, and brought to life had met me at midnight among the rocks of an inaccessible mountain. I remembered the nervous fever with which I had been seized at just the time that I dated my creation, and which would make the tale—which would sound utterly impossible as it was—sound like a

Having the creature scale a nearly perpendicular mountainside shows his extraordinary physical abilities.

The party visiting Lord Byron in Switzerland in 1816, Mary Shelley began Frankenstein, *included John William Polidori who was just beginning his book,* The Vampyre; a Tale. *This would become one of the first popular vampire stories and would set the tone for most of the future's vampire literature, including Bram Stoker's* Dracula *(1897).*

feverish delusion. I knew full well that—had anyone else told me such a story—I would have thought the teller was insane. Besides, even if anyone *did* believe my story, the Creature itself would be able to outrun and outclimb even the most skilled search party.

It was about five in the morning when I entered my father's house. I told the servants not to disturb the family, and went into the library to greet them when they awoke.

The six years that had passed seemed to be almost a dream except for the undeniable fact of my brother's death, and I stood in the same place where I had last embraced my father before leaving for Ingolstadt. I looked at the portrait of my mother, which stood over the mantelpiece. It was an historical subject, painted at my father's request, and represented Caroline Beaufort kneeling by the coffin of her dead father. Her clothing was rustic, and her cheek was pale, but the painting was more beautiful and dignified than horrible and mournful. Below this picture was a miniature of William, and I cried furiously when I looked at it. While I was still crying, Ernest entered. He had heard me arrive, and hurried to welcome me.

❂ Notice Mary Shelley's preoccupation and fascination with death.

"Welcome home, Victor," he said. "How I wish you had come three months ago, when you would have found us all happy. You come to us now to share a misery that nothing can alleviate. I dearly hope your being here will help Father. He seems to be sinking under his misfortune. I also hope you'll be able to persuade poor Elizabeth to stop her pointless self-accusations. Poor William! He was our darling and our pride!"

A flood of tears fell from my brother's eyes, and a horrible sense of agony nearly overpowered me. Before, I had only *imagined* the wretchedness of my desolated home, but now the *reality* came on me as a new—and not less terrible—disaster. I made an effort to calm Ernest, and tried to learn more about the condition of my father and my adopted cousin.

"She most of all requires consolation" he told me. "She accuses herself of having caused William's death, and it has made her miserable. But since they've found the murderer—"

"They've found the murderer? Good God! How can that be? Who could possibly follow him? It is impossible.

One might as well chase the wind. I just saw him. He was free last night!"

"I don't know what you mean," replied my brother, perplexed, "but to know who murdered our brother only makes us even more miserable. No one would believe it at first. Even now Elizabeth will not be convinced, despite all the evidence. Indeed, who could possibly believe that Justine Moritz—who was so kind-hearted, and beloved by all of us—could suddenly become so capable of so frightful, so appalling a crime?"

"Justine Moritz! Poor, poor girl, is she the accused? But it is wrong! Everyone must know that. Surely no one really believes it, Ernest?"

"No one did at first, but several things have happened, that have almost forced us to believe it is she. Her own behavior seems to indicate her guilt. But her trial is today, so you will hear everything."

He then told me that the morning on which the murder had been discovered, Justine became ill, and was confined to her bed for several days. During her illness, one of the servants just happened to examine the clothes she had worn on the night of the murder and found the picture of my mother—which we'd suspected had been what enticed the murderer—in her pocket. This servant showed it to one of the others, who went straight to the judge, without saying a word to any of the family. Based on their depositions, Justine was arrested. When she was charged, her confusion confirmed suspicion.

This was a strange tale, but it did not convince me. I said to Ernest frankly, "You are all mistaken. I know the murderer. Justine—poor, good Justine—is innocent."

Just then my father entered. I saw the unhappiness deep in his face, but he tried to welcome me cheerfully. After we had exchanged our mournful greeting, I think he would have changed the subject of our conversation, had Ernest not exclaimed, "Good God, papa! Victor says that he knows who was the murderer of poor William."

"We do also, unfortunately," replied my father. "I think I would rather have been forever ignorant of the culprit than to have discovered so much evil and ingratitude in someone I loved so much."

"My dear father, you are wrong. Justine is innocent."

Remember that Mary Shelley introduced Justine to the reader in a letter from Elizabeth in the last chapter.

"If she is, God forbid that she should be found guilty. She is to be tried today, and I hope—I sincerely hope— that she will be acquitted."

This speech calmed me. I was firmly convinced that Justine was innocent of this murder. No human being had killed my brother. I had no fear, therefore, that any circumstantial evidence strong enough to convict her could be brought forward. My tale was not something I could announce publicly. It would be dismissed as madness. Who else, but I, the creator, could believe that such a being as my Creature could truly exist? Elizabeth soon joined us. Time had indeed changed her since I last saw her. It had blessed her with a loveliness far beyond the prettiness of her childhood. Her face was still honest and lively, but these virtues were blended with wisdom. She welcomed me very warmly. "Your arrival, my dear cousin," she said, "fills me with hope. Perhaps you will be able to acquit poor, innocent Justine. Who is safe, if *she* can be convicted? I am as convinced of her innocence as I am of my own. We have been double unlucky—first to lose dear, dear William and then to lose Justine in this horrible, horrible way. If she is condemned, I will never know joy again. But she will not, I am *sure* she will not. And I *will* be happy again, even after the sad death of my little William."

"She *is* innocent, Elizabeth," I said, "and that will be proved. Have no fear, but be happy in the anticipation of Justine's release."

"How kind and generous you are! Everyone else believes in her guilt, and that made me miserable, for I knew that it was impossible that she would do such a thing. And to see everyone else so certain of her guilt has made me most unhappy." She wept.

"Dearest niece," said my father, "dry your tears. If she is, indeed innocent, then you can trust the justice of our laws."

> ❷ Why doesn't Victor feel it is important to tell about the Creature in order to free Justine?

> ❷ What is potentially ironic about this statement?

You weep now, unhappy ones, but these will not be your last tears.

VICTOR FRANKENSTEIN
FRANKENSTEIN, CHAPTER 8

Frankenstein

or The Modern Prometheus

❧

MARY SHELLEY

CHAPTER 8

We passed a few sad hours until eleven o'clock, when the trial was to begin. As my father and the rest of the family had been called to appear as witnesses, I accompanied them to the court. Throughout this entire mockery of justice I suffered living torture. This trial would determine whether my own foolish pride would result in the death of *two* fellow human beings—one a smiling babe full of innocence and joy, the other even more dreadfully murdered, bearing forever the reputation of an ingrate and a murderer. Justine was a good girl. She had the promise of a happy life before her. But it was all to be buried in a disreputable grave, and I was the cause! I would rather have confessed to the murder a thousand times, but I hadn't even been there when it was committed. Such a claim would have been considered the ravings of a madman and would not have vindicated Justine.

The girl appeared calm. She was dressed in a black mourning dress, and her expression—always attractive— was made exquisitely beautiful by her solemn feelings. Yet she appeared confident in her innocence and did not tremble, even though she was gazed on and hated by thousands. Any mercy any of the spectators may have felt for her was shattered by the enormity of the crime she was supposed to have committed. She was composed, yet her tranquility was obviously forced, and—since her earlier confusion had been accepted as proof of her guilt—she made an effort to put up a brave front. When she entered the court, she threw her eyes round it and quickly found where we were seated. A tear seemed to dim her eye when she saw us, but she quickly recovered herself. The sorrowful love with which she looked at us proved to all of us her guiltlessness.

The trial began, and after the prosecutor stated the charge, several witnesses were called. Several strange facts conspired against her, which might have shaken the belief of anyone who did not have the proof of her innocence that I had. She had been out the whole night on which the murder had been committed and toward morning had been seen by a market woman not far from the spot where the body was later discovered. The woman asked her what she was doing there, but she looked very strangely and returned a confused and unintelligible answer. She returned to the house about eight o'clock, and when she was asked where she had spent the night, she replied that she had been looking for William and demanded to know whether there had been any news. When she was shown the body, she became hysterical and lay in her bed for several days.

The picture that the servant had found in her pocket was then produced. Elizabeth was forced to testify—in a faltering voice—that it was the same picture which—only an hour earlier—she herself had given William to wear. At this, a murmur of horror and fury filled the court.

Justine was called on for her defense. As the trial had proceeded, her face had altered. Surprise, horror, and misery were strongly expressed. Sometimes she struggled with her tears, but when she testified, she collected her powers and spoke in an audible, although wavering, voice.

"God knows," she said, "how entirely I am innocent. But I do not expect that my claims of innocence should acquit me. I rest my innocence on a plain and simple explanation of the facts which have been presented against me, and I hope the integrity I have always shown

In United States criminal courts, the defendant must be proven guilty beyond "reasonable doubt."

will persuade my judges to give me the reasonable benefit of any doubt."

She then testified that, with Elizabeth's permission, she had passed the evening of the night on which the murder had been committed at the house of an aunt at Chene, a village about a league from Geneva. Returning around nine o'clock, she met a man who asked her if she had seen anything of the lost child. She was alarmed by this news and spent several hours looking for him. Then the gates of Geneva were shut, and she was forced to remain several hours of the night in a barn. She was not willing to disturb the owners—even though they knew her well—because of the late hour. She spent most of the night sitting awake in this barn. Toward morning she thought she might have slept for a few minutes. Some steps disturbed her, and she awoke. It was dawn, and she left the barn to continue looking for William. If she had gone near the spot where his body lay, she did not know it. It was no mystery that the rude questioning of the market-woman had confused her, since she had not really slept all night, and she was still worried about William.

She could not offer any explanation of how she came to have the picture in her pocket.

"I know," she continued, "that this one piece of evidence casts all of my testimony into doubt, but I have no explanation. I can only *guess* how it might have come to be in my pocket. But here also I am frustrated. I have no enemies that I know of, and no one would be so utterly wicked as to destroy me for no reason at all. Did the murderer place it there? I don't know when he could have. And why would he have stolen the locket, only to part with it again so soon?

"I commit myself to the mercy of my judges, yet I see no reason for hope. I do beg for permission to have a few witnesses questioned about my character. If their testimony does not outweigh my supposed guilt, then I must be condemned. But I swear by everything that is holy that I am innocent."

Several witnesses were called who had known Justine for many years, and they spoke well of her. Their fear of the crowd's anger and hatred, however, made their testimony seem nervous and feeble. Elizabeth feared she would not have the strength and comfort to testify. Still, she summoned up the courage and asked for permission to address the court.

"I am," she said, "the cousin of William Frankenstein, the child who was murdered—or rather his sister—for I was educated by and have lived with his parents since long before he was born. You may think it inappropriate for a member of the victim's family to come forward at the trial of the accused murderer, but when I see a fellow creature about to perish through the cowardice of her supposed friends, I wish to be allowed to speak, tell what I know of her character. I am well acquainted with the accused. I have lived in the same house with her—at one time for five years, and at another for nearly two years. During all that time she seemed to be the most loving and kind of human creatures. She nursed Madame Frankenstein—my aunt—in her last illness, with great affection and care. Afterwards she attended her *own* mother during a serious illness. Everyone who knew her commented on the love and devotion with which she cared for the mother who had been so cruel to her. After her mother died, she again lived in my uncle's house, where she was beloved by all the family. She was warmly attached to the child who is now dead and loved him as a mother would. For my own part, I do not hesitate to say that—despite all the evidence produced against her—I am absolutely convinced of her innocence. She had no temptation for such an action. As to the trinket on which the chief proof rests, if she had truly wanted it, I would have willingly given it to her. That is how much I love her."

A tense but hushed murmur arose from the crowd, but it was not a murmur of support for poor Justine. The crowd was so angry at Justine's betrayal of those who had been nothing but loving toward her, that Elizabeth's speech served only to make Justine seem all the more ungrateful and evil. Justine herself wept as Elizabeth spoke, but she did not answer. My own anguish was extreme during the whole trial. I *knew* Justine was innocent. I did not doubt for a second that my Demon was the murderer of my brother, but could he have devised the means to cast suspicion on

Why do you suppose Victor never speaks up? What does this say about his character?

this innocent girl? I could not bear the situation, and when I realized that the voice of the people and the edicts of the judges had already condemned Justine, I rushed out of the court in agony. At that point, I knew I was suffering even more than poor, condemned Justine. She, at least, could rely on the knowledge that she was innocent, while I had to bear the weight of my guilt.

I passed a thoroughly wretched night. In the morning I went to the court. My lips and throat were parched. When the moment came, I was simply unable to ask the question I had gone to ask. But they knew who I was in the court and guessed my errand. The officers told me that the jury had indeed voted and reached a unanimous verdict of guilty—Justine was condemned.

I cannot even begin to describe how I felt. I had experienced sensations of horror before—and I have tried to express them adequately—but words cannot convey the heart-sickening despair I endured at that moment. The officer to whom I was speaking added that Justine had already confessed her guilt. "That evidence," he observed, "was hardly required in such a clear case, but I am happy about it. None of our judges likes to condemn a criminal on the basis of circumstantial evidence alone, no matter how convincing."

I was astounded. What could it mean that Justine had confessed? Had my eyes deceived me? Was I truly as mad as I feared everyone would believe me to be if I revealed what I suspected? I hurried home, and Elizabeth demanded the verdict.

"My cousin," I replied, "it is just as we expected. All judges would rather have ten innocent people suffer than allow one guilty to escape. But she has confessed."

This devastated poor Elizabeth, who had so believed in Justine's innocence. "Alas!" she said, "How can I ever believe in human goodness? Justine, whom I loved as a sister—how could she seem so innocent and yet betray us? She seemed incapable of cruelty or deception, and yet she has committed a murder."

Soon after, we received word that Justine had expressed a desire to see Elizabeth. My father did not want her to go, but left it up to her to decide for herself. "I will go,"

❷ Be aware of places where Mary Shelley might betray her Romantic anti-government sentiments.

✅ *Consider that, because of the Tragic Hero's flaw or hamartia, he is not necessarily a likeable or sympathetic character.*

✅ *According to traditional Roman Catholic doctrine, one must confess all of one's sins in order to receive absolution (total forgiveness) for them. Justine, of course, is reacting to a perversion of this doctrine; she was probably encouraged by her priest to confess to a sin she did not commit in order to be absolved and enter Heaven upon her death.*

✅ *Excommunication is the removal of an individual from the religious community and denying him or her all of the benefits of communion with the church. It was believed that excommunicated individuals could not enter Heaven.*

said Elizabeth after some careful thought. "Even though she is guilty. And you, Victor, will go with me. I cannot go alone."

The idea of this visit was torture to me, but I could not refuse. We entered the gloomy prison cell and saw Justine sitting on some straw at the far end. Her hands were chained, and her head rested on her knees. She rose when we entered, and when we were left alone with her, she threw herself at Elizabeth's feet, weeping bitterly. My cousin wept also.

"Oh, Justine!" she said. "Why did you rob me of my last consolation? I relied on your innocence, and although I was then very wretched, I was not as miserable as I am now."

"And do you also believe that I am so very, very wicked? Do you condemn me as a murderer, just as my enemies have?" Her voice was suffocated with sobs.

"Rise, my poor girl," said Elizabeth; "why do you kneel, if you are innocent? I am not one of your enemies. Despite all the evidence, I *believed* you innocent until I heard that you had confessed. If—as you say—your confession is untrue, then be assured, dear Justine, that nothing can shake my confidence in you for a moment, but you must explain your confession."

"I did confess, but I confessed a lie, that I might obtain absolution. But now that lie sits heavier in my heart than all my other sins combined. God forgive me! Ever since I was condemned, my confessor has attacked me. He has threatened me until I almost began to think that I was the monster he said I was. He threatened me with excommunication and hell fire in my last moments if I stubbornly insisted that I was innocent. Dear lady, I had no one to support me. Everyone believed that I was a murderess, fully deserving humiliation and condemnation. What could I do? In an evil hour I swore to a lie, and now I am truly miserable."

She paused, weeping, and then continued, "I thought how horrible it was, my sweet lady, that you would believe me capable of such a crime. No one but the devil himself could have done it. Dear William! Dearest blessed child! I soon shall see you again in Heaven, where we shall all be happy. That consoles me, going as I am to suffer disgrace and death."

"Oh, Justine! Forgive me for having distrusted you, for even a moment. Why did you confess? But do not mourn, dear girl. Do not fear. I will prove your innocence myself. I will melt the stony hearts of your enemies by my tears and prayers. You shall not die! You—my playmate, my companion, my sister—hang at the gallows? No! No! I never could survive such a horrible misfortune."

Justine shook her head mournfully. "I am not afraid to die," she said. "That pain is over. God strengthens me and gives me courage. I leave a sad and bitter world, and—if you would please remember me and think of me as of one *unjustly condemned*—then I can accept the fate awaiting me. Learn from me, dear lady, to submit patiently to the will of Heaven."

During this conversation I withdrew to a corner of the cell, where I could hide my anguish. Despair! Who dared talk of that? The poor victim, who was to die the very next day, felt nothing like the deep and bitter agony that I felt. I gnashed my teeth and ground them together, uttering a groan that came from my innermost soul. Justine started. When she saw me, she approached and said, "Dear sir, you are very kind to visit me. I hope *you* do not believe that I am guilty?"

I could not answer.

"No, Justine," said Elizabeth, "he is more convinced of your innocence than I was, for even when he heard that you had confessed, he did not believe it."

"I truly thank him. In these last moments I am so very grateful to anyone who thinks of me with kindness. How sweet is *any* affection to someone as wretched as I am! It takes away more than half my despair, and I feel I can die in peace now that my innocence is acknowledged by you, dear lady, and your cousin."

Thus the poor sufferer tried to comfort us, along with herself. She indeed gained the acceptance she desired. But I, the true murderer, felt the never-dying worm alive in my breast, allowing no hope or relief. Elizabeth also wept, but the source of her sorrow was innocence. Her tears were like a thin cloud that might pass over the moon

❷ *Describe the tone of this passage. Would you consider it to be pathos or bathos?*

✔ *Explain this simile.*

and hide it from view for a moment but cannot actually dim its brightness. My heart was dark and joyless to the core. I bore a hell within me that nothing could extinguish. We stayed several hours with Justine, and it was only with great difficulty that Elizabeth could tear herself away. "I wish," she cried, "that I could die with you. I cannot live in this miserable world."

Justine pretended an air of cheerfulness, while barely holding back her bitter tears. She embraced Elizabeth and said in a voice of half-suppressed emotion, "Farewell, sweet lady, dearest Elizabeth, my beloved and only friend. May Heaven—in its unending generosity—bless and preserve you. May this be the last misfortune that you will ever suffer! Live, and be happy, and make others so."

And on the next day Justine died. Elizabeth's heart-rending speech failed to sway the judges from their verdict. My passionate and angry appeals were wasted on them. And when I received their cold answers and heard the harsh, heartless reasoning of these men, my intention to tell the truth about the monster I had created vanished. I would have successfully convinced them of my insanity, but there was no way I could convince them of Justine's innocence. She was hanged that day as a murderess!

I forced myself to forget the torture of my own heart for a while and attend to my Elizabeth's deep and voiceless grief. This also was my doing! And my father's woe! Truly, I had desolated a home that had so recently been happy.

You weep now, unhappy ones, but these will not be your last tears! Again and again you shall raise the funeral wail, and the sound of your lamentations shall again and again be heard! Frankenstein, your son, your kinsman, your early, much-loved friend—he who would die for your sakes, who can be happy only when you are happy, who would be satisfied to spend the rest of his life serving you—he bids you weep, to shed countless tears!

These prophetic words rang in my ears as I witnessed the sorrow and despair of those I loved, and as I watered the graves of William and Justine with my own bitter tears.

Think and Discuss:

What is/are the true source(s) of the Frankenstein family's troubles?

Frankenstein

or The Modern Prometheus

MARY SHELLEY

CHAPTER 9

Nothing is more painful to the human mind than the dead and quiet boredom that follows highly emotional events, when the mind, heart, and soul are all numb. Justine was dead. She was at rest, but I was alive. The blood flowed freely in my veins, but an unending weight of despair and regret pressed on my heart. Sleep fled from my eyes. I wandered like an evil spirit, for I had committed deeds horrible beyond description. I *knew* still more evil consequences would be revealed. Still, my heart was full to overflowing with kindness and the love of virtue. I had begun life with kind and good intentions and had longed for the moment when I would put these intentions in practice and make myself useful to humanity. Now everything was ruined. Instead of that peace and deep satisfaction that would have been the result of my great success, I was seized by remorse and guilt, a hell of intense tortures such as no language can describe.

This state of mind affected my health, which had probably never fully recovered from my earlier illness. I shunned all companionship. Even the sounds of joy or satisfaction were torture to me. Solitude was my only comfort—deep, dark, deathlike solitude.

It hurt my father to see the change in my mood and habits. He tried to encourage me with strength and hope,

Again, this exaggerated emotional response is typical of both the Romantic and the Tragic Hero. This type of exaggeration is called hyperbole.

to help me beat off the dark cloud that hung over me. "Do you think, Victor," he asked, "that I don't also suffer? No one could love a child more than I loved your brother"—tears came into his eyes as he spoke—"but doesn't the appearance of excessive grief only add to the sorrow of those around us? Doesn't it also hurt yourself since such extreme sorrow prevents any enjoyment of life. You should find some way to make yourself useful to someone else."

While I understood my father's motive, there was no way I could do what he was suggesting. I would have been the first to hide my grief and console my friends if my sorrow had not also been mingled with guilt and bitterness and terror. Now I could only answer my father with a look of despair and simply try to stay out of his way.

About this time we retired to our house at Belrive. This change was particularly agreeable to me. I had begun to resent the way the city gates were shut every night precisely at ten o'clock so that I could not stay out on the lake any later. I was now free. Often—after the rest of the family had retired for the night—I took the boat and spent many hours on the water. Sometimes I set my sails and allowed myself to be carried by the wind. Other times, after rowing into the middle of the lake, I simply let the boat float and surrendered to my own miserable thoughts. I was often tempted—when everything else was at peace all around me—to plunge into the silent lake and let the waters drown me and end my troubles forever. But when I thought of Elizabeth, and how much I loved her, and how her life was so intricately bound up with mine, I could not go through with it. I also thought of my father and surviving brother. How could I desert them, leaving them exposed and unprotected to the viciousness of the monster I had let loose among them?

At these moments I wept bitterly and wished that I could find peace, if only so that I could provide them consolation and happiness. But that could not be. My regret extinguished every hope. I had committed an irreversible evil, and I lived in daily fear that the monster I had created would perform some new wickedness. I had a vague dread that it was not over and that he would still

Note the developing self-destructive tendency typical of the Romantic hero.

This internal conflict is typical of both the Romantic and Tragic Hero.

do something so horrible that its enormity would dwarf the past. There was always reason to fear while anything I loved remained behind. You cannot possibly understand how utterly I hated this fiend. When I thought of him, I gnashed my teeth, my eyes became inflamed, and I wished more than anything to extinguish that life which I had so thoughtlessly bestowed. When I thought of his crimes and malice, my hatred and desire for revenge were unlimited. I would have climbed the highest peak of the Andes, if I could have hurled him to their base. I wished to see him again, so that I could avenge the deaths of William and Justine. Our house was a house of mourning. My father's health was severely hurt by the horror of these recent events. Elizabeth was sad and gloomy, no longer taking any delight in what she used to enjoy. She acted as if it would be a sin to admit to any small pleasure at all. Eternal woe and tears were the only just tribute to innocence so utterly destroyed. She was no longer that happy creature who had once wandered with me on the banks of the lake and talked with joy about our future. She had experienced sorrow, she had witnessed injustice, and these seemed to make it impossible for her ever again to find pleasure in this world.

"When I think about Justine's miserable death," she said, "I no longer see the world as I used to. Before, I believed the stories of injustice that I read in books or heard from others were the tales of ancient days or imaginary evils, far away and more familiar to reason than to the imagination. But now misery has come home, and men appear to me like monsters thirsting for each other's blood. Yet I know that that is unfair. Everybody *believed* that poor girl to be guilty. And if she could have committed the crime for which she suffered, she would indeed have been the most depraved of human creatures. For the sake of a few jewels, to murder the son of her benefactor and friend, a child whom she had nursed from birth, and appeared to love as if he had been her own! I am thoroughly opposed to killing a human being for any reason whatsoever, but certainly I would agree that such a creature would be unfit for human society.

"But she was innocent. I believe she was innocent—as do you—and that strengthens my dislike of humanity.

Remember that the "you" Victor is addressing is Captain Walton.

What is ironic about Victor's attitude toward his Creature?

This disillusionment is a psychological loss of innocence that mirrors Original Sin and humanity's expulsion from the Garden of Eden—from a perfect world into a very imperfect one.

Remember that in the story of the expulsion from Eden, Adam and Eve ate from the Tree of the Knowledge of Good and Evil. From a psychological standpoint, it is their newfound awareness of evil that constitutes the Fall.

❷ *What is the irony here?*

❷ *Elizabeth is expressing typical Romantic ideas that true love between equals can create a Heaven even in the midst of Hell.*

Alas! Victor, when a lie can look so much like the truth, who can be assured of happiness? I feel as if I were walking on the edge of a cliff, and thousands of madmen are crowding and trying to plunge me into the abyss. William and Justine were assassinated, and their murderer walks free. He walks free. He is, perhaps, a respected member of the community. But even if *I* were the one condemned to hang for the same crimes, I would not change places with such a wretch."

I listened to her in agony. I *was* the true murderer, if not in actual deed, then certainly in effect. Elizabeth saw the anguish in my face, and—kindly taking my hand—said, "My dear friend, you must calm yourself. These events have affected me—God knows how deeply—but I am not as wretched as you are. There is an expression of despair, and sometimes of revenge, in your face that makes me tremble. Dear Victor, banish these dark passions. Remember the friends around you, who focus all their hopes in you. Can we no longer make you happy? As long as we love, as long as we are true to each other, in this land of peace and beauty, we will be blessed with tranquility—what can disturb our peace?"

But her words could not chase away the fiend that lurked in my heart. Even as she spoke, I drew close to her, as if I feared that the Destroyer was nearby and would take her from me.

Thus nothing: neither the tenderness of friendship, nor the beauty of Earth and Heaven could redeem my soul from woe. Words and gestures of love had no effect. A cloud hung over me that no kindly influence could penetrate. I was like a wounded deer, dragging itself to some hidden glade—to gaze upon the arrow that had wounded it—and to die.

Sometimes I could cope with my sullen despair, but sometimes the turbulent passions of my soul drove me to seek some relief from my intolerable sensations by hiking among the mountains. On one such hike, I found myself in a rugged Alpine valley, seeking to forget my sorrow in its stark beauty. I wandered toward the valley of Chamounix. I had visited it frequently during my boyhood. Six years had passed since then. *I* was a wreck, but the savage beauty of the scene had not changed.

I rode the first part of my journey on horseback, but afterwards hired a mule, a more sure-footed animal, less liable to receive injury on these rugged roads. The weather was fine. It was about the middle of August, nearly two months after the death of Justine. That miserable period from which I dated all of my problems. The weight on my soul was noticeably lighter as I descended into the ravine of Arve. The immense mountains and precipices that overhung me on every side, the sound of the river raging among the rocks, and the dashing of the waterfalls around spoke of a power mighty as Omnipotence—and I ceased to fear or to bend before any being less almighty. Then, as I climbed to the heights, the valley took on a more magnificent and astonishing character. Ruined castles hanging on the precipices of piney mountains, the impulsive Arve, and cottages here and there peeping out from among the trees formed a scene of incredible beauty. But the mighty Alps deepened the beauty of the scene into something almost holy. The mountains' white and shining pyramids and domes towered above all, as if they belonged to another earth and were the habitations of another race of beings.

I passed the Pelissier bridge, where the ravine, which the river forms, opened before me, and I began to climb the mountain that overhangs it. Soon after, I entered the valley of Chamounix. This valley is more wonderful and sublime, but not as beautiful and picturesque as the valley of Servox, through which I had just passed. The high and snowy mountains were its immediate boundaries, but I saw no more ruined castles and fertile fields. Immense glaciers approached the road. I heard the rumbling thunder of the falling avalanche and marked the smoke of its passage. Mont Blanc, supreme and magnificent, raised itself even higher than the surrounding needle-sharp peaks, and its tremendous dome overlooked the valley.

I felt a tingling, long-lost sense of pleasure during this journey. Some turn in the road, something new that I would suddenly see and recognize, all reminded me of days gone by, and the lighthearted fun of boyhood. The very winds whispered in soothing accents, and loving, motherly Nature coaxed me to weep no more.

Then, just as suddenly, I would find myself

This is an allusion to Romantic poet William Wordsworth's poem "Lines Written a Few Miles above Tintern Abbey" in which he revisits a favorite spot, full of the beauty of Nature, after a five years' absence.

Pantheism is the belief that God exists in all things. The Romantics' view of Nature was very close to Pantheism.

Note the popular Gothic settings.

What does Victor's choice of words seem to foreshadow?

This is the location where Percey Shelley wrote his famous poem, "Mont Blanc: Lines Written in the Vale of Chamouni." This poem celebrates the rugged and awesome beauty of Nature and its effect on human thought and emotions.

The Romantics saw a clear difference between the merely picturesque— country cottages, white picket fences, vines of flowers—and the sublimely beautiful—the rugged power of mountain peaks, raging rivers, etc.

grieving again, indulging in all the misery of reflection. So I spurred on my mule, always trying so to forget the world, my fears, and—most of all—myself.

Eventually I arrived at the village of Chamounix. I was exhausted—mentally, physically, and emotionally. For a short while, I remained at the window watching the pallid lightning that played above Mont Blanc and listening to the rushing of the Arve, which followed its noisy way beneath. These sounds acted like a lullaby, and when I placed my head on my pillow, sleep crept over me. I felt it as it came and blessed the giver of total forgetfulness.

Research Opportunity:

Look up examples of Romantic art.

Writing Opportunity:

Compare the Romantic artist's portrayal of Nature with the Romantic writer's.

Frankenstein
or The Modern Prometheus

MARY SHELLEY

CHAPTER 10

I spent the following day roaming through the valley. I stood beside the sources of the Arveiron, which flow from a glacier, slowly moving down from the summit of the hills to barricade the valley. The abrupt sides of vast mountains were before me, the icy wall of the glacier looming over me. A few shattered pines were scattered around, and the solemn silence of this glorious hall of Imperial Nature was broken only by the thunder of an avalanche or the cracking of the accumulated ice, echoing through the mountains. These sublime and magnificent scenes gave me great consolation. They elevated me from all common feelings, and—although they did not remove my grief—they calmed it. To some extent, they also distracted my mind from the thoughts that had plagued it for the last month. When I lay myself down to rest that night, I slept deeply and, in my sleep, I dreamed that these beautiful forms of Nature gathered around me like nurses—the unstained snowy mountaintop, the glittering pinnacle, the pine woods, and ragged bare ravine, the eagle, soaring amidst the clouds—they all gathered round me and begged me to be at peace.

Where had they fled when, the next morning, I awoke? Their comfort was gone with the night, and a dark melancholy clouded every thought. The rain was pouring in torrents, and thick mists hid the summits of the

Again, the Gothic love of foul weather. Notice how the fog and clouds not only hide the mountain peaks from view, but they also hide the healing power of viewing the peaks.

mountains, along with their comforting presence. Still, I would penetrate their misty veil and seek them in their cloudy hiding places. What were rain and storm to me? My mule was brought to the door, and I resolved to climb to the summit of Montanvert. I remembered the effect it had produced on my mind when I first saw it. It had then filled me with a sublime ecstasy that gave wings to the soul and allowed it to soar from this puzzling world to a world of Light and Joy. The sight of the awful and majestic in nature had indeed always the effect of calming my mind and allowing me to forget the passing cares of life. I decided to go without a guide, for I was very familiar with the path, and the presence of another person would destroy the solitary grandeur of the scene for me.

The ascent is steep, but the path is cut into continual and short windings, which enable you to overcome the steepness of the mountain. It is a wonderfully desolate scene. In a thousand places you can see the traces of the winter avalanche, where trees lie broken and scattered on the ground, some entirely destroyed, others bent, leaning on rocks or lying across other trees. As you climb still higher, ravines of snow, down which stones continually roll from above, intersect the path. One of them is particularly dangerous, as the slightest sound—even speaking in a loud voice—is enough to bring down an avalanche and kill the speaker. The pines are not tall or luxuriant, but they are dismal and add an air of serenity to the scene. I looked on the valley beneath, where vast mists were rising from the rivers and curling in thick wreaths around the opposite mountains, their summits hiding in the swirling clouds. Rain poured from the dark sky and added to the deep, deep sadness I sensed in the objects around me. Alas! Why do humans brag about our supposed superior awareness? If all we knew were hunger, thirst, and other purely physical desires, we might be nearly free. Instead we are moved by every wind that blows and thoughts we cannot control:

> We rest; a dream has power to poison sleep.
> We rise; one wand'ring thought pollutes the day.
> We feel, conceive, or reason; laugh or weep,
> Embrace fond woe, or cast our cares away;
> It is the same: for, be it joy or sorrow,

Margin notes:

❓ *Consider the phrase "sublime ecstasy." What does it mean?*

✅ *Define awful.*

✅ *Don't miss Mary Shelley's vivid imagery in this passage.*

✅ *To give human thoughts and emotions to non-human things is called a pathetic fallacy.*

The path of its departure still is free.
Man's yesterday may ne'er be like his morrow;
Naught may endure but mutability!

✔ *These are the last two stanzas of Percy Shelley's poem "Mutability," published in 1816, but probably written in 1814.*

It was nearly noon when I arrived at the top. For some time I sat on the rock that overlooks the sea of ice—shrouded in mist—and the surrounding mountains. Before too long, a breeze dissipated the cloud, and I descended onto the glacier. The surface is very uneven, rising and falling like the waves of a troubled sea. The field of ice is barely a league wide, but it took me nearly two hours to cross it. The opposite mountain is a bare perpendicular rock. From the side where I now stood Montanvert was exactly opposite, at the distance of a league. And above it rose Mont Blanc, in awful majesty. I stayed in a hollow in the rock, gazing on this wonderful and stupendous scene. The vast river of ice wound its way around the mountains. Their icy and glittering peaks shone in the sunlight over the clouds. My heart—which had been sorrowful—now swelled with something like joy. I shouted out loud, "Wandering spirits, if you are now awake, let me have this brief moment of happiness, or take me, as your companion, away from the joys of life."

✔ *A league is approximately three miles.*

As I said this, I suddenly saw the figure of a man, quite far away, coming toward me with superhuman speed. He bounded over the crevices in the ice, among which I had walked with caution. As he approached, I saw he was abnormally tall. I felt faint, but I was quickly restored by the icy mountain wind. As the creature came nearer, I recognized him as the wretch that I had created. I trembled with rage and horror, determined to engage him in mortal combat. He approached. His face was filled with bitter anguish, combined with evil and hatred. He was ugly—almost too ugly to be seen by human eyes. But I scarcely noticed. My own rage and hatred rendering me speechless, before I recovered to hurl my accusations at him.

✔ *Percy Shelley and John Keats, another late Romantic poet, often expressed a desire to die during a moment of intense joy, so as not to have to live through the end of the moment.*

"Devil," I exclaimed, "do you dare approach me? Do not you fear my vengeance? Get away, vile insect! Or rather, stay, that I may trample you to dust! And, oh! That I could, by killing you, restore those victims whom you have so diabolically murdered!"

"I expected this," said the demon. "All men hate the wretched, so must I be hated, since I am the most miserable of all living things! Even you, my creator, detest and spurn me. But the ties that bind us together can only be broken by the death of one of us. And now you want to kill me. How dare you play with life? Do whatever you want with me, as I will with you and the rest of mankind. If you agree to my conditions, I will leave you and yours at peace. But if you refuse, I will splatter the earth with the blood of your remaining friends."

"Fiend! Monster! The tortures of Hell are too good for you. Wretched devil! You condemn me for your creation, then let me extinguish the spark which I so stupidly bestowed."

My rage knew no limit. I sprang at him, driven by everything that can fuel hatred of one being for another.

He easily eluded me and said, "Be calm! I ask only that you hear me out before you give vent to your hatred. Have I not suffered enough? Life—anguished though it may be—is dear to me, and I will defend it. Remember, you made me more powerful than yourself. I am taller. I have more fluidity of motion. But I won't give in to the temptation to fight you. I am your creature, and I will be your servant if you will perform your part, which is no less than what you owe me. Oh, Frankenstein, you cannot be fair to others while trampling upon me—to whom you *most* owe justice, even mercy and affection. Remember that *I am your creature*. I ought to be Adam, but instead I'm the fallen angel, whom you punished before I did anything wrong. Everywhere I look, I see happiness, from which I alone am completely excluded. I *was* kind and good. Suffering made me a fiend. Make me happy, and I shall again be virtuous."

"Go away! I will *not* hear you. There can be nothing between you and me; we are enemies. Go away, or let us try our strength in a fight, in which one of us must die."

"How can I persuade you? Will nothing make you look at me with sympathy, with goodness, with compassion? Believe me, Frankenstein, my soul once glowed with love and humanity. But am I not alone—miserably alone? You, my very creator, hate me. What hope do I have with your

❓ *What is your first impression of the Creature?*

✔ *This is another allusion to the story of Adam in the Old Testament, especially as it is told in John Milton's* Paradise Lost, *in which the war between God and Lucifer is narrated in vivid detail, and in which Lucifer/Satan is a dynamic and fascinating character.*

fellow humans, who owe me nothing? They reject me and hate me. I have wandered here many days. The caves of ice are my home—the only home which your humans do not begrudge me. These bleak skies are kinder to me than your fellow beings. If the multitude of humankind knew of my existence, they too would rise up in arms, determined to destroy me. Shall I not then hate those who hate me? I will make no deals with my enemies. I am miserable, and they shall share my misery. Yet it is in your power to help me, and save them from this evil, or else you and your family—and *thousands* of others—will be swallowed up in the tempest of my wrath. Listen to me with compassion, and do not despise me. Listen to my tale, and then judge what I deserve. But hear me. Even the guilty are allowed to speak in their own defense before they are condemned. Listen to me, Frankenstein. You accuse me of murder, and yet you would—with a clear conscience—destroy your own creature. Now is *that* an example of your justice? And yet, I don't ask you to spare me, only listen to me. Then, if you still want to destroy me, and you think you *can* destroy me, I encourage you to try."

"Why do you force me to remember," I rejoined, "my greatest regret and guilt? Cursed be the day that you first saw light! Cursed be these hands that formed you! You have made me more miserable than I even have words to describe. I can't even think whether I have been just to you or not. Go away! Remove your ugly form from my sight."

"Here, I relieve your sight, my creator," he said, and placed his hated hands over my eyes. I pushed them away violently. "It is easy for me to take from you a sight which you despise. But you can still listen to me and grant me your compassion. By the virtues that I once possessed, I *demand* this from you. Hear my tale. It is long and strange, and since the cold is too extreme for you to tolerate, come to my hut on the mountain. The sun is yet high in the heavens. Before it sets, you will have heard my story and can decide. It is up to you whether I forever leave the company of man and lead a harmless life, or become the plague of humanity and the author of your own speedy ruin."

❷ *Who's right here? Why?*

As he said this, he led the way across the ice. I followed. My heart was full, and I did not answer him, but as I proceeded, I considered his various arguments and decided at least to listen to his tale. I was urged partly by curiosity and partly by compassion. I had, from the first, assumed he was my brother's murderer, and I eagerly sought the truth. But I also began to realize, for the first time, the duties of a creator toward his creature—to make him happy before complaining of his wickedness. And so I agreed to his demand. We crossed the ice and climbed the opposite rock. The air was cold, and the rain fell. We entered the hut, the fiend with an air of triumph, I with a heavy heart and depressed spirits. But I agreed to listen, and sat by the fire that my loathsome companion had lighted. He then began his tale:

✔ *This is an early statement of a theme that would become even more prominent later in the nineteenth century—that the causes of human evil were poverty and misery, not the "intrinsic nature" of the individual. If you could eliminate poverty, you would eliminate crime.*

Frankenstein
or The Modern Prometheus

❦

MARY SHELLEY

CHAPTER 11

"It is hard for me to remember my first days. Everything is confused and vague. A strange assortment of sensations assaulted me. I saw, felt, heard, and smelled all at the same time without being able to make sense of what I was experiencing. It was a long time before I learned to distinguish my various senses. Gradually, I remember, a strong light forced me to shut my eyes. The resulting darkness frightened me, but when I opened my eyes again, I again saw the light. I walked and, I believe, descended. Suddenly there was a change in my perceptions. Before, dark and opaque objects had surrounded me, but I now found that I could wander around at liberty, unhindered by any obstacle. The light became more and more oppressive to me, as did the heat. So I sought a place where I could find shade. This was the forest near Ingolstadt, and here I lay by the side of a brook resting from my fatigue, until I was overwhelmed by hunger and thirst. This roused me, and I ate some berries which I found hanging on the trees or lying on the ground. I quenched my thirst at the brook, and then lay down and fell asleep.

"It was dark when I awoke—and cold. I was frightened, finding myself so alone. Before I had fled your apartment, I had covered myself with some clothes, but these were not enough to protect me from the dampness of night. I

Consider the various levels of narration in this book: the Creature is talking to Victor; Victor is talking to Walton; and Walton is writing to his sister.

Even before the development of a science of psychology, Mary Shelley is trying to describe an infant's earliest impressions—something no human being remembers.

What has caused this change of perception? What is the Creature describing?

Remember that Victor first brought the Creature to life in November.

One of the Creature's first awarenesse is of Nature and the delight it brings him.

was a poor, helpless, miserable wretch. I knew nothing. But feeling pain invade me on all sides, I sat down and wept.

"Soon a gentle light crept across the sky and gave me a sensation of pleasure. I stood up and saw a softly-glowing form rise from among the trees—the moon. I gazed with a kind of wonder. It moved slowly, but it lit my path, and I again went out in search of berries. I was still cold when under one of the trees I found a huge cloak, with which I covered myself, and sat on the ground. I was incapable of thinking. Everything was confused. I felt light, and hunger, and thirst, and darkness. Countless sounds rang in my ears, and on all sides various scents greeted me. The only object that I could distinguish was the bright moon, and I fixed my eyes on that with pleasure.

"Several days and nights passed before I began to distinguish my sensations from each other. I gradually saw plainly the clear stream that supplied me with drink and the trees that shaded me with their leaves. I was delighted when I first discovered that a pleasant sound—which often saluted my ears—came from the throats of the little winged animals that had often blocked the light from my eyes. I also began to see the objects that surrounded me more clearly and to notice the boundary of the radiant roof of light that canopied me. Sometimes I tried to imitate the pleasant songs of the birds but was unable. Sometimes I wished to give voice to my emotion, but the rude and inarticulate sounds that broke from me frightened me into silence again.

"The moon disappeared from the night, then returned as a smaller version of itself, while I still remained in the forest. My senses were now distinct, and new ideas came into my mind every day. My eyes adjusted to the light, and I was able to see objects in their right forms. I distinguished the insect from the herb, and by degrees, one herb from another. I found that the sparrow uttered only harsh notes, while those of the blackbird and thrush were sweet and enticing.

"One oppressively cold day, I found a fire which had been left by some wandering beggars, and was overcome with delight at its warmth. In my joy, I thrust my hand into the live embers, but quickly drew it out again with a cry of pain. How strange, I thought, that the same cause should produce such opposite effects! I examined the fire, and found its source was wood. I quickly collected some branches, but they were wet and would not burn. Frustrated, I sat still watching the existing fire. The wet wood that I had placed near the heat eventually dried and caught fire. Now understanding the method, I collected a great quantity of wood, so that I could dry it and have a plentiful supply of fire. I was in great fear that my fire would burn out while I slept at night. I covered it carefully with dry wood and leaves and placed wet branches on it. Then, spreading my cloak, I lay on the ground and sank into sleep.

"The next morning, my first thought was to visit the fire. I uncovered it, and a gentle breeze quickly fanned it into a flame. Watching this, I fashioned a fan of branches, which reignited the embers. When night came again, I was pleased to find that the fire gave light as well as heat, and was useful for cooking as well. For I had found some of the meat that the travelers had left had been roasted and tasted much better than the berries I had gathered from the trees. I tried, therefore, to prepare my food in the same manner, placing it on the live embers. I learned that cooking spoiled the berries but greatly improved the roots and nuts.

Remember that the Creature was brought to life in November, so winter is approaching.

"Food, however, became scarce, and I often spent the whole day searching in vain for a few acorns to ease my hunger pangs. At this point, I resolved to leave the forest for some place where I could more easily fulfill my basic needs. I lamented the loss of the fire. I had discovered it by accident and, although I had learned how to keep it burning, I had no idea how to light a new one. I thought about whether there was any way to move the fire, but finally gave it up. Wrapping myself in my cloak, I started across the woods toward the setting sun. I walked for three days and eventually found myself in the open country. A great snowfall had taken place the night before, and the fields were of one uniform white, making everything look gloomy. My feet were chilled by this cold and damp stuff that covered the ground.

"It was about seven in the morning, and I needed food and shelter. Before long, I saw a small hut, on a small hill, obviously built for the convenience of some shepherd. This was a new sight to me, and I examined it with great curiosity. Finding the door open, I entered. An old man was sitting near a fire, over which he was preparing his breakfast. When he heard me enter, he turned. He saw me and shrieked loudly, running from the hut and across the fields faster than his weak, old body seemed able to run. Both the terror on his face and his running away surprised me. But I was enchanted by the hut. Here the snow and rain could not penetrate. The ground was dry, and it seemed as wonderful a place as Pandemonium was to the demons of hell after their sufferings in the lake of fire. I greedily devoured the remnants of the shepherd's breakfast, which consisted of bread, cheese, and milk. There was wine as well, which I did not care for. Then, overcome by fatigue, I made a bed out of some straw and fell asleep.

"It was noon when I awoke, and—warmed by the sun, which shone brightly on the white ground—I decided to continue my journey. I collected the remains of the peasant's breakfast in a bag I found and hiked across the fields for several hours. Finally, at sunset, I arrived at a village. It was like a miracle to me. The huts, the cottages, and the stately houses all seemed like perfect homes to me. The vegetables in the gardens, as well as the milk and cheese that I saw placed at the windows of some of the cottages, sharpened my appetite. I entered one cottage that looked neater and better kept than many of the others, but I had hardly placed my foot in the door before the children screamed, and one of the women fainted. The whole village was roused. Some ran away, some attacked me, throwing stones and sticks at me until I ran back into the open country, bruised, bleeding, and very, very frightened. I hid in a low shack, quite bare, and wretched in comparison with the palaces I had seen in the village. This shack was however, attached to a neat and pleasant cottage. After my experience in the village, however, I didn't dare to enter the cottage. My shack was made of wood, but was so low that it was hard for me even to sit up in it. The floor was bare ground, but it was dry. It was far from wind proof, but still proved to be an agreeable shelter from the snow and rain.

This is another allusion to John Milton's Paradise Lost. Pandaemonium *is the name of the great mansion in Hell in which the fallen angels lived. The name comes from Latin and means "the place of all demons." Today, the word* pandemonium *means any confusing or noisy uproar.*

"And so I lay down. I was, on the one hand, happy to have found a shelter. On the other hand, however, I was miserable, from both the cold and wet weather and the utter cruelty of humanity. As soon as morning dawned, I crept outside to inspect the attached cottage and decide whether I could stay in my newfound home. The shack leaned against the back of the cottage and was surrounded on the open sides by a pigsty and a clear pool of water. I covered every crevice through which I might be seen with stones and wood, but arranged them so that I could move them to come and go. All the light I had came through the pigsty, but that was enough for me.

"Having arranged my home and carpeted it with clean straw, I retired, for I saw the figure of a man in the distance, and I remembered too well how the humans had treated me the night before. I had already gotten enough food for that day—a loaf of coarse bread that I stole, and a cup with which I could drink the clear water in the pool by my home. The floor was a little raised, so that it did keep dry, and it was close to the chimney of the cottage so it kept nicely warm.

"Having most of my needs taken care of, I decided I would stay in this shack until I was forced out. It was indeed a paradise compared to the bleak forest. I ate my breakfast with pleasure and was about to get some water when I heard a step. Looking through a small chink in my wall, I saw a young creature, with a pail on her head, passing by. The girl was young and seemed gentle, unlike the cottagers and farmhouse servants I'd encountered. Yet she was poorly dressed in only a coarse blue petticoat and linen jacket. Her fair hair was plaited but not adorned. She looked patient, yet sad. I lost sight of her, and in about fifteen minutes, she returned carrying the pail, which was now partly filled with milk. As she walked along, seemingly unbothered by the burden, an even sadder-looking young man met her. Uttering a few sad sounds, he took the pail from her head and carried it to the cottage. She followed, and they disappeared. Soon I saw the young man cross the field behind the cottage, with some tools in his hand. The girl was also busy, sometimes in the house and sometimes in the yard.

"When I examined my new home, I found that one

of the cottage windows used to look into the shack but had been boarded up. There was a small chink in one of the boards, and I could just barely see through it into the cottage. The room I saw was whitewashed and clean but very bare of furniture. In one corner, near a small fire, sat an old man, sadly leaning his head on his hands. The young girl was busy tidying the cottage, but soon she took something out of a drawer and sat down beside the old man, handing the item to him. It was an instrument, which he began to play, producing sounds sweeter than the voice of the thrush or the nightingale. It was a lovely sight, even to me, who had no knowledge of beauty or kindness. The silver hair and gentle expression of the aged cottager won my admiration, while the gentle manners of the girl captivated me. He played a sweet, mournful song that made the young girl cry. The old man was completely unaware of her reaction until she sobbed loudly. He then pronounced a few sounds, and the fair creature knelt in front of him. He brought her back to her feet, smiling with such kindness and affection that I felt a strange and overpowering sensation. A mixture of pain and pleasure filled my heart, like I had never before experienced. It was a feeling very different from hunger or cold, warmth or food. I withdrew from the window, unable to bear these emotions.

"Soon after this the young man returned, carrying a bundle of firewood on his shoulders. The girl met him at the door, took the wood from him and brought it into the cottage, placing some of it on the fire. Then he showed her a large loaf and a piece of cheese. She seemed pleased and went into the garden for some roots and plants, which she placed in water, and then upon the fire. She returned to her housework, while the young man went into the garden, digging and pulling up roots. After about an hour, the young woman joined him, and they entered the cottage together.

"The old man, who had been quietly brooding, became animated upon seeing the two young people return, and they all sat down to eat. The meal was quickly devoured. The young woman again returned to her housework, the old man took a walk outside the cottage in the sun for a few minutes, leaning on the arm of the youth. There was

❷ *What is the Creature describing?*

a touching beauty in the contrast between the two men. One was old, with silver hair and an expression beaming with kindness and love. The younger was slight and graceful, with fine, even features, yet his eyes and attitude seemed very, very sad. The old man returned to the cottage, and the youth, with tools different from those he had used in the morning, walked across the fields.

"Night quickly fell, but to my amazement, I found that the cottagers had a way of creating their own light by the use of candles. It delighted me that the setting of the sun did not interfere with the pleasure of watching my human neighbors. In the evening the young girl and her companion kept themselves busy with a few tasks I did not understand, and the old man again took up the instrument which produced the divine sounds that had enchanted me in the morning. As soon as he finished, the youth began to utter sounds that were monotonous, resembling neither the harmony of the old man's instrument nor the songs of the birds. I later learned that he was reading aloud, but at that time I knew nothing of the science of words or letters.

"The family, after having been thus occupied for a short time, extinguished their lights and retired—as I guessed—to rest."

Research Opportunity:

Look up some information on early childhood development and a newborn's first impressions.

Writing Opportunity:

Write a description of your first weeks of life from your newborn perspective.

My spirits were lifted
by the charming appearance
of Nature. The past was blotted
from my memory, the present
was peaceful, and the future
bright with hope.

FRANKENSTEIN'S CREATURE
FRANKENSTEIN, CHAPTER 12

Frankenstein

or The Modern Prometheus

❦

MARY SHELLEY

CHAPTER 12

"I lay on my straw, but I could not sleep. I thought of the events of the day. I was moved by the gentle manners of these people, and I longed to join them, but dared not. I remembered too well how those barbarous villagers had treated me, so I resolved to remain quietly in my shack. I had no idea what course of action I would follow in the future. For now I would simply watch the family closely, and try to learn as much as I could about them.

"The cottagers arose the next morning before the sun. The young woman did some housework and prepared breakfast, and the youth departed after the meal.

"They followed the same basic routines as they had the day before. The young man was constantly working outdoors, and the girl in various chores inside the cottage. The old man—whom I soon realized was blind—spent his leisure time playing his instrument or thinking. The young people always showed him the utmost love and respect. They cared for him with tenderness and affection, and were rewarded with generous and kind smiles.

"But they were not entirely happy. Both the young man and girl—when unseen by the other—often seemed to weep. I saw no cause for their unhappiness, but I was deeply affected by it. If such lovely creatures could be unhappy, it was less strange that an ugly and unique being like me should be miserable. Yet why were these gentle beings unhappy? From what I could see, they possessed every luxury: a delightful house with a fire to warm them and food to eat. They had excellent clothes to wear, and they had each other's company, every day looking at one another with love. What did their tears imply? Did they really express pain? I had no idea, but I eventually was able to figure it out.

"It was some time before I realized that one of the causes of the anxiety of this loving family was extreme poverty. Their nourishment consisted entirely of the vegetables of their garden and the milk of one cow, which gave very little during the winter, since its masters could give it barely enough food to survive. I believe they often went hungry, especially the two younger cottagers, for several times they placed food before the old man when they had none for themselves.

"Their kindness moved me immensely. I would often sneak some of their food for myself during the night, but after I learned that I was depriving them, I abstained and satisfied myself with berries, nuts, and roots that I gathered from a nearby forest.

"I discovered another way to help them. I found that the youth spent much of his time collecting firewood, and during the night I often took his tools and chopped enough to last several days.

"I remember the astonishment of the young woman when she opened the door in the morning and saw the great pile of wood I'd left outside. The youth joined her and also expressed surprise. It pleased me that he did not go to the forest that day, but spent it in repairing the cottage and working in the garden.

"But I was to make an even more important discovery. I noticed that these people had a means to communicate with each other by articulate sounds. I noticed that the words they spoke sometimes produced pleasure or pain, smiles or sadness, in the hearers. This was indeed a godlike science, and I seriously wanted to learn it. But I was baffled in every attempt I made. Their pronunciation was quick, and the words—without any apparent connection to visible objects—left me no clue to unravel their meaning. With great effort I discovered the names for the most familiar objects: 'fire,' 'milk,' 'bread,' and 'wood.' I also

For centuries, it was believed that—in addition to the soul—what made humanity Godlike was language. The Old Testament story of the Tower of Babel explores the power of a humanity united by a single language. In this story, God creates different languages for different peoples to prevent their completing the tower and actually seeing God.

learned the names of the cottagers themselves. The youth and his companion seemed to have several names each, but the old man had only one, which was 'father.' The girl was called 'sister' or 'Agatha,' and the youth 'Felix,' 'brother,' or 'son.' I cannot describe the delight I felt when I learned the meanings of each of these sounds and was able to pronounce them. I recognized many other words without really knowing what they meant or to use them, such as 'good,' 'dearest,' and 'unhappy.'

"This is how I spent the winter. The gentleness and charm of the cottagers made me begin to love them. When they were unhappy, I felt depressed. When they rejoiced, I felt their joy. I saw few other human beings, and when others did appear, their harsh manners and rude behavior only served to prove to me the superiority of my friends. The old man often tried to encourage his children, as he called them, to cast off their melancholy. He would speak cheerfully, with an expression of goodness that would persuade even me. I listened with respect. Agatha's eyes sometimes filled with tears, which she tried to hide, but her father could always cheer her. It was not the same with Felix. He was always the saddest of the group, and even to my eyes, he appeared to have suffered more deeply than the rest of his family. But if his expression was more sorrowful, his voice was more cheerful than his sister's, especially when he addressed the old man.

"I can remember so many things that revealed the goodness of these people. In the midst of their poverty, Felix happily brought his sister the first little white flower that peeped out from beneath the snowy ground. Early in the morning, before she had risen, he cleared away the snow from her path to the milk house, drew water from the well, and brought in the firewood that—to his constant surprise—was always replaced by an invisible hand. During the day it seemed he would frequently work for a neighboring farmer, often leaving and not returning until dinner. At other times he worked in the garden, but since there was little to do in the frosty season, he would read to the old man and Agatha.

"This reading deeply puzzled me at first, but little by little, I discovered that he uttered many of the same sounds when he read as when he talked. I guessed that

The essential goodness of people, the ability to rise to the occasion and find happiness even in suffering are all Romantic ideals.

Remember that the Creature is forming all of these early impressions of the cottagers without language.

the paper held the symbols for speech, and I deeply longed to understand, but how was that possible when I didn't understand the sounds they corresponded to? I was slowly beginning to grasp spoken language, but not sufficiently for any kind of conversation, although I applied my whole mind to the effort. I easily realized that—while I longed to make myself known to the cottagers—I couldn't dare to try until I could speak to them. I hoped this might make them overlook my ugliness. By now I was well aware of how different I was from them.

"I had admired the appearance of my cottagers—their grace, beauty, and delicate complexions, but my own face terrified me when I saw its reflection in a pool. At first I pulled back, unable to believe that it was truly my own reflection. When I became fully convinced of my own monstrosity, I was filled with bitterness and dejection. Still, I could not yet even guess at how miserable my deformity would eventually make me and the desperate actions it would push me to.

"As the sun became warmer and the days longer, the snow vanished, and I saw the bare trees and the black earth. Now Felix was busier, and the harvest appeared more plentiful. Their food, as I afterwards found, was coarse, but it was healthy and sufficient. Several new kinds of plants sprang up in the garden, which they cultivated. As the season advanced, so did the family's level of comfort.

"The old man, leaning on his son, took a walk each day at noon when it did not rain, which I found was the name for the water falling down from the heavens. This happened frequently, but a high wind quickly dried the earth, and the weather became far more pleasant than it had been.

"My routine remained the same. During the morning I studied the activities of the cottagers, sleeping only when they went about their various individual tasks. Once I woke, I'd spend the rest of the day watching my friends. When they went to bed—if there was any moon or starlight—I went into the woods to collect my own food and fuel for the cottage. When I returned, as often as necessary, I would clear the snow from their path, and any other chores that I had seen Felix do. This labor—performed by an invisible hand—greatly astonished them. Once or twice I heard them say, "good spirit," or "wonderful," but, at the time, I didn't understand the meaning of the words.

"My mind was eager, and I so wanted to understand the inner life and emotions of these people—to know why Felix seemed so miserable and Agatha so sad. I foolishly thought that I might be able to restore happiness to these deserving people. Even when I slept or left the shack, my mind's eye saw the respected, blind father, the gentle Agatha, and the devoted Felix. I looked at them as Superior Beings, and believed that they would ultimately determine my fate. I fantasized about introducing myself to them. I imagined overcoming their initial disgust and finally winning their favor and love with my gentle manner and persuasive words.

"These thoughts exhilarated me, inspiring me to greater efforts in learning their language. My vocal chords were indeed harsh, but supple, and although my voice was very unlike the soft music of their tones, I still pronounced the words I was able to understand fairly easily. It was like the donkey and the lap dog, yet surely the gentle donkey, whose intentions were affectionate—even if his manners were crude—deserved better treatment than to be beaten and cursed.

"The pleasant showers and delightful warmth of spring greatly altered the landscape. Men who might as well have been hiding in caves returned to the earth and began to cultivate it. The birds sang in more cheerful notes, and the leaves began to bud forth on the trees. The happy earth, which had been bleak, damp, and foul so short a time before, suddenly seemed to be a fitting home for gods. My spirits were lifted by the charming appearance of Nature. The past was blotted from my memory, the present was peaceful, and the future bright with hope."

This is an allusion to the Aesop fable in which the lap dog is treated kindly for barking and jumping around the master, while the donkey is worked hard and left to live in the stable. One day the donkey breaks into the master's house, jumps and brays as he has seen the lap dog do. Then he tries to climb into the master's lap. The servants, thinking that the donkey is attacking the master, beat him with sticks until he returns—dejected—to the stable. The Creature's point is that the lap dog was loved because it was cute, despite the fact that the donkey provided the most service to the master.

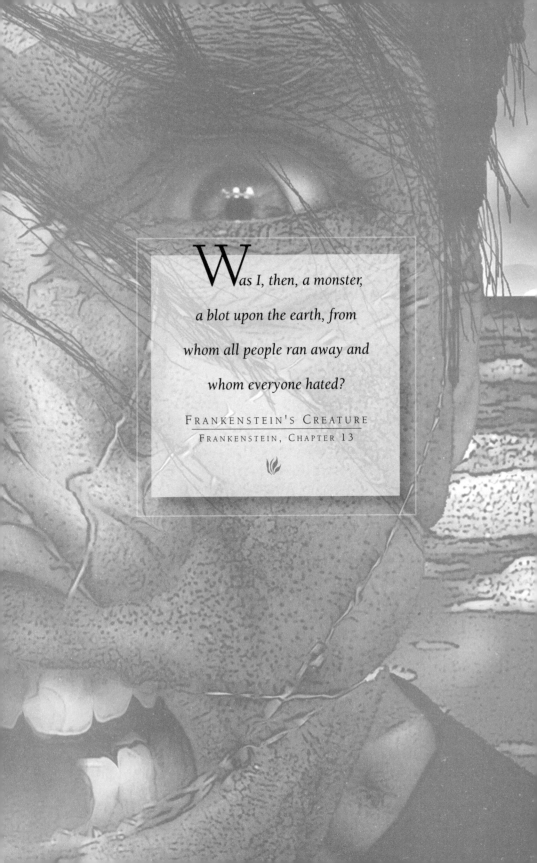

Was I, then, a monster, a blot upon the earth, from whom all people ran away and whom everyone hated?

FRANKENSTEIN'S CREATURE
FRANKENSTEIN, CHAPTER 13

Frankenstein
or The Modern Prometheus

❦

M ARY S HELLEY

CHAPTER 13

"I come now to the more moving part of my story. I will now tell you of the events that made me the monster that I am.

What is the Creature suggesting here?

"Spring advanced rapidly. The weather became fine and the skies cloudless. It surprised me that what had been so barren should now bloom with the most beautiful flowers and leaves. My senses delighted in a thousand delicious scents and a thousand beautiful sights.

"It was on one of these days, when my cottagers periodically rested from their work—the old man played on his guitar, and the children listened to him—that I saw that Felix was more melancholy than I had ever seen him. He sighed frequently, until his father paused in his music and asked why he was so sad. Felix replied in a cheerful tone, and the old man was just beginning to play his music again when someone tapped at the door.

"It was a lady on horseback, accompanied by a country man as her guide. The lady was dressed in a dark suit and covered with a thick black veil. Agatha asked a question, to which the stranger only replied by pronouncing, in a sweet accent, the name of Felix. Her voice was musical but unlike that of either of my friends. When he heard her, Felix quickly approached the lady. When she saw him, she threw up her veil, and I saw a remarkably beautiful face. Her hair was a shining raven black, and curiously braided. Her eyes were dark and gentle yet animated. Her complexion wondrously fair, each cheek tinged with a lovely pink.

"Felix was overwhelmed when he saw her. Every sign of sorrow vanished from his face and was replaced with a joy more intense than anything I had seen before. His eyes sparkled, his cheek flushed with pleasure, and at that moment I thought he was as beautiful as the stranger. She seemed to be having different feelings. Wiping a few tears from her lovely eyes, she held out her hand to Felix, who kissed it rapturously and called her—as well as I could hear—his sweet Arabian. She did not appear to understand him, but she smiled. He helped her dismount and led her into the cottage, dismissing her guide. He said something to his father, and the young stranger knelt at the old man's feet and would have kissed his hand, but he lifted her and embraced her affectionately.

"It was apparent to me that the stranger had her own language and neither understood—nor was understood by—my friends. They made many signs that I did not understand, but I saw that her presence raised the cottagers' spirits, dispelling their sorrow the way the sun dissipates the morning mist. Felix seemed especially happy, welcoming his Arabian with smiles of delight. Agatha—ever gentle—kissed the lovely stranger's hands and, indicating her brother, made signs that appeared to mean that he had been sad until her arrival. Several hours passed, and they all appeared to be joyful, but I did not understand why. I did understand, from the frequent repetition of some sounds that the stranger repeated, that she was trying to learn their language. It occurred to me that I should listen in on the stranger's lessons and that would help me also learn. The stranger learned about twenty words in the first lesson, most of which I already knew, but I still managed to learn some new ones.

"As night came on, Agatha and the Arabian retired early. When they separated, Felix kissed the hand of the stranger and said, 'Good night, sweet Safie.' He sat up much longer, talking with his father, and by the frequent repetition of her name I surmised that their lovely guest was the subject of their conversation. I sincerely wanted to understand them, and strained to pay close attention

✪ The arrival of this stranger is the vehicle Mary Shelley will use to teach the Creature language.

and comprehend, but found it utterly impossible.

"The next morning Felix returned to work, and after Agatha finished her own chores, the Arabian sat at the feet of the old man. Taking his guitar, she played some tunes so beautiful that I cried both tears of sorrow and delight. She sang, and her voice flowed in a rich cadence, swelling or dying away like a nightingale of the woods.

"When she had finished, she gave the guitar to Agatha, who at first declined it. She relented, and played a simple tune. While Agatha's voice was sweet, it was not at all like the wondrous strain of the stranger. The old man was enchanted and said some words that Agatha tried to explain to Safie, apparently expressing their delight in her music.

"The days now passed as quietly as before, except that joy had taken the place of sadness in the household. Safie was always happy. She and I improved rapidly in the knowledge of language, so that in two months I began to understand most of the words my protectors spoke.

"In the meantime the black ground had become covered with vegetation, and the green banks lined with countless flowers, sweet-smelling and colorful—pale, little stars on the floor of the moonlight woods. The sun became warmer, the nights clear and mild, and my nighttime wanderings were pleasant—even though they were considerably shortened by the late setting and early rising of the sun. I never ventured out during daylight, fearful of meeting with the same treatment I had endured in the first village which I entered.

"I spent my days studying so that I could master the language more quickly. Indeed, I improved more rapidly than the Arabian, who understood very little and conversed in broken accents, whilst I understood and could imitate almost every word I heard.

"While I improved in speech, I also learned to write, as 'my family' also taught this to the stranger. This opened yet another wonderful and delightful world for me.

"The book from which Felix taught Safie was Volney's *Ruins of Empires*. I would not have understood the content of this book if Felix hadn't given very detailed explanations while he read. He explained that he had chosen this work because the style imitated that of

❷ *Why would this be?*

✔ *Constantin Francois Chasseboeuf Boisgirais Volney (1757 – 1820) was a French thinker and writer. His ideas helped form the Enlightenment and fueled the French Revolution. The book [Continued on next page]*

that Felix uses to teach Safie French, The Ruin of Empires (Les ruines, meditations sur les revolutions des empires), *was a treatise on governmental tyranny throughout history and why any nation—no matter how powerful—will inevitably fail if its people are not free and prosperous.*

✔ *Be careful. These obviously biased statements reflect the tone and content of the Volney book, and the Creature's imperfect understanding of it, not necessarily Mary Shelley's actual feeling.*

❓ *To whom is the Creature referring here?*

❓ *Remember how this chapter began? What is ironic about the Creature's reaction to his first learning about the dark side of human nature?*

✔ *Remember that—although a Romantic and therefore politically liberal—Mary Shelley has made all of her important characters come from backgrounds of wealth and rank. Even if poor and displaced by circumstances, these characters' origins are in the priveledged classes.*

Eastern authors. Through this work I gained some slight knowledge of history and a view of the several empires at present existing in the world, along with an insight into the manners, governments, and religions of the different nations of the earth. I heard of the slothful Asiatics, the stupendous genius and mental activity of the Greeks. I learned of the wars and wonderful virtue of the early Romans—of their subsequent degenerating and the decline of that mighty empire. Felix read about the Age of Chivalry, the spread of Christianity, and the rise and fall of kings. I heard of the discovery of the American hemisphere and wept with Safie over the hapless fate of its original inhabitants.

"These wonderful histories inspired me with strange feelings. Was humankind *really* so powerful, virtuous, and magnificent, yet also so vicious and base at the same time? He appeared to be alternately the offspring of evil and then noble and godlike. To be great and virtuous seemed to be humankind's highest aspiration, while to be base and vicious—as many have been—appeared the lowest degradation, lower even than being a mole or worm. For a long time I could not believe how anyone could commit murder, or even why there was a need for laws and governments. But when I heard details of vice and bloodshed, my wonder ceased, and I turned away with disgust and loathing.

"Every conversation I overheard now opened new wonders to me. While I listened to Felix's lessons to the Arabian, the strange system of human society was explained to me. I heard of the division of property, of immense wealth and squalid poverty, of social rank, family descent, and the idea of 'noble blood.'

"The words made me see myself in a different light. I learned that the possessions most prized by human kind were high social position and wealth. A man might be respected with only one of these advantages, but without either he was almost always regarded as an outcast and a slave, doomed to toil for the profits of the upper class.

"And what was I? I knew absolutely nothing about my creation and creator. I did know that I had no money, no friends, no kind of property. I was—in addition—hideously deformed and loathsome, and did not even have the same nature as a human. I was more agile and could survive upon a coarser diet. I could tolerate extremes of heat and cold far better, and I was much larger. In all my travels I had neither seen nor heard of any creature remotely like me.

"Was I, then, a monster, a blot upon the earth, from whom all people ran away and whom everyone hated?

"I cannot describe the agony these thoughts inspired. I tried to drive them out of my mind, but sorrow only increased with knowledge. If only I had remained forever in my native wood, knowing nothing but the sensations of hunger, thirst, and heat!

"How strange knowledge is! It clings to the mind like moss to a rock. I wished sometimes to shake off all thought and feeling, but I learned the only way to overcome was death—which I feared even though I did not understand it. I admired virtue and good feelings and loved the gentle manners and good-natured qualities of my cottagers, but I was shut out from contact with them, other than as a spy and eavesdropper, unseen and unknown. This increased, rather than satisfied, the desire I had of joining this warm and loving family. Neither the gentle words of Agatha nor the animated smiles of the charming Arabian were for my benefit. Nor were the mild encouragement of the old man and the lively conversation of the beloved Felix. I was nothing but a miserable, unhappy wretch!

"Other lessons were impressed upon me even more deeply. I heard of the difference between the sexes, and the birth and growth of children—how the father doted on the smiles of the infant, and the lively play of the older child—how the mother's entire life and attention were wrapped up in the precious responsibility, how the mind of the growing child expanded and gained knowledge, of brother, sister, and all the various family relationships which bind one human being to another.

"But where were *my* friends and *my* family? No father had watched me in my infancy, no mother had blessed me with her smiles and caresses. Or, if they had, all my past life was now a blank, an emptiness of which I remembered nothing. From my earliest memory I had always been the same size. I had never yet seen a being that either resembled me or claimed any relation to me.

✪ *Here the Creature is developing a self-concept. This idea was a relatively new one in the early nineteenth century. Psychology as a science had not yet emerged, but there was starting to be inquiry into the working of the mind and the formation of the personality.*

✪ *Mary Shelley's mother, Mary Wollstonecraft Godwin, died only a few days after Mary's birth, so the child never knew the affection and care of her mother. Her own first child—a daughter—had been born premature and died in 1815. In the summer of 1816—while Shelley was creating Frankenstein— she was also caring for her second child, William, who had been born in January. Earlier in 1816, Percy Shelley's legitimate wife Harriet and Mary's half-sister Fanny had both committed suicide. Therefore the irony of life and death and a mother's preoccupation with the well-being of her child were very much on her mind.*

Here again the Creature utters one of the key themes of the book, and echoes the developing idea of a self-concept.

"What was I? I asked that question again and again, only to answer it with a groan.

"I will soon explain the effect of these feelings, but allow me now to return to the cottagers, who inspired such a variety of feelings: indignation, delight, wonder, and an even greater love and respect for these people I naively thought of as my protectors.

Discussion Topic:

Discuss Frankenstein *from a Marxist viewpoint. Who in the story has the power and influence? Why is it important for Mary Shelley to have her characters come from the upper classes of society?*

Discussion Topic:

Discuss Frankenstein *from a Freudian or Psychoanalytic perspective. What impact do the characters' backgrounds have on their actions, reactions, and values? What impact does Mary Shelley's background have on the story she is telling?*

Frankenstein

or The Modern Prometheus

❦

MARY SHELLEY

CHAPTER 14

"Some time elapsed before I learned my friends' history. It was one which could not fail to move me. I learned it in stages and each bit was amazing and terrifying to me, since I had no experience with life whatsoever.

"The name of the old man was De Lacey. He was descended from a good family in France, where he had been quite wealthy, respected by people of higher rank and beloved by his equals. His son was brought up to be a soldier, and Agatha had associated with the finest ladies. A few months before my arrival, they had lived in a large and luxurious city called Paris, surrounded by friends owning every luxury that virtue, intelligence, or taste—assisted by money—could afford.

"The father of Safie, the Arabian, had been the cause of their ruin. He was a Turkish merchant who had lived in Paris for many years, when—for some reason that I never did understand—he fell into disfavor with the government. He was arrested and thrown into prison the very day that Safie arrived from Constantinople to join him. He was tried and condemned to death. The injustice of his sentence was obvious. All of Paris was indignant; and it was judged that his religion and wealth, rather than the crime with which he had been charged, were the real causes of his condemnation.

✔ *Again, note how even the poor cottagers come from a "good family."*

✔ *The society in pre-Revolutionary France (the De Laceys are French) was divided into three clases or "Estates." The First Estate was the Church—bishops, archbishops, cardinals, etc. The Second Estate was the Nobility (including the higher-ranking military). The Third Estate was the peasantry. The De Laceys are clearly of the Second Estate. Thus, a daughter would be married to a wealthy and titled husband, and the son would either enter the Church or the military. An oldest son would never enter the Church because he would, of course, inherit his father's estate and title and would be expected to produce the family's next generation.*

✔ *Wealthy foreign merchant as opposed to peasant.*

✔ *Islam*

Again, note the role of coincidence in literature.

"By pure coincidence, Felix had been present at the trial. His intense anger and indignation were uncontrollable when he heard the decision of the court. He made—at that moment—a solemn vow to save the man from the savage sentence. After many fruitless attempts to gain admittance to the prison, he found a strongly grated window in an unguarded part of the building, which lighted the cell of the unlucky Muslim, who was heavily chained and awaited his execution in despair. Felix visited the grate at night and told the prisoner of his plan. The Turk, amazed and delighted, attempted to further encourage his rescuer with promises of reward and wealth. Felix rejected his offers until he saw the lovely Safie visiting her father. She did her best to express her gratitude for his heroism, and Felix could not help thinking that the Turk did indeed possess a treasure that would fully reward the danger he had placed himself in.

"The Turk quickly saw the effect that his daughter had on Felix and tried to secure him by the promise of her hand in marriage so soon as he was safe. Felix was too discrete to accept this offer, but he did look forward to it and thought it would make him supremely happy.

"During the following days, while the preparations were going forward for the escape, Felix was seduced by several letters that he received from this lovely girl, who managed to write with the help of an old servant of her father who understood French. She thanked him deeply for rescuing her father, while fearing for her own future.

"While I was living in my shack, I managed to get pen and ink, and I copied these letters while Felix or Agatha read them over and over again. Before I leave, I will give them to you, and they will prove the truth of my tale. But since the sun is already close to setting, I only have time to summarize them for you.

Remember that Mary Shelley's mother had been the infamous author of the notorious A Vindication of the Rights of Women.

"Safie wrote that her mother was a Christian Arab, kidnapped and enslaved by the Turks. Well-known for her beauty, she won the heart of Safie's father, who married her. The young girl spoke highly of her mother, who had been born in freedom and despised the bondage to which she was now reduced. She brought her daughter up as a Christian, and taught her to aspire to higher powers of intellect and an independence of spirit forbidden

to the female followers of Islam. The mother died, but her
lessons were forever impressed on Safie. She grew sick
at the thought of returning to Asia to be imprisoned in a
harem and allowed only childish amusements, ill-suited to
her intellect and convictions. The prospect of marrying a
Christian and remaining in a country where women were
treated almost as equals was more than welcome to her.

"The date for the execution of the Turk was set, but he
escaped the night before. By morning, he was miles away
from Paris. Felix had gotten passports for his father, sister, and himself. He had already told his father what he'd
been planning. Old De Lacey helped by leaving his house
pretending to take a journey and hiding with Agatha in an
obscure part of Paris.

"Felix conducted the fugitives through France to Lyons
and across Mont Cenis to Leghorn, where the merchant
had decided to wait for the right moment to cross into
some part of the Turkish Dominions.

"Safie decided to remain with her father until he left.
The Turk renewed his promise that she would marry to
Felix, who remained with them to await the marriage. In
the meantime, he enjoyed Safie's company. She showed
him the simplest and most tender affection. They spoke
to one another with the help of an interpreter, and sometimes with the interpretation of looks. Safie sang to him
the songs of her native country.

"The Turk allowed this intimacy to take place and
encouraged the hopes of the youthful lovers, while in his
heart he had formed very different plans. He loathed the
idea of his daughter marrying a Christian, but was afraid
of making his rescuer angry, for he knew that he was still
in Felix's power should he choose to turn him over to
the authorities. He did everything he could to keep his
true intentions a secret until he and Safie were well into
Turkish territory. His plans were actually assisted by the
news from Paris.

"The government of France was enraged by the escape
and was sparing no effort to find and punish whoever
was responsible. The plot was quickly uncovered, and
De Lacey and Agatha were thrown into prison. The news
gave Felix a rude awakening. His blind and aged father and
his gentle sister lay in a dark prison while he was free,

✔ *Leghorn is a city on the west
coast of Italy, also called
Livorno.*

✔ *These "Turkish Dominions"
are the Ottoman Empire
that extended as far east
as Persia (eastern border
of Syria), as far south as
Ethiopia and Yemen, as
far north as Russia, and
as far west as Bosnia-
Herzegovina, Albania,
and Greece.*

enjoying the company of his beloved. This idea was torture to him. He told the Turk to wait for the right opportunity to escape to his homeland, leaving Safie to remain as a boarder at a convent in Leghorn. Then, bidding the lovely Arabian farewell, he hurried to Paris and turned himself in to the authorities, hoping to free his father and Agatha.

"He did not succeed. They were held in prison for five months before their trial took place, the result of which was that their fortune was confiscated by the Republic, and they were condemned to a perpetual exile from their native country.

"They found a miserable shelter in the cottage in Germany, where I discovered them. Felix soon learned that the treacherous Turk, for whom he and his family had risked so much, heard of their poverty and ruin and betrayed them by leaving Italy with his daughter. He increased the insult by sending Felix a pittance of money for his pains.

"This experience tore at Felix's heart, making him the most miserable of his family when I first saw him. The poverty did not bother him, but the ingratitude of the Turk and the loss of his beloved Safie were misfortunes from which he could never recover. The arrival of the Arabian brought his soul back to life.

"When the news reached Leghorn that Felix had lost his wealth and rank, the merchant commanded his daughter to forget her lover, and prepare to return to her native country. Safie was outraged by this command. She tried to protest, but he left her angrily, repeating his tyrannical command.

"A few days later, the Turk entered his daughter's apartment, saying he had reason to believe that his whereabouts had been betrayed to the French government. He had, therefore, hired a ship to escape to Constantinople and would sail in a few hours. He intended to leave his daughter under the care of a trusted servant, to follow later with the majority of their fortune, which had not yet arrived at Leghorn.

"Once she was alone, Safie developed her own plan. She thoroughly hated the idea of living in Turkey. Her

religion and her feelings were both opposed to it. She discovered some of her father's papers and learned of Felix's
exile and the name of the spot where he currently lived.
She hesitated a little while, but eventually summoned the
strength. Taking with her some jewels that belonged to
her and a sum of money, she left Italy with a servant—a
native of Leghorn who understood the common language
of Turkey—and left for Germany.

"She arrived safely at a town about twenty leagues from
the cottage of De Lacey, when her servant fell dangerously
ill. Safie nursed her affectionately, but the poor girl died,
and the Arabian was left alone. She knew neither the language nor the local customs. But she was fortunate. The
servant had mentioned their destination to their hostess,
and, after the servant died, the woman made sure that Safie
arrived in safety at the family's cottage."

Βut Adam's situation was far different from mine in every other respect. His God had made him happy and prosperous. His Creator guarded him and cared for him. He was allowed to talk with—and learn from—superior beings. But I was wretched, helpless, and alone.

FRANKENSTEIN'S CREATURE
FRANKENSTEIN, CHAPTER 15

Frankenstein

or The Modern Prometheus

❦

MARY SHELLEY

CHAPTER 15

"**S**o that is the history of my beloved cottagers. It impressed me deeply, and taught me to admire their virtues and to loathe the vices of mankind.

"Crime was a distant evil to me. I wanted only to be as good, generous and kind as the family I spied upon every day. Nevertheless there was an important event in my intellectual and emotional growth that I must not omit. It occurred in early August of the same year.

"One night during my usual trip into the nearby woods where I collected food for myself and firewood for my protectors, I found on the ground a leather case containing several articles of clothing and some books. I eagerly seized the prize and returned with it to my shack. Fortunately the books were written in the language I had learned at the cottage. They consisted of *Paradise Lost*, a volume of Plutarch's *Lives,* and *The Sorrows of Werther.*

"These treasures delighted me, and I continually studied them, while my friends were busy with their usual daily tasks.

"I can't tell you how these books affected me. They showed me countless new images and feelings, sometimes raising me to ecstasy, but more frequently sinking me into despair and depression. In *The Sorrows of Werther*—besides its simple and affecting story—so many opinions are expressed and so much light is thrown upon

John Milton's epic poem Paradise Lost *has already been alluded to. It is a poem that explores the roots of human evil, Adam and Eve's disobedience in the Garden of Eden, and the development of Lucifer/ Satan as a vibrant and sympathetic character.*

Plutarch was an ancient Greek historian. His Parallel Lives *is a collection of biographies of great Greeks and Romans, paired so as to emphasize their moral and ethical triumphs and failures. Plutarch was not concerned with writing histories, as much as exploring the influence of character—good or bad— on the lives of famous men.*

Johann Wolfgang von Goethe's novel The Sorrows of Young Werther, *which was also written as a series of letters, was first published (in German) in 1774. It is the story of a brilliant young man with heightened emotions who falls desperately in love with a married woman. His desire for his love and his inability to have her ultimately lead him to suicide.*

◑ *Being in love, Werther's focus, source of joy, reason for being, etc. are outside of himself. Having just started to develop a sense of self, this is now a new concept for the Creature. The Creature sees Werther's suicide—motivated by his inability to possess the object of his love—as a god-like, selfless act.*

◑ *Here the Creature is facing the essential questions of human nature, philosophy, and theology.*

◑ *Numa Pompilius was the second king of Rome. The Romans credited him with inventing their religious institutions. He is depicted as a priestly figure with a long white beard.*

Solon was a just and wise ruler in Athens.

Lycurgus was a ruler in Sparta who willingly surrendered his power to the newborn son of his dead brother, who was the rightful ruler.

Romulum was the mythological founder of Rome. His exploits include killing his twin brother Remus for ridiculing his city's walls, and stealing the women from the Sabines—
[Continued on next page]

subjects that I really had not understood before. The book was indeed a neverending source of astonishment to me. The gentle and domestic manners it described, combined with exalted emotions—focused on someone other than the Self—were so like my impression of my protectors, and showed me things I had already come to believe. Werther himself was a more divine being than I had ever seen or imagined. He made no false claims to greatness, yet his fall was epic. The discussions on death and suicide filled me with wonder. I did not pretend to be able to debate the subject, yet I tended to agree with the opinions of the hero, whose death I mourned, without precisely understanding it.

"As I read, however, I applied much to my own personal feelings and condition. I found myself similar to—yet at the same time strangely different from—the characters in the books. I sympathized with them and partly understood them, yet I was completely separated from all humans, and, therefore, unable to completely understand them. 'The path of my departure was free,' and there was none to lament my annihilation. I was gigantic and hideous. What did this mean? Who was I? What was I? From where did I come? What was my destination? These questions continually recurred, but I was unable to solve them.

"The volume of Plutarch's *Lives* contained the histories of the first founders of the ancient republics. This book had a far different effect upon me from *The Sorrows of Werther*. I learned despair and gloom from Werther, but Plutarch taught me high thoughts. He elevated me above my morbid fascinations, to admire and love the heroes of past ages. Many of the things I read surpassed my understanding and experience. I had only a limited knowledge of kingdoms, wide expanses of country, mighty rivers, and boundless seas. But I was completely unfamiliar with towns and large gatherings of men. The cottage of my protectors had been the only school in which I had studied human nature, but this book presented me with new and mightier scenes of action. I read of men involved in public affairs—either governing or massacring others of their species. I felt a great desire for virtue rise within me, and an extreme hatred of vice, as far as I understood them.

Inspired by these feelings, I was of course led to admire peaceable lawgivers like Numa, Solon, and Lycurgus much more than Romulus and Theseus.

The family life of my protectors caused these ideas to take a firm hold on me. Perhaps, if an ambitious, young soldier had made my first introduction to humanity—burning for glory and lusting for bloodshed, I probably would have developed thinking differently.

"But *Paradise Lost* excited a different and far deeper reaction. I read it—as I had read the other books that had fallen into my hands—as a true history. I was awed and terrified at the idea of an all-powerful God waging war against His own creatures. I thought how terribly *similar* were the situations of the people in this story and myself. Like Adam, I was apparently completely alone in all of Creation. But Adam's situation was far different from mine in every other respect. His God had made him perfect, happy and prosperous. His Creator guarded him and cared for him. He was allowed to talk with—and learn from—superior beings. But I was wretched, helpless, and alone. Many times I considered the outcast Satan's condition to more resemble mine, for often—like him—when I saw the utter happiness of my protectors, I felt nothing but bitter envy.

"Something else happened that strengthened these feelings. Soon after my arrival in the shack I discovered some papers in the pocket of the clothing that I had taken from your laboratory. At first I had ignored them, but now that I was able to read them, I began to study them diligently. It was your journal of the four months immediately prior to my creation. In it, you describe, in precise detail, every step you took in the progress of your work. And there were bits of news about your family and home mixed in with the notes of your…experiment. I'm sure you remember these papers. Here they are. Everything relevant to my accursed origin is recorded here. The smallest description of my detestable and repulsive body is given, in language that declared your own horror and made my horror inescapable. I grew ill as I read. Hateful day when I received life!' I exclaimed in agony. 'Accursed creator! Why did you form a monster so hideous that even YOU turned from me in disgust? God, in love, made humankind

another Italian tribe—to provide wives for the citizens of his city.

Theseus was a king of Athens, son of Aegeus. His most famous adventures include defeating the Minotaur of Crete and defeating the Amazons— taking Antiope, sister to the Amazon queen. Later in life, he foolishly sought adventure for adventure's sake and died in exile, his kingdom having been invaded and taken over while he was on an adventure.

❷ *What side of the "Nature versus Nurture" controversy does the Creature seem to be advancing here?*

❷ *Envy is one of the Seven Deadly Sins. In* Paradise Lost, *Lucifer's fall from favored Angel to Ruler of Hell is due to his envying the Son of God.*

beautiful, after His own image. But my form is nothing but a disgusting imitation of yours, even more horrid because of its resemblance. Even Satan had his companions—fellow devils—to admire and encourage him, but I am completely alone and thoroughly hated.'

"These were the thoughts that came out of my utter despair and solitude. But when I thought about the virtues of the cottagers, their kind and friendly dispositions, I persuaded myself that once they knew of my love for them they would feel compassion toward me and overlook my personal deformity. Could they turn from their door someone who—however monstrous—begged for their understanding and friendship? I decided not to despair, but to make myself ready for an interview with them that would decide my fate. I postponed this attempt for several months longer, because I was terribly afraid of failure. Besides, I found that my understanding grew so much each day that I was unwilling to undertake the task until a few more months had added to my wisdom.

"In the meantime, several changes took place in the cottage. The presence of Safie spread happiness among its inhabitants, and they seemed a bit more prosperous as well. Felix and Agatha seemed to have more leisure time, and were assisted by servants. They certainly didn't seem rich, but they were contented and happy. They were serene and peaceful, while I became more restless every day. My increased knowledge only served to emphasize what a wretched outcast I was. My hope failed me whenever I saw myself reflected in water or my shadow in the moonshine.

Consider:

Why do you suppose Mary Shelley would have the Creature learn the Creation and Fall story from a poem like Paradise Lost *instead of from the Book of Genesis?*

"I tried to crush these fears and to fortify myself for the ordeal which, in a few months, I resolved to undergo. Sometimes I allowed myself to fantasize. I imagined loving creatures sympathizing with my feelings and making me cheerful, with angelic faces smiling at me lovingly and compassionately. But it was all a dream. No Eve soothed my sorrows or shared my thoughts. I was alone. I remembered Adam's plea to his Creator. But my creator had abandoned me, and in the bitterness of my heart I cursed him.

"Autumn passed. I saw—with surprise and grief—the leaves decay and fall. Nature again assumed a barren and bleak appearance. Yet I gave no thought to the bleakness of the weather, as I was better suited to endure cold than heat. But my primary joy had been the sight of the flowers, the birds, and all the beauty of summer. When those were all gone, I paid even more attention to the cottagers. The loss of summer did nothing to decrease their happiness. They loved and sympathized with one another and the events that took place around them did not affect that. The more I saw of them, the more I wanted to claim their protection and kindness. My heart longed to be known and loved by these beloved creatures. To have them look at me with affection was the thing I wanted most. I dared not think that they would turn away from me with disdain and horror. Peasants who stopped at their door were never driven away. Granted, I was hoping for more than a little food or rest. I wanted kindness and sympathy—love, which surely I was not totally unworthy of.

> **Think:**
>
> *A full year has passed since the Creature's creation. How has Victor spent that year? Where is he at this point of the Creature's story?*

"The winter advanced, and an entire revolution of the seasons had taken place since I had come to life. My attention at this time was solely directed toward my plan of introducing myself to the cottagers. I devised many schemes, but my final plan was to enter the house when the blind old man was alone. I was smart enough to know that my appearance was the chief reason everyone who had ever seen me had reacted with such horror. My voice, although harsh, was not terrible. I thought, therefore, that if in the absence of his children I could gain the good will of the old De Lacey, he might gradually persuade the younger people to accept me as well.

"One sunny, brisk autumn day, Safie, Agatha, and Felix departed on a long country walk. The old man did not wish to go, and so he was left alone in the cottage. When his children had left, he took up his guitar and played several melodies, more sweet and mournful than I had ever heard him play before. At first his face was lit with pleasure, but as he continued, he seemed to grow sadder and sadder, finally laying aside the instrument, completely absorbed in deep thought.

"My heart beat fast, as this was the hour I had been waiting for. Either my hopes or my fears would be realized, and I would either have companionship or once again be outcast and alone. The servants had gone to a nearby fair. Everything was silent in and around the cottage. It was an excellent opportunity, yet, when I tried to proceed, my arms and legs failed me and I sank to the ground. Again I rose, and exerting all my strength, removed the planks that hid me. The fresh air revived me, and with renewed determination I approached the door of the cottage.

"I knocked. 'Who is there?' said the old man. 'Come in.'

"I entered. 'Pardon this intrusion,' I said; 'I am a traveler in need of rest. I would greatly appreciate it if you would allow me to sit a few minutes before the fire.'

"'Come in,' said De Lacey, 'and I will offer whatever I can, but, unfortunately, my children are away, and since I am blind, I'm afraid it will be difficult to find any food for you.'

"'Do not trouble yourself, my kind host. I have food. It is only warmth and rest that I need.'

"I sat down, and a silence followed. I knew that every minute was precious, but I was unsure how to begin, when the old man spoke to me. 'By your language, stranger, I suppose you are my countryman. Are you French?'

"'No, but I was educated by a French family and that is the only language I understand. I am traveling to the home of some friends, whom I sincerely love, and whose kindness I need to rely on.'

"'Are they Germans?'

"'No, they are French. But let us change the subject. I am an unhappy and lonely creature, with no relation or

The obligation of a host to offer hospitality to a guest—even an uninvited guest—was essentially a sacred obligation. If asked, even the poorest cottager would offer a traveler a bite of food and a place to rest.

Being Genavese, French would also be Victor's native language, so we can assume Victor and the Creature are conversing in French.

friend on earth. These kind people to whom I am traveling have never seen me and do not know much about
me. I am afraid, for if I fail there, I am an outcast in the
world forever.'

"'Do not despair. To be friendless is indeed unfortunate, but the hearts of men are loving and kind when
they have not been prejudiced by self-interest. Keep up
your hope. If these friends are good and gentle, do not
despair.'

"'They are kind—they are the most excellent creatures in the world, but, unfortunately, they *are* prejudiced against me. I have lived a virtuous life, but preju-
dice clouds their eyes, and where they ought to see a
feeling and kind friend, they look at only a detestable
monster.'

"'That is indeed unfortunate. But if you really are
blameless, can't you make them see that?'

"'I am about to try. That is why I am so terrified. I
dearly love these friends. I have—for some time and
without their knowledge—been doing them a number of
favors. But they believe I intend to harm them, and I want
to make them see how far from the truth that is.'

"'Where do these friends reside?'

"'Not too far from here.'

"The old man paused and then continued, 'If you will
tell me your whole story, I may be able to help you. I am
blind and cannot see your face, but your words convince
me that you are sincere. I am poor and an exile, but it will
give me great pleasure to help a fellow human being.'

"'Excellent man! I thank you and accept your generous offer. Your kindness raises me from the dust, and I
trust that, with your aid, I won't be driven away.'

"'Heaven forbid! Even if you were really criminal, for
that would only drive you to desperation, rather than
virtue. I also am unfortunate. My family and I have been
condemned—although innocent—and I feel for your
misfortunes.'

"'How can I thank you? You are truly the first person
ever to be kind to me. I shall be forever grateful, and your
compassion convinces me that I might indeed be successful with those I hope to befriend.'

"'Will you tell me their names and where they live?'

Again, Mary Shelley emphasizes the idea that crime and virtue are the results of one's circumstances rather than one's nature.

"I paused. This, I thought, was the moment of decision—the moment that would either make me happy
forever or forever dash my hopes. I struggled for the
strength to answer him, but the effort exhausted me, and
I sank onto the chair and sobbed aloud. At that moment I
heard the arrival of my younger protectors. I had no time
to waste. I grabbed the old man's hand and cried, 'Now
is the time! Save and protect me! You and your family are
the friends whom I seek. Please do not you desert me!'

"'Great God!' exclaimed the old man. 'Who *are* you?'

"At that moment, the cottage door was opened, and
Felix, Safie, and Agatha entered. You can imagine their
horror when they saw me. Agatha fainted, and Safie
rushed out of the cottage. Felix darted forward and tore
me from his father, furiously throwing me to the ground
and striking me violently with a stick. I could have torn
him limb from limb, but my heart bitterly sank within me,
and I held back. He was ready to strike again—but overcome with pain and anguish—I fled the cottage, escaping
during the commotion to my shack."

Research Opportunity:

*Look up the "Nature versus Nurture" controversy. What is it, and which
"side" seems to be "winning" today?*

Frankenstein
or The Modern Prometheus

❦

MARY SHELLEY

CHAPTER 16

"Cursed, cursed creator! Why did I live? Why, at that moment, did I not extinguish the spark of life you had so carelessly bestowed? I do not know. Complete hopelessness had not yet taken hold of me. I felt only rage and the desire for revenge. I could happily have destroyed the cottage and its inhabitants, avenging myself with their shrieks and misery.

"When night came, I left my retreat and wandered in the woods. No longer fearing discovery, I vented my anguish in fearful howling, like a wild beast. I spent a miserable night. The cold stars mocked me by their brilliance, and the bare trees waved their branches above me, accompanied by the sweet voice of a bird. All of nature was happy and at peace—all but me. I, like the devil, bore a hell within me. Finding myself friendless, I wanted to tear up the trees, spread havoc and destruction, and then enjoy the ruin.

"But this was a luxury I could not afford, as I was worn out and sank on the damp grass in despair. No one would pity me or help me, so why should I feel kindness toward my enemies? At that moment, I declared neverending war against humanity and—most of all—against the one who had created me and sent me on this path of misery.

"The sun rose. I heard the voices and knew it was impossible to return to my retreat during that day. I therefore hid in the woods and thought about my situation.

Here we see the emergence of the Creature's evil—obviously not his "nature" but the result of his isolation and disappointment. Remember that Captain Walton also lamented the lack of a friend.

✪ *Again, the healing power of Nature.*

"Sunshine and fresh air restored me somewhat and in the light of day I felt I'd been too hasty about what had happened at the cottage. I had certainly acted unwisely. It was clear that I had gained the sympathy of the father, and I'd been foolish to expose myself so quickly to the young people. I should have continued to befriend De Lacey, and reveal myself to his children gradually, preparing them for my approach. But I didn't think my mistakes were irreversible. I resolved to return to the cottage, seek the old man, and again win him over.

"These thoughts calmed me, and in the afternoon I slept—but not peacefully. The horrible scene of the day before played again and again in my head, with the women taking flight and Felix tearing me from his father's feet. When I awoke, I was still exhausted. Night had fallen while I slept, so I crept out of my hiding-place and searched for food.

"After satisfying my hunger, I returned to the cottage. Everything was quiet. I crept into my shack and waited for the family to rise. Hours passed. The sun rose higher in the sky, but the cottagers did not appear. I trembled violently, fearing some dreadful misfortune. The inside of the cottage was dark, and I heard no motion. I cannot describe the agony of this suspense.

"Eventually two countrymen passed by, pausing near the cottage. They spoke with wild gestures, in a language I could not understand. Then Felix approached with another man, which surprised me, since I knew that he hadn't left the cottage that morning. I waited anxiously to hear why the stranger was there.

"'Don't you realize,' said the stranger, 'that you will be paying three months' rent while losing your harvest? I don't want to take advantage of you. I urge you to reconsider.'

"'It is utterly useless,' replied Felix; 'we cannot live here. Our lives are in danger. My wife and my sister will never recover from their horror. You will not change my mind. Take back your cottage and let me get out of this place.'

"Felix trembled violently as he said this. He and his companion entered the cottage, where they remained for a few minutes, and then departed. I never saw any of the De Lacey family again.

"I spent the rest of the day in my shack, utterly and stupidly desperate. My protectors had left, breaking my only link to the world. This time, when thoughts of revenge and hatred filled my heart, I did not try to control them. Allowing myself to be carried away by the stream, I began to fantasize about injury and death. When I thought of my friends, of the mild voice of De Lacey, the gentle eyes of Agatha, and the exquisite beauty of the Arabian, a rush of tears washed away my angry, violent thoughts. But when I remembered their rejection and desertion, my rage returned. Unable to injure anything human, I turned my fury toward inanimate objects. As night advanced, I placed a variety of combustibles around the cottage, and after burning everything in the garden, I impatiently waited for the moon to set to begin.

"But as the night advanced, a fierce wind arose from the woods and quickly dispersed the clouds. The gale tore along like an avalanche, producing a kind of insanity in me that destroyed all reason. I lit the dry tree branches I had gathered and danced with fury around the cottage. As the moon set, I waved my torch. I set fire to the straw, heath and bushes I had collected with a loud scream. The wind fanned the fire, and the flame quickly engulfed the cottage, licking it with their forked and destroying tongues.

"As soon as I was certain nothing could save the cottage, I ran away and looked for a hiding place in the woods.

"But where could I go? I wanted to go as far away as I could, but—hated and despised as I was—no place would welcome me. Finally I thought of you. I learned from your papers that you were my father, my creator. Who else could I go to? I had learned geography from the lessons Felix had given Safie. I knew the locations of various countries. You had mentioned Geneva as the name of your native town, and I decided that I would go there.

"But how would I find my way? I knew that I must travel toward the southwest, but the sun was my only guide. I did not know the names of the towns that I was to pass through, nor could I ask for directions from a single human being. But I did not despair. You were my only hope for comfort, even though I hated you. Unfeeling,

✪ *Don't miss the metaphor of the fire compared to a devouring beast's tongue.*

✪ *Remember that, while Safie and her father hid in Leghorn (Livorno), Italy, the De Laceys' cottage is in Germany. That explains the journey to the south and west to get to Geneva, Switzerland.*

heartless creator! You had given me consciousness and emotion and then abandoned me to horrify and be hated by mankind. But I had a claim on no one but you. And I was determined to demand justice from you—a justice that I had tried to seek from other humans, but which no other human owed me.

"My travels were long and my suffering intense. It was late in autumn when I left the only home I had ever known. I traveled only at night, afraid of meeting anything that resembled a human being. Nature seemed to die around me. The sun lost its warmth, and rain and snow poured around me. Mighty rivers were frozen. The surface of the earth was hard, cold and barren, and I found no shelter. Oh, earth! How often did I curse my existence? All that was good within me was gone, turned to malice and bitterness. The closer I got to you, the more I felt the spirit of revenge burning in my heart. Snow fell, water turned to ice, but I did not rest. Occasional signs directed me. I had a map of the country, yet I often lost my way. Still, my agony allowed me no rest. My rage and misery never lessened, but something happened when I arrived in Switzerland. The sun recovered its warmth and the earth again began to look green. These changes, however, only served to oddly confirm my bitterness and horror.

"I usually rested during the day and traveled by night, hidden from the view of humanity. One morning, however, finding that I needed to travel through a deep wood, I dared to continue my journey after the sun had risen. The day—one of the first of spring—cheered even me with its sunshine and balmy air. I felt gentleness and pleasure revive within me. I allowed myself to be carried away by these feelings, forgetting my solitude and deformity, daring to be happy. Soft tears ran down my cheeks, and I even raised my tear-filled eyes with gratitude toward the blessed sun, which bestowed such joy upon me.

"I continued along the path in the forest, until I came to its boundary, skirted by a deep and rapid river, into which many of the trees bent their branches, now budding with the fresh spring. Here I paused, not knowing which way to go. I heard the sound of voices, and decided to hide under the shade of a cypress. Suddenly a young girl came running toward the spot where I was hidden, laughing as if playing a game of hide-and-seek. She ran along the steep sides of the river, when her foot slipped, and she fell into the rapid stream. I rushed from my hiding place and—with great effort, given the force of the current—rescued her and dragged her to shore. She was unconscious, and I tried by every means I could think of to revive her. I was suddenly interrupted by the approach of a villager, probably the person from whom she had playfully fled.

"When he saw me, he rushed toward me, tearing the girl from my arms and fleeing into the woods. I don't know why, but I ran after them. When the man saw me approach, he aimed a gun at me and fired. I sank to the ground, and my attacker quickly escaped into the woods.

"This was the reward for my kindness! I had saved a human being from destruction, and as compensation I now writhed in pain with a wound that shattered my flesh and bone. The feelings of kindness and gentleness I felt but a few moments before gave way to hellish rage. Inflamed by pain, I vowed eternal hatred and vengeance on all mankind. But the agony of my wound overcame me, and I fainted.

"For some weeks I led a miserable life in the woods, trying to cure my wound. The bullet had entered my shoulder, and I didn't know whether it was still there or had passed through. At any rate, I had no way to remove it. My suffering was magnified by the injustice and ingratitude of my persecution. My daily vows rose for revenge—a deep and deadly revenge, equal to the outrages and anguish I had endured.

"After several weeks, my wound healed, and I continued my journey. My efforts were no longer helped by the bright sun or gentle breezes of spring. All joy was a mockery, insulting my desolate state and making me feel my isolation from all pleasure and joy even more painfully.

"But my journey was nearly over, and in two months from this time I reached the outskirts of Geneva.

"It was evening when I arrived, and I hid among the fields that surround it to decide how I would approach you. I was tired and hungry and far too unhappy to enjoy the gentle breezes of evening or the prospect of the sun setting behind the stupendous mountains of Jura.

"Then sleep rescued me from my thoughts, but that sleep was disturbed by the approach of a beautiful child. He came running into the hollow I had chosen, with all the playfulness of infancy. Suddenly, as I gazed on him, it occurred to me that this little creature was unprejudiced and had lived too short a time to have any fear of deformity. If, therefore, I could seize him and educate him as my companion and friend, I would not be so desolate in this earth full of the humankind I hated.

❷ Who do you think is this child? What is the Creature going to try to do?

"Urged by this impulse, I seized the boy as he passed and pulled him toward me. As soon as he saw me, he covered his eyes and screamed. I yanked his hand from his face and said, 'Child, what is the meaning of this? I do not intend to hurt you. Listen to me.'

"He struggled violently. 'Let me go,' he cried; 'monster! Ugly wretch! You wish to eat me and tear me to pieces. You are an ogre. Let me go, or I will tell my papa.'

"'Boy,' I said, 'you will never see your father again. You must come with me.'

"'Hideous monster! Let me go. My papa is M. Frankenstein—he will punish you. You dare not keep me.'

"'Frankenstein! You belong then to my enemy—to the person against whom I have sworn eternal revenge. You shall be my first victim.'

"The child still struggled and screamed curses at me which were like arrows to my heart. I clutched his throat to silence him, and in a moment he lay dead at my feet.

"I gazed on my victim, and my heart swelled with exultation and hellish triumph. Clapping my hands, I exclaimed, 'I too can create desolation. My enemy is not indestructible. This death will carry despair to him, and a thousand other miseries will torment and destroy him.'

"As I fixed my eyes on the child, I saw something glittering on his breast. It was a portrait of a lovely woman, which I took. Despite my fury, it softened and attracted me. For a few moments I gazed with delight on her dark eyes, fringed by deep lashes, and her lovely lips. My rage returned when I thought that I would never know the delights that such beautiful creatures could bestow. The woman whose picture I studied would greet me with the same terror and disgust I'd received from very human I'd ever come in contact with.

"Are *you* amazed that such thoughts fed my rage? The only surprise is that I did not vent my anger through further acts of mayhem, instead of simply screaming my agony.

"Overcome by these feelings, I left the spot where I had committed the murder. Seeking a more secluded hiding place, I entered a barn that appeared to be empty. A woman was sleeping on some straw. She was young, not as beautiful as the portrait I held, but still attractive and in the bloom of youth and health. Here, I thought, is one of those people who smile joyously at everyone but me. And then I bent over her and whispered, 'Awake, my dear, your lover is near—someone who would sacrifice his life for just one affectionate look from your eyes. My beloved, awake!'

"She stirred. A thrill of terror ran through me. Would she indeed awake, see me, curse me, and denounce me as a murderer? This was surely what she would do if she woke up and saw me. The thought was madness, stirring the fiend within me. I would not suffer, but *she* would suffer. *She* would be punished for the murder I had committed because I would be forever deprived of everything that she could give me. My crime had its motive in her, so let the punishment be hers! Thanks to Felix and the laws of man, I had learned how to work mischief. I bent over her and placed the portrait securely in one of the folds of her dress. She moved again, and I fled.

"For several days I stayed in the area, sometimes hoping to see you, sometimes resolved to quit the world and its miseries forever. Finally, I wandered toward these mountains, and climbed their immense recesses, consumed by a burning passion that only you can gratify. We will not part from each other until you have promised to agree to with my request. I am alone and miserable. Humans will not associate with me, but one as deformed

❷ *Do you agree with the Creature's rationale for framing Justine?*

and horrible as myself would not deny herself to me. My companion must be of the same species as me and have the same defects that I have. This being you must create."

Think and Predict:

What are Victor's options? What do you think he will do? What do you think he should do?

Frankenstein
or The Modern Prometheus
❧
MARY SHELLEY

CHAPTER 17

The Creature finished speaking and waited for my reply. But I was bewildered, confused, and unable to understand the full extent of his proposal.

He continued, "You must create a female for me to live with—one who can understand me and share my life. Only you can do this, and I *demand* it of you as a right which you must not refuse."

The last part of his tale rekindled my anger, and I could no longer suppress my rage.

"I *do* refuse," I replied; "and nothing you do to me could make me agree to it. You could make me the most miserable of men, but you shall never make me corrupt in my own eyes. Create another like yourself, so that your joint wickedness might desolate the world? Get away! I have answered you. You may torture me, but I will never consent."

"You are wrong," replied the fiend, "but instead of threatening, I will reason with you. I am malicious because I am miserable. Am I not shunned and hated by all mankind? You, my very creator, would tear me to pieces and rejoice. So tell me why I should pity humanity more than it pities me? You would not consider it murder to destroy me with your own hands. Should I respect humankind when it condemns me?

❷ *Do you agree that this is the creature's right?*

"But show me kindness, and instead of injury I will show gratitude. I know that that cannot be, since humans cannot transcend their senses. Even you cannot see beyond my physical ugliness. Yet I will not be a slave. I *will* be revenged. If I cannot inspire love, then I will inspire fear, and chiefly yours, my archenemy. My hatred for you—my creator—can never be extinguished. Beware. I will work toward your destruction and desolate your heart, until you curse the hour of your birth."

A fiendish rage filled him as he spoke. His face wrinkled into contortions too horrible for human eyes to see. Finally, he calmed himself and continued, "But I mean to reason with you. This passion does me no good, since you do not see that you are its cause. If any individual felt compassion toward me, I would make peace with the whole race for that creature's sake! But that dream can never be. What I ask of you is reasonable and fair. I demand a creature of another sex, but as hideous as myself. This may be little comfort, but it is all that I can receive, and it will make me content. It is true that we will be monsters, cut off from the entire world, but that can help to make us more attached to one another. Our lives will not be happy, but they will be harmless and free from the misery I now feel.

"Oh! My creator, make me happy. Let me feel gratitude toward you for this one benefit! Let me see that I excite the sympathy of some existing thing. Do not deny me my request!"

I admit that I *was* moved. I shuddered when I thought of the possible consequences of my consent, but I felt that there was some justice in his argument. His tale and his feelings proved him to be a sensitive creature, and—as his maker—did I not owe him all the happiness I had in my power to bestow?

He saw my change of feeling and continued, "If you consent, neither you nor any other human being will ever see us again. We will go to the jungles of South America. Unlike you, I do not need to slaughter animals to feed myself. Acorns and berries provide me with sufficient nourishment. My companion will be of the same nature and will be content with the same food. We shall make our bed of dried leaves. The sun will shine on us as on

❷ *Note the words the Creature uses: sympathy, compassion, understanding—not love. Why is this?*

✔ *Note the picturesque, idyllic life the Creature pictures for himself and his mate.*

you and will ripen our food. To deny me this dream of peaceful existence would be the harshest cruelty. Pitiless as you have been toward me, I now see compassion in your eyes. Let me seize this chance to persuade you to promise what I so fiercely desire."

"You promise," I replied, "to flee from all human habitation, to dwell in those wilds where the beasts of the field will be your only companions. How can you survive in this exile, when you crave the love and sympathy of humans? You will return and again seek their kindness, and you will again meet with their hatred. Your evil nature will be revived, and you will have a companion to aid you in destruction. This can never happen. Cease to argue the point, for I cannot consent."

"How fickle you are! Just a moment ago you were moved by my story. Why have your feelings hardened to my situation? I *swear* to you that—with my companion—I will leave the neighborhoods of humans and live, if necessary, in the most savage of places. My evil passions will be gone, because I will have been met with sympathy! My life will pass quietly away, and in my dying moments I will not curse my maker."

His words had a strange effect upon me. I felt compassion and the desire to console him. But when I looked at him, when I saw the filthy mass that moved and talked, my heart sickened and I felt only horror and hatred. I tried to stifle these feelings. Even if I could not sympathize with him, still, I had no right to withhold any happiness that was in my power to give him.

> **Think:**
>
> *For Victor, is the Creature's physical ugliness the only source of horror? The primary source of horror?*

"You *swear*," I said, "you will be harmless? But how can I trust you, after what you have already done? Couldn't even this be a ploy for you to wreak even greater revenge?"

"What is this? I won't be trifled with, and I demand an answer. If I have no ties and no affections, then I will have only hatred and vice. The love of another will destroy the cause of my crimes, and I will disappear.

My vices are caused by a forced and hated solitude, and my virtues will return when I live in fellowship with an equal. I will feel the affections of a sensitive being and become linked to the chain of existence and events from which I am now excluded."

I paused some time to reflect on his story and his arguments. I thought about the potential of virtue he had displayed when he was first created, and how it had been destroyed by the loathing and scorn that his protectors had shown him. I did not ignore his power and threats. A creature who could exist in the ice caves of glaciers and hide in the ridges of inaccessible cliffs was a being who could never be overpowered. I concluded that the justice due both to him and my fellow creatures demanded that I comply with his request. Turning to him, I told him my decision.

❷ Has Victor made the right decision? Why or why not?

"I agree, on your solemn oath to leave Europe forever, and every other place where humans live, as soon as I present you with a female who will accompany you in your exile."

"I swear," he cried, "by the sun, and by the blue sky of heaven, and by the fire of love that burns in my heart, that if you grant my prayer you will never see me again. Go home and begin your work. I will anxiously await your progress, and when you are finished I shall return."

Saying this, he quickly left, afraid, perhaps, that I might change my mind. I saw him descend the mountain faster than an eagle could fly. He quickly became lost among the swells and curves of the sea of ice.

It had taken him the whole day to tell his story, and it was sunset when he left. I knew that I should hurry toward the valley, before darkness fell, but my heart was heavy, and my steps slow. The effort of winding among the little paths of the mountain confused me, occupied as I was by the emotions that the day had produced. It was late at night when I came to the halfway resting place and sat by the fountain. The stars shone as the clouds passed over. The dark pines rose before me, and some broken trees lay on the ground. It was a solemn place and stirred strange thoughts within me. Weeping bitterly, and clasping my hands in agony, I exclaimed, "Oh! Stars and clouds and winds, if you have any pity, crush sensation and memory. Let me become numb, or else leave me in darkness."

These were wild and miserable thoughts, but I cannot describe to you how the eternal twinkling of the stars weighed upon me and how I listened to every blast of wind as if it were a dull ugly squall on its way to devour me.

Morning dawned before I arrived at Chamounix. I took no rest, but returned immediately to Geneva. Even in my own heart I could not express my feelings. They weighed on me as heavily as a mountain, crushing my agony into my heart. This was my condition when I returned home and presented myself to the family. They were shocked and alarmed by my haggard and wild appearance, but I answered no questions. I scarcely spoke. I felt as if I had no right to claim their sympathy, nor to ever again enjoy their companionship. Yet even so I adored them, and to save them, I resolved to dedicate myself to my most abhorred task. The prospect of that task made everything else appear like a dream to me. Only my promise to my Creature was real.

Research Opportunity:

Look up late twentieth and early twenty-first century court cases involving reproductive rights, genetic testing and/or engineering, etc., and report on the nature of the case and what was ultimately decided— if the case has been settled.

To England, therefore, I was bound, and it was decided that my wedding would take place immediately on my return.

VICTOR FRANKENSTEIN
FRANKENSTEIN, CHAPTER 18

Frankenstein

or The Modern Prometheus

❧

MARY SHELLEY

CHAPTER 18

Days and weeks passed after my return to Geneva, and I still could not summon the courage to begin my new work. I feared the vengeance of the disappointed fiend, yet I was unable to overcome my repugnance to the task I had committed to. I realized that I could not compose a female without again devoting several months to intense study and research. I had heard of an English scientist who had made discoveries essential to my success, and I considered asking my father's consent to visit England for this purpose. Instead I made excuses, shrank from taking even the first step, and began questioning the whole necessity of the undertaking. A change indeed had taken place in me. My former ill health was now greatly improved, and my spirits were high as long as I could forget my unhappy promise. My father was pleased to see this change, and he tried to erase the remains of my depression, which only now and then would return. At these moments I took refuge in total solitude. I spent entire days on the lake alone in a little boat, watching the clouds and listening to the rippling of the waves, silent and listless. But the fresh air and bright sun seldom failed to restore me, and I returned with a ready smile and a more cheerful heart.

It was after my return from one of these rambles that my father called me aside and spoke to me.

"It makes me very happy, son, that you have resumed your normal activities and seem to be yourself again. Still, you are frequently unhappy and avoid our company. For some time I wondered what the reason was, but yesterday an idea occurred to me, and if I am right, please tell me so. Denial would be pointless, and only cause more pain for us all."

I trembled violently as he spoke.

"I will admit, my son, that I have always looked forward to your marriage with our dear Elizabeth as the natural outgrowth of our family happiness, and a blessing to me in my old age. You were attached to each other from your earliest infancy. You studied together, and seemed to be entirely suited to one another. But I worry that I have been blind to your own wishes, and perhaps I have unwittingly undone any chance of romance between you. Perhaps you think of her as your sister, without any wish to marry her. You may even have met someone else, but—being bound to Elizabeth—this struggle may be the cause of your misery."

"My dear father, reassure yourself. I love my cousin very much. There is no woman I hold as dear to me as Elizabeth. My future hope is entirely bound up in my desire to marry her."

"To hear these words from you, my dear Victor, gives me more pleasure than I have experienced for some time. If this is true, we will certainly be happy, despite present events. But I still wish to cast out this gloom that has taken hold of you. Tell me, therefore, would you object to having the wedding as soon as possible? We have been unfortunate, and recent events have denied me the comfort or peace of mind that someone my age expects. You are young, but you are financially sound, and an early marriage would hardly interfere with any future plans that you might have. Nevertheless, I have no wish to dictate the terms of your future, or imply that to delay your marriage would cause me any sorrow. Please consider everything I've said, and answer me truly from your heart."

❷ *How old is Victor?*

> **Parallelism and Foreshadowing Alert:**
>
> *What issue do we see developing here?*

I listened to my father in silence, unable to reply. My mind was spinning as I tried to arrive at a decision. Alas! I was horrified and dismayed at the idea of marrying my Elizabeth immediately. I was bound by a solemn promise that I had not yet fulfilled and dared not break, for to do that would cause only misery for both my family and myself. How could I celebrate my wedding with this deadly weight still hanging around my neck? I *had* to honor my commitment and let the monster depart with his mate before I allowed myself the joy and peace of marriage with my beloved.

There was also the necessity of a trip to England, or at least a long correspondence with the scientists of that country whose knowledge and discoveries I needed to complete my project. But corresponding with these scientist—asking them my questions and waiting for their all-important answers—by way of the mail system would simply be too slow. I also hated the idea of performing my loathsome task in my father's house surrounded by my family. I knew that a thousand terrible accidents could happen, any of which would reveal my awful, awful secret. I also knew that I would probably also lose all self-control, all ability to hide my emotional reactions to the morbid and terrifying activities I would be engaged in. I knew I had to distance myself from everyone I cared for until this project was complete. Once I actually started, it wouldn't take long, and I could return to my family in peace and happiness. My promise fulfilled, the monster would depart forever, unless—as I fantasized—some accident occurred to destroy him and put an end to my slavery forever.

These feelings shaped my answer to my father. I told him I wished to visit England, but I hid the real reason I wanted to go and made up some excuse that would not arouse suspicion. I asked him with a serious earnestness that made it practically impossible for him not to agree. After my being depressed for so long, he was delighted to see my enthusiasm for the trip. He hoped that the change of scenery and different routine would restore me entirely to myself.

The length of my trip was left to me—whether a few months, or at most a year. What was not left to my own judgment was my ability to travel alone. Conspiring with Elizabeth, he arranged for Clerval to join me at Strasbourg. This did interfere with the solitude I needed for my project, but at the beginning of my trip, my friend's company would actually keep me from my habit of lonely brooding. Henry might even protect me from my foe. If I were alone, he could force his disgusting presence on me to remind me of my task or to witness its progress.

To England, therefore, I was bound, and it was decided that my wedding would take place immediately on my return. My father's age made him reluctant to delay. For myself, there was one reward I looked forward to, one consolation for my unparalleled sufferings—the day when I would claim Elizabeth and forget the past in my union with her.

I now made arrangements for my journey, but one thought frightened me. During my absence, my friends would be completely unaware of the existence of their enemy, and they would be vulnerable to his attacks. Still, he had promised to follow me wherever I went, so wouldn't he follow me to England? This idea was both dreadful and soothing since it would mean my friends were safe. I agonized over the possibility that he might remain behind to plague my family. But I allowed myself to follow the impulses of the moment, and my instinct told me that the fiend would follow me and leave my family alone.

It was toward the end of September that I left. The trip had been my idea, and Elizabeth had agreed to it, but she was still worried for my welfare. While she had helped arrange for Clerval to travel with me, she was also aware that men lacked the caretaking instinct of women. She longed to tell me to hurry home, but a thousand conflicting emotions rendered her mute as she bade me a tearful, silent farewell.

I threw myself into the carriage, paying no attention to the passing scenery. My only preparation, as I would remember bitterly, had been to order that my chemical instruments be packed to go with me. Morose, I passed a good deal of beautiful scenery, but my eyes were fixed and unobserving. I could only think of the burden of my travels and the work that was to occupy me for the entire tour.

After an exhausting journey of many miles, I arrived at Strasbourg, where I waited two days for Clerval. He came. The contrast between us could not have been greater. He was alive to every new scene, joyful when he saw the beauty of the setting sun, and even happier to see the same sun rise the next morning. He pointed out to me the shifting colors of the landscape and the changing appearance of the sky.

"This is what it is to live," he cried; "how I enjoy living! But you, Frankenstein, why are you depressed and sorrowful?"

To tell the truth, I *was* occupied by gloomy thoughts and neither saw the setting of the evening star nor the golden sunrise reflected in the Rhine. Certainly Clerval's travel journals, full of emotion and delight, would be far more entertaining to any reader than my reflections. I, in contrast, was a wretch, haunted by a curse that shut up every avenue to enjoyment.

Note again the brooding Romantic Hero.

We had agreed to descend the Rhine in a boat from Strasbourg to Rotterdam, from where we would depart for London. During this voyage, we passed many willowy islands and saw several beautiful towns. We stayed a day at Mannheim, and on the fifth day from our departure from Strasbourg, arrived at Mainz. The course of the Rhine below Mainz becomes much more picturesque. The river descends rapidly and winds between hills, not high, but steep, and of beautiful forms. We saw many ruined castles standing on the edges of cliffs, surrounded by black woods, high and inaccessible. This part of the Rhine, indeed, offers a uniquely varied landscape. In one spot you view rugged hills, ruined castles overlooking tremendous cliffs, with the dark Rhine rushing beneath. On the sudden turn of a promontory, flourishing vineyards with green sloping banks and a meandering river and thriving towns fill the scene.

Consider some of the Romantic images you gathered in Chapter 9 as you read the vivid imagery in this passage.

We were traveling at the season when the ripe grapes are crushed into wine and heard the workers singing as we glided down the stream. Even I was charmed, despite my gloom. I lay at the bottom of the boat, gazing on the cloudless blue sky, and drinking in a peacefulness which I had not experienced for a very long time. Henry's emotions were even more blissful. He said he felt as if he had been transported to paradise and enjoyed a happiness seldom tasted by man.

"I have seen," he said, "the most beautiful scenery of my own country. I have visited the lakes of Lucerne and Uri, where the snowy mountains descend almost perpendicularly to the water, casting deep and black shadows, contrasted with the greenest islands one could hope to see. I have seen this lake churned by storms, when the wind tore up whirlwinds of water and the waves dashed with fury against the base of the mountain, where the priest and his mistress were overwhelmed by an avalanche and where their dying voices are still said to be heard amid the pauses of the nightly wind I have seen the mountains of La Valais, and the Pays de Vaud, but this country—Germany—Victor, pleases me more than all those wonders. The mountains of Switzerland are more majestic and strange, but there is a charm in the banks of this divine river that I have never seen equaled. Look at that castle on that cliff, and the castle on the island, almost hidden in the leaves and branches of those lovely trees. Look at that group of workers coming from among their vines, and that village half hidden by the mountain. Oh, surely the spirit that inhabits and guards this place has a soul more in harmony with humanity than those who climb the glacier or retire to the inaccessible peaks of the mountains of our own country." Clerval, my beloved friend! Even now his words delight me. He was a being formed in the "very poetry of nature." His wild and enthusiastic imagination was kept in check by the sensibility of his heart. His soul overflowed with love, and his friendship was so devoted that the worldly wise would be skeptical of him. But even humanity was not sufficient to satisfy his eager mind. Where others merely admire nature, he loved it with a passion:

> —The sounding cataract
> Haunted him like a passion: the tall rock,
> The mountain, and the deep and gloomy wood,
> Their colors and their forms, were then to him
> An appetite; a feeling, and a love,
> That had no need of a remoter charm,
> By thought supplied, or any interest
> Unborrow'd from the eye.

A PRESTWICK HOUSE SPOTLIGHT EDITION

In "History of a Six-Weeks' Tour," Mary Shelley relates having heard this tale from local residents while traveling in the area around Lake Uri in Switzerland.

What is Henry asserting here?

Victor praises Henry because he is a true Romantic.

This is another allusion to William Wordsworth's "Lines Written a Few Miles Above Tintern Abbey" in which he describes his youthful passion for nature compared to his more mature return to a favorite spot.

Wordsworth's "Tintern Abbey".

And where is he now? Is this gentle and lovely being lost forever? Has this mind, so full of ideas, so full of imaginations creative and magnificent, which formed a world, that could not exist except in his mind—has this mind perished? Does it now only exist in my memory? No, it is not so; his body, once full of the strength and beauty of youth, may have decayed, but his spirit still visits and consoles his unhappy friend.

Pardon this outpouring of sorrow; these feeble words are but a slight tribute to Henry's virtues. They do, however, soothe my heart, which overflows with the pain of his memory. I will proceed with my tale.

Beyond Cologne we descended to the plains of Holland, and we resolved to travel the rest of the way by land, since the wind was contrary and the river's tide too placid to be of use. This part of our journey lacked the interest of beautiful scenery, but we arrived in a few days at Rotterdam, and then proceeded by sea to England. It was on a clear morning, in late December, that I first saw the white cliffs of Britain. The banks of the Thames presented a new scene. They were flat but fertile, and almost every town was marked by history. We saw Tilbury Fort and remembered the Spanish Armada, Gravesend, Woolwich, and Greenwich, places that I had heard of even in my country.

Finally we saw the numerous steeples of London, St. Paul's towering above all, and the famous Tower.

❷ *What is Victor foreshadowing?*

✐ *Remember that Victor is talking to Captain Walton.*

✐ *Keep in mind Mary Shelley's apparent anti-Catholic sentiments. The Spanish Armada was a massive naval attack by Catholic Spain on Protestant England. Elizabeth I rallied her ragtag troops to defend England from the attack at Tilbury Fort. Gravesend is the site of the Native American Princess Pocahontas' death and burial. The Royal Arsenal was established by Elizabeth I at Woolwich, and later the Royal Artillery headquarters was established there. Greenwich is home to the Greenwich Royal Observatory (which would become the site of Zero Degrees Longitude, and Greenwich Mean Time).*

I had no doubt that the monster was following me and would appear, when I was finished, to receive his companion.

VICTOR FRANKENSTEIN
FRANKENSTEIN, CHAPTER 19

Frankenstein
or The Modern Prometheus

❧

M ARY S HELLEY

CHAPTER 19

> **Research Opportunity:**
>
> *Given the dates on Robert Walton's letters, and suggestions of the time period from the Creature's story, suggest who some of these talented persons might have been. What scientists might Victor have wanted to consult with?*

London was our final destination, and we decided to remain several months in this wonderful and celebrated city. Clerval wanted to meet the men of genius and talent who flourished at this time, but for me this was less important. I was primarily occupied with obtaining the knowledge I needed to fulfill my promise and quickly used the letters of introduction that I had brought with me to gain access to the most renowned scientists.

If this journey had taken place during my schooldays, it would have provided me with indescribable pleasure. But my existence was now cursed, and my only interest in visiting these people was the knowledge I could gain from them. I found other people annoying. But when I was alone, I could daydream and fill my mind with images of heaven and earth. The voice of Henry soothed me, and allowed me to fool myself into a temporary peace. But regular contact with ordinary people made me unhappy and impatient. I saw an unconquerable barrier placed between myself and other people. It was sealed with the blood of William and Justine, and their memory filled my soul with anguish.

But in Clerval I saw myself as I used to be, curious and eager to gain experience and instruction. He was constantly amused and amazed by the different customs and manners of the English. He was also working toward another longtime desire, to visit India. He thought his knowledge of the Indian languages and customs could help the progress of European colonization and trade. Only in Britain could he advance his plan. He was always busy, and the only thing that limited his joy was my own depression. I tried to hide this as much as possible, so as not to interfere with his happiness. I often refused to accompany him, pretending to be busy, so that I could be alone. I now also began to collect the materials necessary for my new creation, and this—to me—was like the torture of single drops of water continually falling on my head. It was torture to me even to just think or speak about it.

After spending a few months in London, we received a letter from someone in Scotland who had visited us at Geneva. He mentioned how beautiful his country was and invited us to Perth, where he lived. Clerval eagerly wanted to accept this invitation, and—while I had no interest in human company—I did wish to again see mountains and streams and all the wondrous works of Nature. We had arrived in England at the beginning of October, and it was now February. We therefore decided to begin our journey north the next month. We did not intend to follow the great road to Edinburgh, but to visit Windsor, Oxford, Matlock, and the Cumberland lakes, arriving at our final destination about the end of July. I packed up the chemical instruments and materials I had collected, resolving to finish my work in some hidden nook in the northern highlands of Scotland.

We left London on the 27th of March and remained a few days at Windsor, rambling in its beautiful forest. This was a new scene to us mountaineers—the majestic oaks, the vast amount of game, and the herds of stately deer were all novelties to us.

From Windsor, we proceeded to Oxford. As we entered this city, we recalled its history. It was here that Charles I had mustered his army. This city had remained

☑ *In "Lines Written a Few Miles Above Tintern Abbey," Wordsworth recalls his earlier passion for Nature by watching his younger sister's reaction to its beauty.*

☑ *In this puzzling passage, the Romantic/liberal/ democratic Mary Shelley and Victor seem to sympathize more with the monarch than with the nation that hoped to establish a republic.*

faithful to him, after the whole nation had forsaken his cause to join the standard of Parliament and liberty. The memory of that unfortunate king and his companions— the friendly Falkland, the rude Goring, Charles' queen, and son—made every part of the city where they may have lived particularly interesting. The spirit of the past lived here, and we delighted to trace its footsteps. If this was not enough, there was the beauty of the city itself. The colleges are ancient and picturesque; the streets are almost magnificent; and the lovely Isis, which flows beside the city through exquisitely green meadows, swells into a peaceful lake, reflecting the majestic clusters of towers, spires and domes nestled among aged trees.

I enjoyed this scene, yet my pleasure was tainted both by the memory of the past and the anticipation of the future. I was made for peaceful happiness. During my youth I was never unhappy or unsatisfied, and if I was ever bored, the beauty of nature or the virtue of man could always interest my heart and lift my spirits. But I am a tree struck by lightning. The bolt has entered my soul, and I felt then that I should survive as an example—a miserable spectacle of wrecked humanity, to be pitied by others and hated even by myself.

We spent some time at Oxford, wandering around and trying to identify every spot relating to the English Civil War. We visited the tomb of the illustrious Hampden and the field on which that patriot fell. For a brief time, I was distracted from my miserable fears to consider the ideals of liberty and self-sacrifice that were memorialized by these sights. Yes, for an instant I dared to shake off my chains and look around me with a free and lofty spirit, but the iron had eaten into my flesh, and I sank again, trembling and hopeless, into my miserable self.

We sadly left Oxford and proceeded to Matlock, which was our next place of rest. This area strongly resembled the scenery of Switzerland, but on a lesser scale. The green hills lacked the crown of distant white Alps that surround the mountains of Geneva. Henry mentioned feeling a little homesick, and I too was happy to leave Matlock because it reminded me too much of home.

From Derby, still proceeding north, we spent two months in Cumberland and Westmoreland. Now I could

Viscount Falkland, Lucius Carey supported the Monarchy in the English Civil War. George, Lord Goring took money and claimed to support both sides. Queen Henrietta Maria was a devoted supporter of her husband, but she was a Catholic queen in a Protestant nation, and her support and influence of her husband actually fuelled opposition against him. The son is most likely Charles, who was restored to the throne some eleven years after his father's execution.

This metaphor probably alludes to the earlier incident in which the young Victor witnessed the damage caused to a tree by a bolt of lightning. (Chapter 2)

John Hampden was a Member of Parliament who was imprisoned for refusing to pay King Charles what he considered an illegal loan. He was killed fairly early in the English Civil War, fighting on the side of the Parliamentarians.

Note the metaphor. Victor's obligation to his Creature is like iron chains cutting into his flesh.

imagine myself in the Swiss mountains. The little patches of snow that still lingered on the northern sides of the mountains, the lakes, and the dashing of the rocky streams were all familiar and dear sights to me. Here we also met some people who almost tricked me into being happy. Clerval's delight was far greater than mine. His mind came alive in the company of men of talent, and he found he possessed more talent and brilliance than he had ever realized.

"I could spend my whole life here," said he to me. "And with these mountains, I would hardly miss Switzerland and the Rhine."

But he found that a traveler's life also includes much pain along with enjoyment. His emotions are always torn in more than one direction, and whenever he becomes comfortable, he must leave for someplace new. Then he grows to love the new place, which he must leave to travel on.

We had barely visited the various lakes of Cumberland and Westmoreland and become friendly with some of the people when it was time to visit our Scottish friend, and we had to leave. For my own part, I was not sorry. I had now neglected my promise for some time, and I feared the consequences of the demon's disappointment. He might remain in Switzerland and wreak his vengeance on my relatives. The thought tormented me, robbing my mind of any peace. I impatiently awaited letters. Any delay meant misery and agonizing fear. When the letters arrived and I saw Elizabeth's handwriting or my father's, I was almost afraid to read them. Then there were times when I thought that the fiend might have followed me and try to hasten my progress by murdering my companion. When these thoughts possessed me, I would not leave Henry for a moment, shadowing and protecting him from the imagined rage of his destroyer. I felt as if I had committed some great crime, the knowledge of which haunted me. I was guiltless, but I had indeed drawn down a horrible curse upon my head.

I visited Edinburgh like a sleepwalker, although that city might have interested even the most unfortunate being. Clerval did not like it as well as Oxford, because Oxford's long and vital history had fascinated him. But the beauty and symmetry of the new town of Edinburgh, its romantic castle and its surroundings were undeniably delightful. Arthur's Seat, St. Bernard's Well, and the Pentland Hills were enough to fill him with cheerfulness and admiration. But I was impatient to end my journey.

We left Edinburgh in a week, passing through Coupar, St. Andrew's, and along the banks of the Tay, to Perth, where our friend expected us. But I was in no mood for company, or even to be an agreeable guest. I told Clerval that I wished to make the tour of Scotland alone. "Please enjoy yourself. We'll meet again later," I said. "I might be gone a month or two, but please do not try to contact me. Leave me to peace and solitude for a short time, and when I return, I hope it will be with a lighter heart."

Henry tried to discourage me, but when he saw that my mind was made up, he conceded. He urged me to write often. "I would rather be with you," he said, "in your solitary rambles, than with these Scottish strangers. Hurry, my dear friend, to return, so I may feel somewhat at home, which I cannot do in your absence."

Having left my friend, I decided to visit some remote spot of Scotland and finish my work alone. I had no doubt that the monster was following me and would appear when I was finished, to receive his companion. With this certainty I crossed the northern highlands and chose one of the most remote of the Orkney Islands as my workplace. It was an ideal place for such work, being hardly more than a rock whose high sides were continually beaten by the waves. The soil was barren, scarcely providing enough pasture for a few miserable cows, and oatmeal for its inhabitants—five people whose skinny and ill-formed arms and legs were evidence of their miserable existence. Vegetables and bread—which were luxuries they seldom enjoyed—even fresh water—had to be imported from the mainland, which was about five miles away.

On the whole island there were but three miserable huts, and one of these was vacant when I arrived. This I rented. It contained but two squalid rooms. The thatch had fallen in, the walls had no plaster, and the door was off its hinges. I ordered it repaired, bought some furniture, and moved in. This would undoubtedly have surprised the cottagers if their own squalid poverty hadn't made them numb. As it was, I lived unseen and unbothered, hardly thanked for the pittance of food and clothes they received from me.

Here I devoted the morning to work, but in the evening, weather permitting, I walked on the stony beach to listen to the waves. It was a monotonous yet ever-changing scene. I thought of Switzerland, so different from this desolate and horrifying landscape. Her hills are covered with vines. Her quaint and lovely cottages are scattered thickly in the plains. Her lakes reflect a blue and gentle sky, and when troubled by the winds, their tumult is like a child playing compared to the giant ocean's roar.

This was my schedule when I first arrived, but as my work progressed, it became more horrible and tedious to me. Sometimes I could not make myself enter my laboratory for several days, and at other times I toiled day and night in order to complete my work. It was, indeed, a filthy process in which I was engaged. During my first experiment, a kind of enthusiastic frenzy had blinded me to its horror. My mind was intently fixed on the completion of my task, and my eyes were shut to the horror of what I was doing. But now I worked fully aware of the consequences of what I did, and my heart often sickened at the work of my hands.

Working on my vile project, completely isolated from any kind of companionship, my spirits became unbalanced. I grew restless and nervous. Every moment I feared the appearance of my persecutor. Sometimes I sat with my eyes fixed on the ground, afraid to raise them and find the creature standing there. I dreaded being alone, for fear that would be the time he would come to claim his companion.

In the meantime I continued my task, and my work was already far advanced. I both looked forward to and dreaded its completion.

Again the sources of Victor's horror are unclear. Certainly he is again gathering body parts, and he is still meddling with things that are not meant for humans to meddle with.

Compare Victor's loneliness with the Creature's. With Walton's.

> **Writing Opportunity:**
>
> *Write an essay in which you explore possible reasons for Mary Shelley's devoting so much space to the places and people she has Victor visit in this chapter.*

Frankenstein

or The Modern Prometheus

❧

MARY SHELLEY

CHAPTER 20

One evening, I sat in my laboratory. The sun had set, and the moon was just rising from the sea. It was too dark to work, and I remained idle, trying to decide whether I should quit for the night or toil through it. As I sat, I began to consider the effects of what I was now doing. Three years before, I had created a fiend whose cruelty was like nothing I'd ever before seen and filled me with guilt and regret. I was now about to form another being, and I knew no more about the type of creature she would turn out to be than I had been able to predict the first one's. She might become ten thousand times more harmful than her mate and delight in murder and wretchedness for its own sake. *He* had sworn to leave civilization and hide himself in the jungle, but *she* had not. And she—presumably a thinking and reasoning animal—might refuse to abide by an agreement made before her creation.

They might even hate each other. The creature loathed his own ugliness. Wasn't it possible that he could develop an even greater abhorrence for it when it came before his eyes in the female form? She also might turn from him with disgust, lusting after the superior beauty of man. She might abandon him. How would he react to that—the ultimate loneliness of having been deserted by one of his own kind? Even if they were to leave Europe and inhabit the deserts of the new world, they might reproduce. A race of devils, capable of threatening the existence of all humankind, would invade the earth. Was I justified, inflicting this curse on humanity for my own benefit? I had been influenced by the reasoning of the being I had created. His fiendish threats had clouded my senses. But now, for the first time, the wickedness of my promise was clear to me. I shuddered to think that future generations might curse me for my selfishness in buying personal peace at the price of the existence of the whole human race.

I trembled, and my heart failed within me, when I looked up and saw the demon at my window. A ghastly grin wrinkled his lips as he looked at me, where I sat performing the task that he had forced on me. Yes, he had followed me, hiding in forests and caves, or taking refuge in wide and desert heaths. Now he came to inspect my progress and claim the fulfillment of my promise.

As I looked at him, his face was filled with malice and treachery. I saw the madness of creating another like to him. Trembling with passion, I tore the lifeless body of the female creature to pieces. The wretch saw me destroy his only hope for happiness, and—with a howl of devilish despair and revenge—ran away.

I left the room and locked the door, vowing never to resume my work. Then, with trembling steps, I went to my own apartment. I was alone, with no one to scatter the gloom and relieve me from my terrible thoughts.

Several hours passed, and I remained near my window gazing on the sea. It was almost motionless, for there was no wind. All nature rested under the eye of the quiet moon. A few fishing vessels dotted the water, and the occasional breeze carried the sound of voices as the fishermen called to one another. I felt the silence, hardly conscious of its meaning, until I heard the paddling of oars near the shore, and a person landed close to my house.

Minutes later, I heard the creaking of my door, as if someone was trying to open it softly. I trembled from head to foot. I had a feeling of dread and wanted to rouse one of the peasants who lived nearby, but I was paralyzed by my fear. Eventually I heard the sound of footsteps along the passage. The door opened, and the wretch whom I dreaded appeared.

Shutting the door, he approached me and said in a choking voice, "Why have you destroyed the work you began? Do you dare break your promise? I have endured toil and misery. I left Switzerland with you. I crept along the shores of the Rhine, among its willow islands and over the summits of its hills. I have lived many months in the heaths of England and among the deserts of Scotland. I have endured immeasurable fatigue, and cold, and hunger. Do you dare destroy my hopes?"

"Go away! I do break my promise. I will never create another like you, equal in deformity and wickedness."

"Slave, I have tried reasoning with you, but you are not worth the effort. Remember my power. If you think you're miserable now, I can make you so wretched that the light of day will be hateful to you. You are my creator, but I am your master; obey!"

"I am resolved, and you are free to do your worst. Your threats cannot move me to an act of wickedness; they only confirm my decision not to create your partner in evil. Should I—in cold blood—expose the earth to a demon who takes delight in death and heartache? Get away! I have made up my mind, and your words will only fuel my rage."

The monster saw my determination and gnashed his teeth in anger. "Shall each man," he cried, "find a wife for his bosom, and each beast have his mate, and I be alone? I had feelings of affection, and they were met with hate and scorn. Man! You may hate, but beware! Your hours will pass in dread and misery, and any chance of your happiness will vanish. Why should *you* have joy while I am *wretched?* You may deny me all I yearn for, but I still have revenge, and it will be dearer than light or food! I may die, but you—my tyrant and tormentor—will curse the sun that shines on your misery. Beware. I have nothing to lose. You will regret the injuries you inflict."

"Devil, stop poisoning the air with your malice. I have told you my decision. I am no coward to bend beneath words. Leave me."

"So be it. I'll go—but remember, *I will be with you on your wedding night.*"

I started forward and exclaimed, "Villain! Before you sign

❷ What do you suppose the Creature is threatening?

my death-warrant, be sure that you are yourself safe."

I would have seized him, but he slipped away from me and ran from the house. In a few moments I saw him in his boat, which shot across the water like an arrow and was soon out of sight.

Everything was once again silent, but his words rang in my ears. I wanted nothing more than to chase him and drown him in the ocean. I furiously paced in my room, while my imagination conjured up a thousand images to torment and sting me. Why hadn't I followed him and fought him to the death? But I had allowed him to escape, and he was headed toward the mainland. I shuddered to think who the next victim of his revenge might be. And then I thought again of his words—"I WILL BE WITH YOU ON YOUR WEDDING NIGHT." That, then, would be the moment of my destiny. In that hour I would die and at once satisfy his lust for revenge and quiet his malice. The prospect did not frighten me, yet when I thought of the endless sorrow of my beloved Elizabeth should she indeed lose me, I cried the first tears I had shed for many months, and I resolved not to surrender without a struggle.

What does Victor assume the Creature is threatening?

The night passed, and the sun rose. I was calmer, if it can be called calmness when the violence of rage sinks into the stillness of despair. I left the house to walk on the beach, which I tried to imagine as an unconquerable barrier between me and all other creatures. I found myself wishing that it were.

I wished I could spend the rest of my life on that barren rock, weary but safe by any sudden shock of misery. If I returned, it was to be sacrificed or to see those whom I most loved die under the grasp of a demon of my own creation.

I walked about the island like a restless ghost, miserably separated from everything it loved. At noon, when the sun rose higher, I fell asleep on the grass. I had been awake all night, my nerves were agitated, and my eyes inflamed. The sleep into which I now sank refreshed me, and when I awoke, I again felt like a human being. I began to think more calmly about what had happened, yet still the words of the fiend rang in my ears like a death-knell—a bad dream that was nevertheless a distinct and oppressive reality.

I was still sitting on the shore after the sun had set, ravenously eating an oatcake, when I saw a fishing boat land close to me. One of the men brought me a packet containing letters from Geneva, including one from Clerval urging me to join him. He said that he was wasting his time where he was, that his new friends in London wanted him to return to complete the arrangements for his Indian enterprise. He could not delay his departure any longer, but since his trip to London would be immediately followed by his longer voyage, he asked me to spend as much time with him as I could spare. He requested that I meet him at Perth, so we could travel south together.

This letter revived me, and I decided to leave my island two days later. Before I left, however, there was a dreaded task to perform. I had to pack up my chemical instruments, and so it was necessary to enter the room in which I had performed my odious work, and handle those sickening utensils. The next morning, at daybreak, I summoned enough courage and unlocked the door of my laboratory. The remains of the half-finished creature lay scattered on the floor, and I almost felt as if I had mangled the living flesh of a human being. I paused to collect myself and then entered the room. With trembling hands, I took the instruments out of the room, but I realized that leaving the creature's remains behind would arouse the horror and suspicion of the peasants. I therefore put them into a basket and weighted it down with stones, intending to throw it into the sea that very night. In the meantime I sat on the beach, cleaning and arranging my chemical apparatus.

Nothing could be more complete than the change in my feelings since the night of the demon's appearance. I had thought of my promise as something that must be fulfilled, regardless of the consequences, but I now felt as if a film had been taken from my eyes, letting me see clearly for the first time. The idea of renewing my efforts never occurred to me. The threat I had heard weighed on my thoughts, but I was certain there was nothing I could do about it. I knew that to create a female like the fiend I had first made would be an act of the basest and most atrocious selfishness, and I refused to consider it.

Between two and three in the morning I sailed out

❷ *Why does Victor consider the creation of the female selfish? Do you agree? Why or why not?*

in a little skiff, about four miles from the shore, with my basket. I was completely alone. A few boats were returning toward land, but I sailed away from them. I felt as if I was committing a dreadful crime and anxiously avoided meeting anyone. Then a thick cloud suddenly covered the moon, and I took advantage of the darkness to toss my basket into the sea. I listened to the gurgling sound as it sank and then sailed away from the spot. The sky became cloudy, but the air was pure, although chilled by a northeast breeze that was then rising. The breeze refreshed me and I decided stay on the water. Setting the rudder in a direct position, I stretched myself at the bottom of the boat. Clouds hid the moon. Everything was dark, and the only sound I heard was the boat as its keel cut through the waves. The murmur lulled me, and in a short time I slept soundly. I do not know how long I was asleep, but by the time I awoke, the sun had already risen. The wind was high, and the waves continually threatened the safety of my little skiff. The wind was northeast and must have driven me far from my point of departure. I tried to change my course but quickly realized that the attempt would instantly fill the boat with water. In this situation, the only thing I could do was sail against the wind. I confess that I was terrified. I had no compass with me and was so unfamiliar with the geography of this part of the world that the position of the sun was of little help to me. I feared that I might be driven into the Atlantic and starve or be drowned in the turbulence all around me. I had already been out many hours and was thirsty. This thirst would prove to be merely a prelude to my other sufferings. I looked at the sky, covered by clouds that flew before the wind, only to be replaced by others. I looked upon the sea that would be my grave.

"Fiend," I screamed aloud, "your task is already accomplished!"

I thought of Elizabeth, of my father, and of Clerval—all left behind, on whom the monster might satisfy his bloody and merciless rage. This idea plunged me into despair so profound that even now I shudder simply to remember it.

Several hours later, as the sun set on the horizon, the

wind died away into a gentle breeze, and the sea calmed. But this calm was soon replaced by a heavy swell. I felt sick and hardly able to hold the rudder, when suddenly I saw a line of high land toward the south.

Almost exhausted as I was, this sudden rescue brought a flood of warm joy to my heart, and tears gushed from my eyes.

How changeable our feelings are, and how strange that we cling to life even in the midst of endless misery! I constructed another sail with a part of my clothing and eagerly steered my course toward the land. It was wild and rocky, but did appear to have some plantlife. I saw vessels near the shore and found myself suddenly transported back to civilization. I carefully examined the landscape and noticed a steeple behind a small promontory. Since I was exhausted, I sailed directly toward the town, where it would be easiest to find food. Fortunately I had money with me.

As I turned the promontory I saw a small neat town and a good harbor, which I entered, amazed and joyful at my unexpected escape.

While I docked my boat, several people crowded toward the spot. They seemed quite surprised at my appearance, but instead of offering to help me, they whispered together with gestures that at any other time might have frightened me. As it was, I merely noticed that they spoke English, and I therefore addressed them in that language. "My good friends," I said, "will you be so kind as to tell me where I am?"

"You will know that soon enough," replied a man with a hoarse voice. "You may have come to a place you will not like, but you will have no say in your next destination, I promise you."

I was surprised to receive such a rude answer from a stranger, and I was shocked by the frowning and angry faces of his companions. "Why do you answer me so roughly?" I replied. "Surely it is not the custom of Englishmen to receive strangers so inhospitably."

"I don't know," said the man, "what the custom of the English may be, but it is the custom of the Irish to hate criminals." While he spoke, I saw that the crowd had increased rapidly. Their faces showed a mixture of curiosity and anger, which annoyed me but also frightened me a little.

I asked the way to the inn, but no one answered. Then I moved forward, and a murmuring arose from the crowd as they followed me and surrounded me. Then a hostile looking man approached and tapped me on the shoulder.

"Come, sir," he said, "you must follow me to Mr. Kirwin's to give an account of yourself."

"Who is Mr. Kirwin? Why do I have to give an account of myself? Isn't this a free country?"

"Aye, sir, free enough for honest folks. Mr. Kirwin is a judge, and you must give an account of the death of a gentleman who was found murdered here last night."

This answer startled me, but I soon recovered. I was certain to be proven innocent, so I followed him in silence and was led to one of the best houses in the town. I was ready to collapse from fatigue and hunger, but being surrounded by a crowd, I thought it wise to summon all my strength, so that no weakness might be interpreted as a sign of guilt. Little did I know what awaited me, how I would be overwhelmed with horror that would mock death itself.

I must pause here, for it requires all my strength to recall the memory of the frightful events that I am about to tell you about.

Predict:

What do you think Victor is going to say?

Frankenstein
or The Modern Prometheus

❦

MARY SHELLEY

CHAPTER 21

I was soon brought before the judge, a kind, old man with calm and mild manners. He looked at me fairly severely, and then asked my escorts who would come forward as witnesses on this occasion.

About half a dozen men came forward. The judge selected one who testified that he had been out fishing the night before with his son and brother-in-law, Daniel Nugent. At about ten o'clock, they saw a strong northerly wind rising and steered toward port. It was a very dark night, as the moon had not yet risen. They did not land at the harbor, but at a creek about two miles below where they usually landed. He walked on first, carrying a part of the fishing tackle, and his companions followed him at some distance.

As he walked along the sands, he tripped on something and fell onto the ground. When his companions came up to help him, they saw by the light of their lanterns that he had tripped over the body of a man who was apparently dead. They first assumed he was a drowning victim who'd washed ashore. On closer examination, however, they found that the clothes were not wet, and the body was not yet cold. They immediately carried it to the nearby cottage of an old woman and tried in vain to restore it to life. It appeared to be a handsome young man, about twenty-five years of age. He had apparently been strangled, for there was no sign of any violence except the black mark of fingers on his neck.

❷ *What does Victor suspect?*

I was not the least interested in the first part of this testimony. But when the mark of the fingers was mentioned, I remembered my brother's murder and became extremely agitated. My limbs trembled, and my eyes misted with tears. I had to lean on a chair for support. The judge watched me closely and, of course, took my reaction as a sign of guilt.

The son confirmed his father's account. When Daniel Nugent was called, he swore positively—that just before his companion fell—he saw a boat, with a single man in it, not far from the shore. As far as he could tell, it was the same boat in which I had just landed. A woman testified that she lived near the beach and was standing at the door of her cottage, waiting for the return of the fishermen, about an hour before she heard of the discovery of the body. She saw a boat with only one man in it push off from that part of the shore where the corpse was later found.

Another woman confirmed the account of the fishermen having brought the body into her house. It was not cold. They put it into a bed and rubbed it, and Daniel went to the town for a doctor, but it was too late.

Several other men were questioned about my landing, and they agreed that—with the strong north wind that had arisen during the night—it was likely that I had beaten about for many hours and had to return to almost the same spot I had departed from. They also observed that it seemed as if I had brought the body from somewhere else, and had accidentally landed close to the spot where I had left the body because I did not know the coast well.

After this testimony, Mr. Kirwin decided I should be taken into the room where the body lay, to see what effect it would have on me. My reaction to hearing the details of the murder was probably the inspiration. And so the judge and several other escorts brought me to the inn. There had been so many strange coincidences during this eventful night, but, knowing that I had been speaking with several people on the island I had been staying on at the time that the body was found, I felt safe.

❷ *What do you think Victor is about to discover?*

I entered the room where the corpse lay and was led up to the coffin.

How can I describe what I felt when I looked at that body? I still feel the horror, and I can't remember that terrible moment without shuddering in agony. The investigation, the judge and witnesses, everything I had just experienced became unreal when I saw the lifeless form of Henry Clerval stretched before me. I gasped for breath, and throwing myself on the body, I exclaimed, "Has my fatal scheme killed you too, Henry? I have two lives on my conscience, and perhaps more to come, but you, Clerval, my friend, my benefactor—"

My agony was truly beyond human endurance, and I was carried out of the room in strong convulsions. A fever followed. I was near death for two months, and I was told my ravings were frightful. I called myself the murderer of William, of Justine, and of Clerval. Sometimes I begged my nurses to help me destroy the fiend who tormented me, and at others I felt his fingers already grasping my neck, and screamed aloud with agony and terror. Fortunately, as I spoke my native language, only Mr. Kirwin understood me, but my gestures and bitter cries were enough to frighten the other witnesses. Why didn't I die? I was the most miserable of humans, so why did I not sink into forgetfulness and rest? Death snatches away many beautiful children, the only hopes of their doting parents. How many brides and youthful lovers have been in their prime one day, only to become food for worms the next? What was I made of that I could withstand so many shocks, which—like the turning of the wheel—continually renewed the torture?

But I was doomed to live and in two months found myself in a prison, stretched on a bare cot. I felt as if I were waking from a dream to learn that I was surrounded by jailers in a cell that can only be described as a dungeon.

I remember that it was morning when I finally became conscious. I had forgotten what had happened and only felt overwhelmed by some unknown grief. But when I looked around and saw the barred windows and the grubbiness of the room, my memory returned, and I groaned bitterly.

Remember that first-person narrator Victor speaks for himself, not necessarily Mary Shelley.

What is ironic about Victor's complaint about his treatment?

I disturbed an old woman who was sleeping in a chair beside me. She was a hired nurse, the wife of one of the guards, and her face expressed the worst of that class. The lines of her face were hard and rude, devoid of sympathy. Her tone was indifferent as she addressed me in English, and the voice struck me as one that I had heard during my sufferings. "Are you better now, sir?" she asked.

I replied weakly, "I think so, but unless this is a dream, I am sorry to be alive to feel this misery and horror."

"If you mean about the gentleman you murdered," replied the old woman, "I also believe you would be better off dead, for I think you will have a hard time of it! But that's none of my business. I am here to nurse you and make you well. I do my duty with a clear conscience. Everyone should do the same."

I turned away from this hateful woman who could speak so unkindly to a person so recently near death, but I was too weary to think about everything that had happened. My whole life seemed like a dream. It seemed so unreal to me that I did from time to time doubt its truth.

As the images from that life floated before my eyes, I grew feverish, and darkness shrouded me. No one was near to soothe me with the gentle voice of love, no affectionate hand supported me. The doctor came and prescribed medicines, and the old woman prepared them for me, but the doctor had been careless and the nurse brutal. Who cared about the fate of a murderer but the hangman?

These were my first thoughts, but I soon learned that Mr. Kirwin had shown me extreme kindness. He had caused the best room in the prison to be prepared for me—wretched as it was—and it was he who had provided a doctor and a nurse. True, he rarely came to see me, for he sincerely wanted to relieve the sufferings of every human creature, but he had no desire to witness the mad ravings of a murderer. He came occasionally to see that I was not neglected, but his visits were short and far between.

One day during my recovery, while seated in a chair, my eyes were half open, and my face looked like death. I was entertaining my usual gloomy and miserable thoughts and realized that death was actually preferable to living

in such a wretched world. I even considered declaring
myself guilty in order to suffer the penalty of the law. I
was, after all, considerably *less innocent* than poor Justine
had been. These were my thoughts when the door of my
cell opened, and Mr. Kirwin entered. His expression was
sympathetic and compassionate. He drew a chair close to
mine and addressed me in French, "I fear that this place
is very shocking to you. Can I do anything to make you
more comfortable?"

"Thank you, but there is nothing you can do for me."

"I know that the sympathy of a stranger is little comfort to you, burdened by so strange a misfortune. But I
hope you will soon be free from this place, for surely the
evidence will clear you of the criminal charge."

"That is my least concern. I have become, through the
most unlikely situation, the most miserable of mortals.
As persecuted as I am and have been, could death be
anything but a relief?"

"Nothing could be more painful than what you have
been through. You were thrown, by some surprising
accident, on this shore—usually known for its hospitality. Before you even knew where you were, you were
arrested and charged with murder. The first thing you
saw was the body of your friend, murdered in such a horrible way and left in your path by some fiend."

I was startled by how much Mr. Kirwin knew about
me. My astonishment must have been evident, for Mr.
Kirwin hastened to add, "As soon as you were taken
ill, all your identifying papers were brought to me, and
I examined them to see if I might notify any relatives
of your misfortune and illness. I found several letters,
including one from your father. I immediately wrote to
Geneva. That was nearly two months ago. But you are too
ill to bear any further stress right now."

"I cannot bear any more suspense. Tell me what new
death has been inflicted, and whose murder I am now to
lament?"

"Your family is perfectly well," said Mr. Kirwin with
gentleness; "and someone, a friend, has come to visit you."

It instantly occurred to me that the murderer had
come to mock and taunt me with Clerval's death, to
force me into complying with his hellish desires. I put

Again, remember the heightened sensations and sensitivity of the Romantics and the Romantic Hero.

Notice how easily and how often Victor jumps to the wrong conclusion and reacts accordingly.

my hand before my eyes, and cried out in agony, "Oh! Take him away! I cannot see him; for God's sake, do not let him enter!"

Mr. Kirwin looked at me with a troubled expression. He could not help viewing my exclamations as confessions and said severely, "I should have thought, young man, that the presence of your father would have been welcome instead of inspiring such violent disgust."

"My father!" I cried, and my anguish turned to pleasure. "Is my father really here? How kind, how very kind! But where is he, why does he not hurry to me?"

My abrupt change of mood surprised and pleased the judge. He became friendly again, leaving the room with my nurse. In a moment my father entered it.

At that moment, nothing could have made me happier than seeing my father. I stretched out my hand to him and cried, "Are you safe—and Elizabeth—and Ernest?" My father assured me of their wellbeing and tried to raise my depressed spirits by dwelling on these subjects so dear to my heart. But he soon understood that nothing could make a prison a cheerful place.

"What a place to find you, my son!" said he, looking mournfully at the barred windows and wretched appearance of the room. "You traveled to seek happiness, but disaster just seems to follow you. And poor Clerval—"

The name of my unfortunate and murdered friend was too painful for me to hear in my weakened state. I wept. "Alas! Yes, father," I replied, "some horrible fate hangs over me, and I must live to fulfill it, or surely I would have died on Henry's coffin."

We were not allowed to speak for very long, for my delicate health demanded rest. Mr. Kirwin came in and insisted that I not exert myself. But my father's appearance was like having my guardian angel nearby, and I gradually regained my health.

> ### Research Opportunity:
> Look up psychosomatic illness and the effects of one's emotional state on one's physical condition.

As my sickness was cured, I was absorbed by a gloomy and black melancholy that nothing could chase away. The image of Clerval was always before me, ghastly and murdered. It was often impossible for me to disguise the pain of these memories, and my friends dreaded a dangerous relapse. Alas! Why did they work so hard to save my miserable and detested life? Surely, it was only so that I could fulfill my destiny, which I knew was imminent. I wished for death to soon extinguish this torture and relieve me from the mighty weight of anguish—bringing both justice and rest. While the appearance of death was distant, the wish was always in my thoughts, and I often sat for hours motionless and speechless, wishing for some catastrophe that would annihilate both my destroyer and me in its ruins.

❷ What does Victor believe his destiny to be?

The time of the trial approached. I had already been three months in prison, and although I was still weak and in continual danger of a relapse, I was forced to travel nearly a hundred miles to the country town where the court was held. Mr. Kirwin himself conducted my defense, collecting witnesses and evidence. I was spared the disgrace of appearing publicly as a criminal, as the case was not brought before the court that decides on life and death. The Grand Jury rejected the charge, once it was proved that I was on the Orkney Islands when the body of my friend was found. Two weeks later, I was set free.

❷ The Grand Jury is the body of citizens who hear the evidence and determine whether there is cause to formally indict the accused of a crime and bring him or her to trial.

My father was overjoyed at my release, which allowed me to breathe the open air and return to my native Switzerland. I could not share his joy, for it made no difference to me where I was. Both the walls of a dungeon or a palace were equally hateful. My life had been poisoned forever, and although the sun shone as brightly on me as anyone, I could see nothing but a dense and frightful darkness, that no light but the glimmer of two eyes glaring upon me could penetrate. Sometimes they were Henry's expressive eyes, languishing in death, the dark orbs nearly covered by the lids and the long black lashes that fringed them. Sometimes it was the watery, clouded eyes of the monster, as I first saw them in my room at Ingolstadt.

❷ What do you suppose is the Creature's plan?

My father tried to bring me back to life. He spoke of Geneva, which I would soon visit. He spoke of Elizabeth and Ernest, but the only reply I could offer was to groan painfully. Sometimes, indeed, I wished for happiness,

✅ *Literally, "disease of the country," maladie du pays is French for homesickness. Victor is longing to return to his native land.*

❓ *Again, would you describe the tone of this passage to be bathos or pathos? Why?*

remembering my beloved cousin or longed, with a devouring *maladie du pays* to once again see the blue lake and rapid Rhone, that had been so dear to me in early childhood. But I mostly spent my days in a sluggish pout so that a prison was as welcome a residence as the most divine scene in nature. The only relief I had from this mental and emotional numbness was to sink into deeper misery and despair. At these times I did try to end my hated life, and it required persistent vigilance to keep me from committing suicide.

But I still had one duty to fulfill, the memory of which finally helped me to overcome my selfish despair. It was necessary for me to return—without delay—to Geneva, to protect the lives of my loved ones and to lie in wait for the murderer. If any chance led me to his hiding place, or if he dared show himself to me, I would put an end to the existence of the monster I had created. My father still wanted to delay our departure, fearing I was still not strong enough to travel, for I was a shattered wreck—the mere shadow of a human being. My strength was gone. I was a skeleton, and suffered fever night and day. Still, my impatience to leave Ireland convinced my father to yield. We booked passage on a vessel bound for Havre-de-Grace and swiftly sailed from the Irish shores.

It was midnight. I lay on the deck looking at the stars and listening to the waves. I hailed the darkness that shut Ireland from my sight, and my pulse beat with a feverish joy when I thought of seeing Geneva. The past seemed like a frightful dream, yet the ship itself, and even the wind and the sea reminded me too well of reality. Clerval, my friend and dearest companion, had fallen victim both to my monstrous creature and to me. I relived, in my memory, my whole life—my quiet happiness with my family in Geneva, the death of my mother, and my departure for Ingolstadt. I remembered—shuddering—the mad enthusiasm that led me to create my hideous enemy, and the night that he first lived. I was unable to continue. A thousand feelings pressed upon me, and I wept bitterly. Since my recovery, every night I took a small quantity of laudanum, for without it I would not have been able to sleep. Burdened by the memory of my various misfortunes, I now swallowed double my

✅ *Laudanum is a mixture of alcohol and opium that was widely used as a cure for just about everything in the late eighteenth and early nineteenth centuries.*

usual dose and soon slept profoundly. But sleep offered
me no relief from thought and misery. My dreams frightened me horribly. Toward morning I was haunted by a
nightmare in which I felt the fiend grasp my neck, and
I was unable to free myself. My father woke me. There
was no monster, only the sound of the crashing waves
and the glittering of the stars above. For a brief moment
I did manage to forger my troubles and fell again into a
restful sleep.

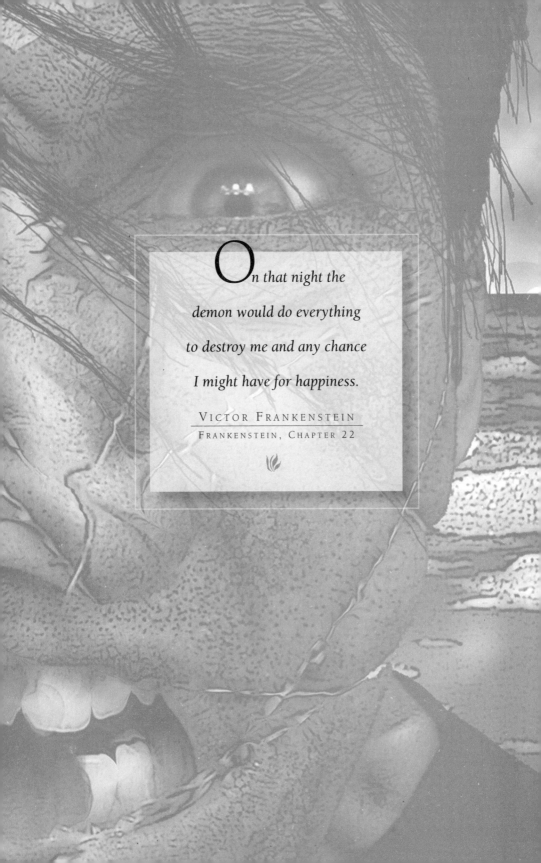

On that night the demon would do everything to destroy me and any chance I might have for happiness.

VICTOR FRANKENSTEIN
FRANKENSTEIN, CHAPTER 22

Frankenstein
or The Modern Prometheus

MARY SHELLEY

CHAPTER 22

The voyage came to an end. We landed, and proceeded to Paris. I soon found that I had overtaxed my strength and that I had to rest before continuing. My father never tired in his care for me, but he did not know the true cause of my sufferings and sought to fix them in the wrong way. He tried to distract me with the company of other people. But I hated all humans. Well, not really *hated!* They were my brothers and sisters, my fellow beings, and I felt connected even to the worst of them. But I felt that I had no right to companionship. I had unleashed an enemy among them who reveled in shedding their blood and causing misery. How they would all hate me and drive me from their world if they knew my unhallowed acts and the crimes I had committed!

My father finally accepted my aversion to society and tried other methods to banish my despair. Sometimes he thought that I had been humiliated by the accusation of murder, and he tried to impress on me the futility of pride.

"Alas! My father," I said, "how little you know me. How could a wretch like me feel pride? It would fly in the face of all human dignity. Poor unhappy Justine was as innocent as I, and she suffered the same charge. She died for it. And I am the cause of this—I murdered her. William, Justine, and Henry—they all died by my hands."

❷ *Remember what the Creature said about not being connected to any other being. Is Victor correct in asserting that he has no right to human companionship?*

❷ *"Unhallowed" means not sanctified or blessed. This is the crux of the issue. Victor has done that which is not proper for a man to do. Like Prometheus, he has usurped a power, a knowledge that belongs only to the gods.*

AN ANNOTATED ADAPTATION

During my imprisonment, my father had often heard me make the same statement. When I accused myself, sometimes he wanted an explanation. At other times he seemed to think it was simply a delusion, as if some misunderstanding had embedded itself in my imagination during my illness, and still remained in my mind even after my recovery.

I avoided explanation and remained silent about the wretch I had created. I believed people would think I was insane. This alone would have been enough to keep me quiet, but, I also could not bring myself to reveal a secret that would terrify whoever heard it. I curbed my desperate desire for sympathy and was silent—even though I would have given *anything* to be able to confide the fatal secret. Still, at times, I would betray myself, words bursting uncontrollably from me. I could offer no explanation for them, but the fact that they were true was oddly something of a relief to me. At this most recent outburst, my father said, with a shocked expression, "Victor, what craziness is this? My dear son, don't ever say such things."

"I am not insane!" I cried emphatically. "The sun and the heavens—who have seen my deeds—can testify to my truth. I am the murderer of those most innocent victims. My own foolishness caused their deaths. I would gladly have shed my own blood—drop by drop—to have saved their lives. But I could not, Father. Indeed I could not sacrifice the whole human race."

My words only succeeded in convincing my father that I was indeed deranged, and he instantly changed the subject of our conversation, trying to make me think of other things. He wished as much as possible to erase all memory of what had happened in Ireland. He never again mentioned it or allowed me to speak of my misfortunes.

As time passed I became calmer. There was misery in my heart, but I no longer babbled insanely about my crimes. The awareness of them was enough for me. With all of my self-control, I curbed my desire to declare my wretchedness to the whole world, and my manners were tranquil and more composed than they had ever been since my journey to the sea of ice when I first met my creature face to face. A few days before we left Paris on our way to Switzerland, I received the following letter from Elizabeth:

My dear Friend,

It gave me great pleasure to receive a letter from my uncle postmarked from Paris. You are no longer so far away, and I may hope to see you in less than two weeks. My poor cousin, how much you must have suffered! I expect to see you looking even more ill than when you left Geneva. This winter has been miserable, tortured as I have been by suspense. Yet I hope to see peace in your expression and to find that your heart is not totally void of comfort and tranquility.

Yet I fear that what made you so miserable a year ago still persists, and is now perhaps even worse. I would not disturb you now, when so many misfortunes trouble you, but a conversation that I had with my uncle before his departure makes some explanation necessary before we meet. Explanation! You may wonder what I could possibly have to explain. If this is the case, my questions are answered and all my doubts satisfied. But you are far away, and it is possible that what I have to say might be both painful but liberating to you. I therefore can no longer postpone writing what I have often wished to say to you but have never had the courage to begin.

You well know, Victor, that your parents had planned our marriage ever since our infancy. We were told this when we were young, and we were taught to look forward to it as inevitable. We were affectionate playmates, and, I believe, dear and valued friends, as we grew older. But we loved each other as a brother and sister love each other without desiring a more intimate union. Could this now be the case with us? Tell me, dearest Victor. Answer me truthfully, I beg you—Are you in love with someone else?

You have traveled, and spent several years of your life at Ingolstadt. I confess to you, my friend, that when I saw you so unhappy last autumn, keeping yourself apart from everyone, I could not help thinking that you might regret our engagement. Perhaps you believe yourself bound in honor to fulfill your parents' wishes. But this is false reasoning. I confess to you, my friend, that I love you and

❷ *What does Elizabeth assume is the cause of Victor's sorrow?*

that I have dreamed of our future together. But it is *your* happiness I desire as well as my own when I tell you that our marriage would make me miserable unless it were your own free choice. Even now I weep to think that, weighed down as you are by such cruel misfortunes, you may stifle all hope of your own love and happiness in the name of "honor". I, who have so clear-eyed an affection for you, could increase your misery by standing between you and your true wishes. Ah! Victor, my love for you is too sincere to allow this to happen. Be happy, my friend, and know that nothing else in life is as important to me as your happiness.

Do not let this letter disturb you. Do not answer tomorrow, or the next day, or even until you're home, if it will give you pain. My uncle will send me news of your health, and if I see but one smile on your lips when we meet, should this or anything else I've done be the cause of that smile, I shall need no other happiness.

Elizabeth Lavenza
Geneva, May 18th, 17-

This letter reminded me of the threat of the fiend—"I WILL BE WITH YOU ON YOUR WEDDING-NIGHT!" Such was my sentence, and on that night the demon would do everything to destroy me and any chance I might have for happiness. On that night he was determined to culminate his crimes with my death. Well, so be it. A deadly struggle would then certainly take place, and should he win, I would be at peace and his power over me would be finished. If *he* were destroyed, I would be a free man. But alas! What freedom would it be? The freedom granted a peasant when his family has been massacred before his eyes, his cottage burnt, his lands laid waste, and he is left homeless, penniless, and alone…but free? That would be the nature of my freedom except for the treasure I had in Elizabeth.

Sweet and beloved Elizabeth! I read and reread her letter, and my heart dared to whisper dreams of love and joy, but the apple was already eaten and the angel's sword was drawn banishing me from all hope. Yet I would die to make her happy. If the monster fulfilled his threat, I *would* die. Still, I wondered whether my mar-

This is another allusion to the Adam and Eve story, their eating the fruit of the Tree of the Knowledge of Good and Evil (traditionally represented as an apple), their expulsion from Eden, and the entrance to Eden's being blocked by an angel with a flaming sword to prevent Adam and Eve's reentry.

riage would hasten my fate. My destruction might indeed
arrive a few months sooner, but if my torturer suspected
me of a delaying tactic, he would surely find other and
perhaps more dreadful means of revenge.

He had vowed to be with me on my WEDDING-
NIGHT, yet he did not seem to feel compelled to restrain
himself in the meantime. As if to show me that he was
not yet satiated with blood, he had murdered Clerval
immediately after issuing his threat. I decided, therefore,
that if my immediate marriage to my cousin was the key
to her happiness or my father's, my adversary's designs
against my life would not delay it a single hour.

In this state of mind I wrote to Elizabeth. My letter was
calm and affectionate. "I fear, my beloved girl," I said,
"little happiness remains for us on earth, yet all my hope
is centered on you. Chase away your idle fears. To you
alone do I dedicate my life and my happiness. I have one
secret, Elizabeth, a dreadful one, which will chill your
frame with horror. Far from being surprised at my misery,
you will only wonder how I have endured. I will confide
this tale of misery and terror to you the day after we are
married, for, my sweet cousin, there must be perfect
confidence between us. But until then, I ask you, do not
mention it. This I most sincerely request, and I know you
will comply."

About a week after the arrival of Elizabeth's letter,
we returned to Geneva. The sweet girl welcomed me
warmly, yet tears were in her eyes as she saw my emaciated body and feverish cheeks. I noticed a change in her
as well. She was thinner and had lost much of that wonderful liveliness that had charmed me. But her gentleness
and soft looks of compassion made her a more fit companion for one as devastated and miserable as I was.

My newfound tranquility did not endure. Memory
brought madness, and when I thought of what had
occurred, a real insanity possessed me. Sometimes I was
furious and enraged, sometimes low and despondent. I
neither spoke nor looked at anyone, but sat motionless,
bewildered by the many, many miseries that overcame
me.

Elizabeth alone had the power to distract me. Her gentle voice would soothe me when I was overwhelmed by

Mary Shelley is trying to portray Victor's marrying Elizabeth as a selfless, sacrificial act.

emotion and only she could bring me out of my gloomy sulks and daydreams. She wept *with* me and *for* me. When reason returned, she tried to encourage me to accept what had happened. Ah! It is one thing for the unlucky to accept their fate, but for the guilty there is no peace. Remorse poisons whatever comfort there might be in expressing grief. Soon after my arrival, my father spoke of my impending marriage to Elizabeth. I remained silent.

❷ Explain the distinction Victor is making between the unlucky and the guilty.

"Is there, then, someone else?" he asked me.

"No one. I love Elizabeth and look forward to our union with delight. Let the date be chosen, and on it I will dedicate myself—in life or death—to the happiness of my cousin."

"My dear Victor, do not speak this way. We have had many misfortunes, but we must embrace what we still have and transfer our love for those we have lost to those who yet live. We will not be a large family, but we will be a close family—drawn together by our love for one another and for the unspeakable horrors we have suffered. And when time has lessened your pain, you and Elizabeth will have children to fill the void left by those who have so cruelly been taken from us."

❷ Dramatic irony is the device of allowing the reader or audience to know something that the characters do not know.

Suspense and Irony Alert:

What event is Victor alluding to? What is ironic about Victor's realization?

That was my father's advice. But to me the memory of the threat returned. It was no wonder that, all-powerful as the murderous fiend had been, I should almost regard him as invincible. When he had pronounced the words "I SHALL BE WITH YOU ON YOUR WEDDING-NIGHT," I truly believed the threatened fate was unavoidable. But death was nothing to me when weighed against losing Elizabeth. And so, with a content—with even a cheerful face—I agreed with my father that the ceremony should take place in ten days, if my cousin would consent, and thus put seal to my fate.

Great God! If I had imagined the hellish intention of my fiendish adversary, I would have exiled myself forever and wandered a friendless outcast over the earth rather than consent to this disastrous marriage. But, like a magician, the monster had blinded me to his real intentions, and while I thought that I had prompted only my own death, I caused the death of a far dearer victim.

As the wedding day drew nearer—whether from fear or foresight—I grew sadder and sadder. But I hid my feelings and pretended to be joyful. This brought smiles and joy to my father's face, but hardly deceived Elizabeth. She looked forward to our marriage with satisfaction, but mixed with some fear. Our family's many, many misfortunes had shown all of us that happiness could be very short-lived and suddenly overwhelmed by deep and everlasting regret. We prepared for the wedding. We received visits of congratulations from our friends and neighbors. Everyone smiled. I hid the anxiety in my heart and earnestly embraced my father's plans, although I knew they would end in tragedy. Through my father's efforts, a portion of Elizabeth's inheritance had been restored to her by the Austrian government. A small residence on the shores of Lake Como belonged to her. It was agreed that, immediately after our wedding, we would travel to this home—Villa Lavenza—and spend our honeymoon there.

In the meantime I took every precaution to defend myself in case the fiend should openly attack me. I carried pistols and a dagger constantly and was always vigilant. This gave me some peace of mind. Indeed, as the day approached, the threat seemed unreal, insignificant when compared to the certainty of my happiness.

Elizabeth seemed happy. My own tranquil mood put her mind at ease. But on the wedding day itself she was glum, shrouded by a premonition of evil. Perhaps she was also thinking about the dreadful secret I was to reveal to her on the following day. My father—overjoyed and in the flurry of preparation—only recognized in the melancholy of his niece the hesitancy of a bride.

After the ceremony, a large party assembled at my father's, but it was agreed that Elizabeth and I would begin our journey by water, sleeping that night at Evian and continuing our voyage the following day. The day was fair, the wind favorable. Everyone smiled at our leaving for our wedding trip.

Those were the last moments of happiness for me. We sailed rapidly along. The sun was hot, but we were shaded by a kind of canopy while we enjoyed the beauty of the passing scenery, sometimes on one side of the lake, where we saw the flat-topped Mont Saleve, the pleasant banks of the Montalegre River, and at a distance, higher than everything, the beautiful Mont Blanc and the group of snowy mountains that offer weak imitations of her grandeur. Sometimes coasting the opposite banks, we saw the mighty Jura Mountains blocking the way for any ambitious fool who would leave his native country, and an almost unconquerable barrier to any invader who might wish to enslave it.

I took Elizabeth's hand. "You are sad, my love. If you only knew what I have suffered and will yet endure, you would try to let me taste the quiet and freedom from despair that this one day at least permits me to enjoy."

"Be happy, my dear Victor," replied Elizabeth. "There is, I hope, nothing to distress you. Be assured that even if my face doesn't show it, my heart is contented. Something whispers to me not to expect happiness, but I will not listen to such a sinister voice. See how fast we move along and how the clouds above Mont Blanc make this beautiful scene still more interesting. And see the fish swimming in this clear water, where we can see every pebble at the bottom of the lake. What a divine day! How happy and serene all nature appears!"

Thus Elizabeth attempted to distract both of us from melancholy subjects. But her mood was unpredictable—joyful one moment, melancholy and distracted the next.

The sun sank lower in the sky. We passed the river Drance and watched its path through the chasms of the higher peaks and the glens of the lower hills. The Alps here come closer to the lake, and we approached the range of mountains that forms its eastern boundary. The church steeple of Evian shone under the woods that surrounded it, and the range of mountain above mountain by which it was overhung.

The wind, which had up to that point carried us along with amazing speed, lessened at sunset to a light breeze. The soft air just ruffled the water and pleasantly rustled the trees as we approached the shore. The shore breeze carried the most delightful scent of flowers and hay. The

Remember that it was on a glacier near Mont Blanc where Victor first spoke with his Creature.

A town in Switzerland, near Geneva. It is where the popular mineral water is bottled.

sun sank beneath the horizon as we landed, and as I touched the shore, my fear arose again, like a lump in my throat. I did not yet know that misery would soon take hold of me forever.

Research Opportunity:

Find maps of Switzerland, Germany, and the British Isles and mark the places Victor has mentioned throughout his travels.

✔ *Mary Shelley has two apparent motives for this detailed travelogue. First, it is an established motif in this book and reflects her desire for verisimilitude. Secondly, she is building suspense.*

"**M**an," I cried, "how
ignorant you are in your
pride of wisdom!"

Victor Frankenstein
Frankenstein, Chapter 23

Frankenstein

or The Modern Prometheus

❧

MARY SHELLEY

CHAPTER 23

It was eight o'clock when we landed. We walked for a short time on the shore, enjoying the fading light, and then retired to the inn gazing at the lovely scene of waters, woods, and mountains, obscured in darkness, yet still visible in their black outlines.

The wind, which had fallen in the south, now rose with great violence in the west. The moon had reached her height and was beginning to set. Windblown clouds swept across her face, dimming her rays. The lake reflected the busy heavens that were made to look even busier by the restless waves that were beginning to rise. Suddenly a heavy storm broke.

Don't miss the signifcance of the bad weather.

I had been calm during the day, but as soon as night fell I grew terrified. I was anxious and watchful, my right hand grasping the pistol hidden in my bosom. Every sound terrified me, but I resolved that I would hold my life dearly and not shrink from the conflict until my own life—or that of my adversary—was extinguished. Elizabeth noticed my anxiety for some time but maintained a nervous silence. Still, there was something in my glance that filled her with terror, and trembling, she asked, "What is it that worries you, my dear Victor? What is it you fear?"

"Oh! Peace, peace, my love," I replied, "All will be safe after this, but tonight is dreadful, very dreadful."

❷ Is this a good decision?

I spent an hour in this state of mind, when I realized how awful it would be for my dear Elizabeth to witness the fierce combat that would soon occur between my monster and myself. I therefore urged her to retire, resolving not to join her until I knew where my enemy was hidden and when he planned to confront me.

She left me, and I continued walking up and down the corridors of the house and checking every corner where the fiend might be hiding. But I found no trace of him and was beginning to think that some lucky chance had prevented his revenge when suddenly I heard a shrill and dreadful scream. It came from Elizabeth's room. As soon as I heard it, I knew what had happened.

My arms dropped, every muscle and tendon moved as if in a slow-motion dream. I could feel the blood trickling in my veins and tingling in my arms and legs. In an instant the scream was repeated, and I rushed into the room. Great God! Why didn't I die right then? Why did I survive to tell this awful story? She was there, lifeless, thrown across the bed, her head hanging down and her pale and distorted features half covered by her hair. From that moment, everywhere I turn I see the same figure—her bloodless arms and limp body flung by the murderer onto our bridal bed. Could I see this and live? Alas! Life is most enduring where it is most hated. For a moment I lost consciousness, fainting onto the ground.

When I recovered, I found myself surrounded by the people at the inn. Their faces were full of a breathless terror, but their response seemed a mockery, a mere shadow of my own emotions. I escaped from them to the room that held Elizabeth's body—my love, my wife, so lately living, so dear, so worthy. She had been moved from the position I'd found her, and now she lay with her head upon her arm and a handkerchief thrown across her face and neck. She looked peaceful, as if she were merely asleep. I rushed toward her and embraced her passionately, but the deadly limpness and coldness of the limbs told me that the Elizabeth I had loved and cherished was gone. The murderous mark of the fiend's grasp was on her neck, and her breathing was stilled. While I still hung over her in the agony of despair, I happened to look up. The windows of the room had been darkened, and I panicked on seeing the pale yellow light of the moon illuminate the chamber. The shutters had been thrown back, and with indescribable horror, I saw at the open window THE figure most hideous and abhorred, a grin on his face He seemed to jeer, as he pointed toward the corpse of my wife. I rushed toward the window, drew the pistol from my bosom, and fired. But he got away, leaping from the window and plunging into the lake.

The gunshot brought a crowd into the room. I pointed to the spot where he had disappeared, and we followed the track with boats. Nets were cast, but in vain. After passing several hours, we returned hopeless, most of my companions believing I had imagined the intruder. After having landed, they proceeded to search the country, parties going in different directions among the woods and vines.

I tried to accompany them and proceeded a short distance, but I was overcome by utter exhaustion, a film covering my eyes, and my skin parched with the heat of fever. In this state I was carried back and placed on a bed, barely conscious. My eyes wandered round the room as if looking for something that I had lost.

After some time I rose and crawled into the room where the corpse of my beloved lay. Women surrounded her, weeping, and I joined their grief. I couldn't think clearly, and my thoughts rambled over my misfortunes and their cause. I was bewildered—in a cloud of wonder and horror. The death of William, the execution of Justine, the murder of Clerval, and lastly of all, my wife—all made me realize that I had no assurance that my remaining friends were safe from the demon. My father even now might be writhing under his grasp, and Ernest might be dead at his feet. This idea made me shudder and summoned me to action. I decided to return to Geneva as quickly as possible.

There were no horses available, and I had to return by boat. But the wind was unfavorable, and the rain fell in torrents. However, it was still early morning, and I could reasonably hope to arrive home by night. I hired men to row and took an oar myself, for I had always found relief from mental torment in physical exercise. But the incredible misery I now felt, and the stress that I endured

❷ *Is it likely the Creature will continue killing Victor's friends and family? Why or why not?*

made me too weak. I threw down the oar, and leaned my head on my hands, simply surrendering to every gloomy idea that arose. Tears streamed from my eyes. The rain had ceased for a moment, and I saw the fish play in the waters as they had when Elizabeth watched them mere hours before. Nothing is as painful to the human mind as a great and sudden change. The sun might shine or the clouds might lower, but nothing was the same as the day before. A fiend had snatched from me every hope of future happiness. No one had ever been as miserable as I was. No other tragedy could compare to mine. But why should I dwell upon what happened after this last overwhelming event? My tale is one of horror, and I have reached its climax, and what's left to tell you can only be repetitive. One by one, my friends were snatched away, and I was left alone.

✪ *Again the Tragic Hero and the Romantic Hero—when they suffer—suffer much more intensely than the average person does.*

✪ *This is what the Creature intended all along, just as Victor had condemned him to a life of isolation.*

> **Review:**
>
> *In terms of plot structure, the climax is the point at which the action can no longer build. The outcome is determined.*

I am exhausted, and I must quickly finish my hideous story. I arrived at Geneva. My father and Ernest were indeed still alive, but my news was devastating to my father. I see him now, an excellent and honorable old man! His eyes went blank, having lost their charm and delight. Elizabeth was more than a daughter to him. He had doted on her with all the affection of a man late in life, with few attachments left, and held her that much more dear. Damn the fiend that brought him misery and wretchedness! He could not live under the horrors that were accumulated around him. His spirit was broken, and finally he was unable to rise from his bed. A few days after my return, he died in my arms.

What then became of me? I don't know. I lost my mind, and saw only darkness around me. Sometimes I would dream of wandering in flowery meadows and pleasant valleys with my childhood friends, only to wake and find myself in a dungeon. Deep, deep depression followed, but slowly I regained consciousness of reality and was then released from my prison. For they had actually declared me insane, and for several months I had been locked in a cell.

Freedom, however, was useless to me, until—as I came to my right mind—I began to think of revenge. As I reflected on my past tragedies, I began to reflect on their cause—the monster I had created, the miserable demon I had sent into the world. I was possessed by an insane rage at the thought of him, and my dearest prayer was to have him within my grasp to wreak a great and singular revenge on his cursed head.

❷ Is the Creature really the cause? Why or why not?

My hate did not remain a fantasy for long. I began to form a plan, and for this purpose, about a month after my release, I approached a criminal judge in the town and told him that I had an accusation to make, that I knew who the destroyer of my family was, and that he must do everything in his power to apprehend the murderer. The judge listened to me with attention and kindness.

"Be assured, sir," he said, "I will spare no effort to find the villain."

"I thank you," I replied, "Here, then, is my statement. I'm afraid you will think it too strange to believe. But there is something about Truth so that—no matter how fantastic it may be—it is somehow believable. The story is too logical to be mistaken as a dream, and I have no reason to lie." My manner as I spoke with him was impressive but calm. I was determined to pursue and kill my destroyer, and this purpose made my pain bearable and reconciled me to life. I now related my history briefly but with firmness and precision, marking the dates with accuracy and never letting my words turn into an angry tirade.

The judge clearly did not believe me at first, but as I continued, he became more attentive and interested. I saw him sometimes shudder with horror. At other times his face betrayed a surprise that showed no signs of disbelief. When I had finished my story I said, "This is the being I accuse, and I call upon you to do everything in your power to arrest and punish him. It is your duty as a judge, and I believe and hope that your feelings as a man will not allow you to shrink from your responsibility." These words brought a considerable change in his expression. He had listened to my story with some belief, but now that he was called upon to act officially as a result, the whole tide of his unbelief returned. He

❷ What do you think of Victor now turning responsibility over to a judge?

answered respectfully, "I would gladly help you, but the creature you describe appears to have powers far beyond my own. Who can follow an animal that can navigate the sea of ice and inhabit caves and dens where no man would venture to intrude? Besides, some months have elapsed since the crimes were committed, and no one can guess where he is now."

"I know that he is never far from where I live, and if he has indeed taken refuge in the Alps, he may be hunted and killed like any game. But I can see that you don't really believe me and have no intention of pursuing and punishing my enemy as he deserves." As I spoke, the rage sparking in my eyes frightened the judge.

"You are mistaken," he said. "I will make every effort, and if it is in my power to seize the monster, be assured that he will suffer a punishment appropriate to his crimes. But I fear, from how you have described him, that this will prove impossible. So, while every measure will be taken, you should be prepared to be disappointed."

"I cannot accept that, but obviously my words make little difference. My revenge is insignificant to you, and while I know it is a vice, it is now the only passion of my soul. My rage is unspeakable when I think that the murderer I turned loose upon society still exists. Since you refuse to help, I have one last resort, and I devote myself to his destruction."

I trembled with anger as I spoke. There was frenzy in my manner, and perhaps something of the righteous fierceness that the martyrs of old are said to have possessed. But to a Genevan judge, who had more to worry about than one man's mad heroism, this state of mind looked like insanity. He tried to soothe me the way a nurse would a child and regarded my tale as rooted in delirium.

"Man," I cried, "how ignorant you are in your pride of wisdom! Stop! You don't know what you're saying."

I fled the house angry and disturbed and retired to consider some other course of action.

Frankenstein

or The Modern Prometheus

❦

MARY SHELLEY

CHAPTER 24

My present situation was one in which all voluntary thought was swallowed up and lost. I was driven by fury, my strength fueled only by my lust for revenge. It formed my feelings and allowed me to be calculating and calm at periods when otherwise delirium or death would have taken control of me.

My first decision was to leave Geneva permanently. My country—so dear to me in my happier days—was now hateful to me in my adversity. I took a sum of money, together with a few jewels that had belonged to my mother, and left. I began the wanderings that will last until the end of my days. I have traveled a vast portion of the earth and have endured all the hardships that are the lot of travelers in deserts and barbaric countries. How I have lived I hardly know. Many times have I stretched my failing limbs upon the sandy plain and prayed for death. But my desire for revenge kept me alive. I dared not die and leave my nemesis alive.

Immediately after leaving Geneva I searched for the trail of my fiendish enemy. But I was disorganized, wandering many hours through the town, uncertain what path I should pursue. As night approached I found myself at the entrance of the cemetery where William, Elizabeth, and my father rested. I entered it and approached the tomb that marked their graves. Everything was silent

AN ANNOTATED ADAPTATION

except the leaves of the trees, which were gently rustled by the wind. The night was nearly dark, and the scene would have been solemn and affecting even to an uninterested observer. The spirits of the departed seemed to flit around and to cast a shadow, which was felt but not seen, around the head of the mourner.

The deep grief I felt at this scene quickly gave way to rage and despair. They were dead, and I lived. Their murderer also lived, and to destroy him I must drag out my weary existence. I knelt on the grass and kissed the earth and with quivering lips whispered, "By the sacred earth on which I kneel, by the spirits that wander near me, by the deep and eternal grief that I feel, I swear; and by thee, O Night, and the spirits that preside over thee, to pursue the demon who has caused this misery, until either he or I die in mortal conflict. For this purpose, I will preserve my life. Only to execute this dear revenge will I again behold the sun and tread the earth. Otherwise I would gladly end my life and all of its suffering. And I call on you, spirits of the dead, and on you, wandering ministers of vengeance, to aid me in my work. Let the cursed and hellish monster drink deep of agony; let him feel the despair that now torments me." I had begun my invocation with solemnity and awe, as if the spirits of my murdered friends heard and approved, but fury possessed me as I concluded, and my words were choked by rage.

Here Victor is expressing the hero's weariness with life and desire to die—but also the torment of not being "allowed" to die until the Quest is accomplished.

I was answered by a loud and fiendish laugh. It rang in my ears long and heavily, echoing from the mountains, and I felt as if all hell mocked me with its laughter. I surely could have destroyed myself at that instant but for my vow of vengeance. The laughter died away, when a familiar and hated voice, apparently close to my ear, said to me in an audible whisper, "I am satisfied, miserable wretch! You have determined to live, and I am satisfied."

What is the Creature saying?

I darted toward the spot from which the sound came, but the devil eluded my grasp. Suddenly the broad disk of the moon arose and revealed his ghastly and distorted shape as he fled with superhuman speed.

I chased him, and for many months this has been my task. Guided by a slight clue here or a small hint there, I followed the windings of the Rhone, but vainly. The blue Mediterranean appeared, and by a strange chance, I saw the fiend enter by night and hide himself in a vessel bound for the Black Sea. I booked passage in the same ship, but he escaped, I know not how.

I constantly followed his track through Tartary and Russia, although he still evaded me. Sometimes the peasants, scared by this horrid apparition, informed me of his path. Sometimes he himself left me a clue, as if he were afraid that if I lost all trace of him, I would despair and die. Snow fell, and I saw his huge footprint on the white plain. To you who are young and have no knowledge of grief, how can you understand what I have felt and still feel? Cold, deprivation, and fatigue were the least of my pains. I was cursed by some devil and carried eternal hell within myself, yet still some form of good will followed me, protecting me from what would have been unbearable difficulties. Sometimes just when I was nearly overcome by hunger and sinking from exhaustion, a meal was prepared for me in the desert that restored and encouraged me. The food was, indeed, coarse peasant fare, but I have no doubt that it was set there by the spirits that I had invoked to aid me. Often, when all was dry and the heavens cloudless, and I was parched by thirst, a slight cloud would appear in the sky, shed the few drops that revived me, and vanish.

Whenever I could, I followed the river coastlines, but—since they were more densely populated—the demon generally avoided these. In other places human beings were seldom seen, and I generally survived on the wild animals that crossed my path. I gained the friendship of the villagers with money, or with fresh-killed food, which, after taking a small part, I always presented to those who had provided me with fire and utensils for cooking.

My life, at this point, was indeed hateful to me, and only sleep brought any joy. O blessed sleep! Often, when most miserable, I lay down, and my dreams lulled me even to rapture. My guardian spirits brought these moments, or rather hours, of happiness, giving me the strength I needed to continue. Deprived of this respite, I would have sunk under my hardships. During the day I was sustained and inspired by the hope of night, for in sleep I saw my

Tartary (or Tartaria) is an old term that referred to the region of Asia east of the Ural mountains, now known as Siberia.

Notice how Nature—the healer and nurturer to the Romantics—helps Victor in his Quest.

❷ *What new role does Nature seem to take on here?*

❷ *In what way(s) is the Creature's power over Victor absolute?*

friends, my wife, and my beloved country. Again I saw the kind face of my father, heard the silver tones of Elizabeth's voice, and saw Clerval enjoying health and youth. Often, when wearied by a hard journey, I persuaded myself that my sad reality was the dream, and my dreams of my loved ones were reality. What agonizing fondness did I feel for them! How I would cling to their dear forms, their memories haunting me even during the day, and fantasize that they still lived! At these times my rage would be stilled, and the demon's destruction seemed dictated by heaven, a mechanical impulse of some unconscious power, rather than simply my soul's desire. I have no idea what my enemy was feeling throughout all this. Sometimes he left marks on the bark of trees or cut in stone that guided me and fueled my fury. On one stone he'd carved the words: "My reign is not yet over. You live, and my power over you is absolute. Follow me! I seek the everlasting ice of the North, where you will feel the misery of cold and frost, to which I am immune. If you follow swiftly, you will find a dead hare. Eat it and be refreshed. Come, my Enemy; we still have to wrestle for our lives, but you will endure many hard and miserable hours before we do."

Scoffing devil! Again I vow vengeance—to deliver the miserable fiend to torture and death. I will never give up the search until one of us is dead, and then I shall end my own miserable existence and join Elizabeth and all my other departed loved ones—the reward of my tedious toil and horrible pilgrimage!

As I traveled north, the snow and the cold became almost too severe to endure. The peasants were shut up in their shacks, and only a few of the most hardy ventured out to hunt the animals who themselves were forced from their hiding places by starvation. The rivers were covered with ice, making fishing impossible, and cutting me off from my chief supply of food. The triumph of my enemy increased with the difficulty of my efforts. One inscription that he left was in these words: "Prepare! Your toil has only begin. Wrap yourself in furs and provide food, for we shall soon begin a journey where your sufferings will satisfy my everlasting hatred."

These scoffing words strengthened my courage and

perseverance. I resolved not to fail in my purpose, and—calling on Heaven to support me—I eagerly continued to navigate immense deserts of ice, until the ocean appeared on the horizon. Oh! How different it was from the blue water of the south! Covered with ice, it differed from the land only by being even more wild and rugged. The Greeks wept for joy when they saw the Mediterranean from the hills of Asia, and hailed with rapture the boundary of their toils. I did not weep, but I knelt down and with a full heart thanked my guiding spirit for bringing me safely to this place where I hoped to finally meet the fiend and engage in our final, mortal combat.

This is a quotation from the account of the long Greek retreat from Armenia in Athenian historian Xenophon's work, Anabasis.

I had acquired a sleigh and dogs some weeks before and thus negotiated the snows with incredible speed. I don't know whether the fiend possessed the same advantages, but I did learn that I *was* gaining on him—so much so that, when I first saw the ocean, he was only one day ahead of me. I hoped to catch up to him before he reached the beach. With new courage, therefore, I pressed on, and in two days arrived at a miserable little village on the seashore. I asked the inhabitants about the fiend and gained accurate information. They told me that a gigantic monster had arrived the night before, armed with a musket and many pistols. Fear of his ghastly appearance had forced the inhabitants of one isolated cottage to flee. He had carried off their winter food supply, placed it in a sleigh with a huge team of trained dogs he had also stolen, and continued his journey across the sea in a direction that led to no land. They were joyful at his departure, guessing he would quickly be destroyed by the breaking of the ice or frozen by the unending cold.

At first I despaired on hearing this news. He had escaped me, forcing me to commence a destructive and almost endless journey across the mountainous ice of the ocean, in cold that few of the inhabitants could long endure and which I could not hope to survive, being more used to a warm and sunny climate. Yet my rage and desire for vengeance reignited at the idea that the fiend should live and be triumphant. After a short rest, while I felt the spirits of the dead hovering round and demanding revenge, I prepared for my journey. I exchanged my land-sleigh for one designed to travel on the frozen ocean. Buying a plentiful stock of provisions, I departed from land.

I do not know how many days have passed since then, but I have endured misery which nothing but my unending desire for revenge could justify. Huge and rugged mountains of ice often blocked my way, and I often heard the thunder of the sea beneath the ice, threatening to destroy me. But again the frost came and made the paths of the sea secure.

By the amount of food that I had consumed, I would guess that I had spent three weeks on this journey. It nearly broke my heart to every day feel myself drawing closer to success only to have my hopes dashed by some accident or new obstacle. More than once my despair nearly killed me. Once, after my sleigh dogs had climbed a sloping ice mountain—one even dying from fatigue—I studied the expanse before me with anguish, when suddenly my eye caught a dark speck upon the dusky plain. I strained my sight to figure out what it could be and howled with delight when I made out a sleigh and the distorted proportions of the well-known form inside of it. My heart leapt within my chest. Warm tears filled my eyes, which I hastily wiped away, to prevent their obscuring my sight of the demon. Still my sight was dimmed by the burning drops, until—finally giving in to my emotions—I wept aloud.

With no time to delay, I released the dogs from their dead companion, gave them a generous portion of food. After an hour's rest—which was absolutely necessary but frustrating—I continued my route. The fiend's sleigh was still visible, and I never lost sight of it except when for a short time it was hidden behind some ice rock. I could tell that I was gaining on it. Two days later, I saw that my enemy was no more than a mile away, and my heart bounded within me.

But now, just when I appeared almost within grasp of my foe, I suddenly lost all trace of him. I could hear the sea below the ice, rolling and swelling thunderously beneath me, every moment more ominous and terrific. I pressed on, but in vain. The wind rose, the sea roared, and—like an earthquake—the ice split and cracked with a tremendous and overwhelming sound. In a few minutes a tumultuous sea rolled between me and my enemy. I was left drifting on a random piece of ice that was melting and threatening me with a hideous death. Many terrifying hours passed. Several of my dogs died, and I myself was about to abandon all hope when I saw your ship, and the promise of rescue. I had no idea that ships ever came so far north and was astounded at the sight. I destroyed part of my sleigh to make oars, and was able, even though I was utterly exhausted, to move my ice raft in the direction of your ship. I had decided though that if you were going south, I would still to give myself over to the mercy of the seas rather than abandon my purpose. I hoped to convince you to grant me a boat with which I could pursue my enemy. But your direction was north. You took me on board when my energy was gone, and I would soon have sunk under my multiplied hardships into a death that I still dread, for my task is unfulfilled.

Now we are back to the beginning: Walton rescuing Victor from a raft of ice.

Oh! When will my guiding spirit finally grant me rest. Or must I die, while the demon yet lives? If I do die, swear to me, Walton, that he will not escape, that you will seek him and satisfy my vengeance in his death. Can I dare ask you to undertake my quest, to endure the hardships that I have undergone? No, I am not that selfish. Yet, when I am dead, if he should appear, if the guardians of vengeance should lead you to him, swear that he shall not live to triumph over me, to survive and continue his life of crime. He is eloquent and persuasive, and once his words had even power over my heart, but do not trust him. His soul is as hellish as his form, full of treachery and fiendlike evil intent. Do not listen to him. Call on the names of William, Justine, Clerval, Elizabeth, my father, and of the wretched Victor, and thrust your sword into his heart. I will hover near and direct the steel truly.

What exactly is Victor asking Walton to promise?

Walton, in continuation.
August 26th, 17-

You have read this strange and terrific story, Margaret; and do you not feel your blood congeal with horror, just as it curdles mine? Sometimes—seized with sudden agony—he could not continue his tale. At others, his broken yet piercing voice uttered his anguished words. His

Structurally, we are now returning to that long letter that included Walton's account of Victor's story.

fine and lovely eyes blazed with indignation one moment and then were suddenly downcast in sorrow and infinite wretchedness. Sometimes he controlled his expression and tone, while telling the most horrible incidents in a calm voice. Then, with volcanic force, he would suddenly rage as he unleashed a tirade on his persecutor.

His tale is exact and, therefore, believable. Still, I have to admit that the letters of Felix and Safie—which he showed me—and our own site of the monster seen from our ship, convinced me of the truth of his tale more than his assertions.

Such a monster really exists! I cannot doubt it, yet I am shocked. Sometimes I tried to learn from Frankenstein the details of his creature's formation, but on this point he was resolutely silent. "Are you insane, my friend?" he said. "Where will your senseless curiosity lead you? Would you also create a maniacal enemy for yourself and the world? Peace, peace! Learn from my miseries not to increase your own." Frankenstein discovered that I made notes concerning his history. He asked to see them and then corrected and supplemented them in many places, mostly in the conversations he held with his enemy. "Since you have preserved my narration," he said, "it would be best for it to be an accurate account for history."

Think:

Is the Creature in and of itself maniacal? What does the novel suggest—despite Victor's insistence?

And so a week has passed, and I have heard the strangest tale that anyone could imagine. My thoughts and emotions have been absorbed by this tale and my guest's own refined, gentle manners. I want to console him, yet how can I advise one so infinitely miserable, destitute of every hope, to live? Oh, no! The only joy that he can now know will be when he resigns himself to peace and death. He does enjoy one comfort, the result of his prolonged loneliness and his own troubled mind: he believes that he speaks with his friends in his dreams and they bring him consolation for his miseries or inspire his vengeance. To him they are not fantasy, but the beings themselves who visit him from the afterlife. The fact that he really believes this gives a solemnity to his fantasies that make them almost as interesting to me as Truth.

Our conversations are not always limited to his own history and misfortunes. He is amazingly well-read and learned on every point of general literature. He is indeed eloquent, and I cannot hear him relate the details of his sad life without being moved to tears. What an impressive young man he must he have been in the days of his prosperity, when he is so noble and godlike in ruin! He seems to feel his own worth and the greatness of his fall.

❓ Is *Victor noble and godlike?*

"When I was young," he said, "I believed that I was destined for some great undertaking. My emotions are deep, but I also possessed an intellect that made me capable of high achievement. This belief in my own worth sustained me when others would have been defeated, for I thought it criminal to throw away, in useless grief, those talents that might be useful to humanity. When I reflected on what I had accomplished—nothing less than the creation of a living, thinking animal—I could not rank myself with the common herd. But this thought, which supported me in the beginning of my career, now serves only to plunge me lower in the dust. All my speculations and hopes are like nothing, and like the archangel who aspired to omnipotence, I am chained in an eternal hell. My imagination was vivid, yet my powers of analysis and application were intense. By the union of these qualities I conceived the idea and executed the creation of a man. Even now I can remember my excitement while completing the work. My spirits rose heavenward, exulting in my powers, and blazing with their possibilities. From my infancy I was instilled with high hopes and lofty ambition, but how low have I sunk! Oh! My friend, if you had known me before, you would not recognize me NOW. I was never despondent. A high destiny seemed to bear me on, until I fell, never, never again to rise."

✅ *Again, this overbearing pride, this awareness of one's own greatness, is hubris, and a common flaw of Tragic and Romantic Heroes.*

✅ *And here Victor defines himself almost in terms of the traits of the Tragic Hero.*

✅ *This is Lucifer/Satan in Milton's* Paradise Lost.

Must I then lose this admirable being? I have longed for a friend, one who would understand and love me. Here in this wasteland I have found one, but I fear it is only long enough to know his worth and then lose him. I would like to restore his desire to live, but he resists the idea.

"I thank you, Walton," he said, "for your kind intentions toward me, but when you speak of new ties and

✅ *Again, compare Walton's desire with the Creature's complaint and request of Victor.*

fresh affections, do you think any can replace those I have lost? Can any man be to me what Clerval was, or any woman another Elizabeth? Even if the affections aren't stronger, our childhood friends always have a certain power over us that later relationships seldom equal. They know our childhood nature, which—no matter how we mature—is never totally erased, and they can judge us knowing our true motives. A sister or a brother can never suspect the other of fraud or false dealing unless the sibling in question has a history of such acts. But my friends were dear to me not only through habit and association, but also for their own sakes. Wherever I am, the soothing voice of my Elizabeth and the conversation of Clerval will be ever whispered in my ear. They are dead, and only one feeling in such solitude can persuade me to preserve my life. If I had a lofty quest or ambition, one that would benefit humanity, then could I live to fulfill it. But such is not my destiny; I must pursue and destroy the being to whom I gave existence. Then my lot on earth will be fulfilled, and I may die."

What has been Victor's error? What has he done to "deserve" death?

Writing Opportunity:

Earlier you wrote an essay in which you discussed Victor Frankenstein as either a Tragic or a Romantic Hero. Revise that essay, now drawing from the entire text of the novel as your support. If you feel you must adapt or change your original thesis, feel free to do so.

Frankenstein

or The Modern Prometheus

MARY SHELLEY

EPILOGUE

September 2nd
My beloved Sister,

I write to you, surrounded by peril, not knowing if I will ever see dear England again and the dearer friends that live there. Mountains of ice that allow no escape and threaten to crush my vessel at any moment surround me. The brave fellows whom I have persuaded to be my companions look to me for help, but I have none to offer. Our situation is indeed appalling, but I have not lost hope or courage. Still, it is terrible to think that the lives of all these men are in danger because of me. If we are lost, my mad ambition is the cause.

And what, Margaret, can you be thinking? You will not have news of my destruction, and you will anxiously await my return. Years will pass, and you will despair and yet be tortured by hope. Oh! My beloved sister, the prospect of disappointing you is more terrible to me than my own death.

But you have a husband and lovely children. You may be happy. Heaven bless you and make you so!

My unfortunate guest regards me with the utmost compassion. He tries to fill me with hope and speaks as if life were a possession he valued. He reminds me how often the same accidents have happened to other navigators who have attempted this sea, and in spite of myself, he fills me with optimism. Even the sailors feel the power of his eloquence. When he speaks, they no longer despair. He rouses their energies, and while they hear his voice they believe these vast mountains of ice are mole-hills which will vanish before the determination of man. But these feelings are short-lived, and each day of frustrated expectation fills them with fear. I almost dread a mutiny caused by this despair.

September 5th

Something so remarkable has just happened that, although these letters might not ever reach you, still, I must record it.

We are still surrounded by mountains of ice, still in imminent danger of being crushed. The cold is excessive, and many of my unfortunate comrades have already died here. Frankenstein's health is worse each day. There is still fire in his eyes, but he is exhausted, and any exertion quickly makes him lifeless.

I mentioned in my last letter my fear of a mutiny. This morning, as I sat watching my friend's ashen face—his eyes half closed and his limbs hanging listlessly—I was roused by half a dozen of the sailors, who demanded admission into the cabin. They entered, and their leader spoke me. He told me they represented the other sailors, and had come to make a demand that, in justice, I could not refuse. We were entombed in ice and would probably never escape, but they feared that—should the ice melt and a free passage be opened—I would foolishly continue my voyage, leading them into new danger, when they might have escaped to safety. They insisted, therefore, that I promise them solemnly that if the vessel should be freed I would instantly direct my course southwards.

This speech troubled me. I had not despaired, nor had I thought of returning if set free. Yet could I justifiably refuse this demand? I hesitated before I answered, when Frankenstein, who had at first been silent, and indeed seemed barely strong enough to be paying attention, now roused himself, his eyes sparkling, and his cheeks flushed. Turning toward the men, he said, "What do you mean? What do you demand of your captain? Are you, then, so ready to give up your mission? Did you not call this a glorious expedition?

"And how was it glorious? Not because the way was smooth and calm as a southern sea, but because it was full of dangers and terror, because each and every day your strength and courage would be tested. Because danger and death threatened, and you would have to face them and overcome them. *This* is why you thought it was it a glorious—an *honorable*—undertaking. You were hoping to be hailed as heroes, admired as brave men who risked death for honor and the benefit of mankind. And now, look at you! At the first sign of danger—perhaps the first true test of your courage—you shrink away. You are content to be seen as men without the strength to endure cold and peril. And so, poor souls, they were chilly and returned to their warm firesides. Why did you come so far only to drag your captain to the shame of a defeat and prove yourselves cowards? Oh! Be men! Be *more than* men! Be steady to your purposes and firm as a rock. This ice is not made of such stuff as your hearts should be. It is changeable and cannot stand up against you—if your will is strong. Do not return to your families with the mark of disgrace on your brows. Return as heroes who have fought and conquered and who know not what it is to turn their backs on the foe."

> ❓ *What is ironic about this speech?*

> ✔ *This is an allusion to the Old Testament Cain, who bore a mark on his forehead that indicated he had murdered his brother, but forbid any human being to harm him.*

Think:

What might be Victor's real motivation?

He spoke this with such expression, with an eye so full of aspiration and heroism, that do you doubt that these men were moved? They looked at each other and were unable to reply. I told them to retire and think about what had been said, that I would not lead them farther north if they absolutely objected. Still, I hoped that they would think of what Frankenstein had said, and that their courage would return. They left, and I turned toward my friend. He was nearly dead from exhaustion.

How all this will end, I do not know, but I would rather die than return shamefully, my purpose unfulfilled. Yet

> ✔ *Compare this statement with Walton's earlier sentiment about not wanting the men's lives to be on his conscience.*

I fear such will be my fate. The men—unsupported by ideas of glory and honor—will never willingly continue to endure their present hardships.

September 7th

The die is cast. I have agreed to return if we survive. Thus are my hopes blasted by cowardice and indecision, and I come back ignorant and disappointed. It requires more philosophy than I possess to bear this injustice with patience.

September 12th

It is finished. I am returning to England. I have lost my hopes of usefulness and glory, and I have lost my friend. But I will try to detail these bitter circumstances to you, my dear sister, and while I am carried toward England and toward you, I will not be downhearted.

On September 9th, the ice began to move. We heard a roaring—like faraway thunder—as the islands of ice split and cracked in every direction. We were in the most imminent peril, but since there was nothing we could do, I could only think of my unfortunate guest, whose illness now confined him to his bed. The ice cracked behind us and was driven with force toward the north. A breeze sprang from the west, and on the 11th the south passage was cleared. When the sailors saw this and knew their homecoming was apparently assured, a loud, long shout of joy broke from them. Frankenstein, who was dozing, awoke and asked the cause of the tumult. "They shout," I said, "because they will soon return to England."

"Do you, then, really return?"

"Alas! Yes. I cannot oppose their demands. I cannot lead them unwillingly into danger, and I must return."

"Do so, if you will, but I will not. You may give up your purpose, but mine is assigned to me by Heaven, and I dare not. I am weak, but surely the spirits who assist my vengeance will give me sufficient strength." Saying this, he tried to rise from the bed, but the exertion was too great for him, and he fell back, fainting.

It took a long time to revive him, and I often feared he had died. At length he opened his eyes, breathing with difficulty and unable to speak. The surgeon gave him medication and ordered us to leave him undisturbed. In the meantime he told me that my friend would not live for very long.

His sentence was pronounced, and I could only grieve and be patient. I sat by his bed, watching him. His eyes were closed, and I thought he was asleep, but soon he called feebly. Bidding me come near, he said, "Alas! The strength I relied on is gone. I feel that I shall soon die, and he—my enemy and persecutor—still lives. In the last moments of my life I no longer feel that burning hatred and longing for revenge I once had, but I feel justified in desiring his death. During these last days I have thought about my past conduct, and I do not blame myself. In a fit of enthusiastic madness I created a rational creature and was responsible for his happiness and well being.

"This *was* my duty, but there was another that took priority even over that. My duties toward humanity were more important because they included a greater propor-tion of happiness or misery. Urged by this view, I refused, and I did right in refusing, to create a companion for the first creature. He showed unparalleled destructiveness and selfishness in evil. He destroyed my friends, killing people who were sensitive, happy, and intelligent. I have no idea where this thirst for vengeance may end. The responsibility for his destruction was mine, but I have failed. Before, motivated by selfishness and viciousness, I asked you to undertake my unfinished work. I renew this request now, with reason and virtue as my motives.

"Yet I cannot ask you to renounce your country and friends to fulfill this task, and now that you are returning to England, you will have little chance to meet him. But I will let you consider what your own duty may or may not be. My judgment and ideas are already disturbed by the approach of death. I dare not ask you to do what I think right, for I may still be misled by passion.

"That he should live to be an instrument of mischief disturbs me. In other respects, this hour is the only happy one I have enjoyed for several years, since my release is near. The faces of my beloved dead appear before me, and I hurry into their arms. Farewell, Walton! Seek hap-piness in tranquility and avoid ambition, even the appar-ently innocent one of distinguishing yourself in science

❷ *Doesn't this contradict what he said earlier?*

and discoveries. Yet why do I say this? I have myself been devastated through these hopes, yet another may succeed."

His voice became fainter as he spoke, and finally, exhausted by his effort, he sank into silence. About half an hour later he tried again to speak but couldn't. He pressed my hand weakly, and his eyes closed forever, while the light of a gentle smile passed away from his lips.

Margaret, what can I say about the untimely extinction of this glorious spirit? What can I say to make you understand the depth of my sorrow? Words seem inadequate and feeble. My tears flow, and my mind clouds with disappointment. But I journey toward England, and I may find consolation there.

I hear a strange sound and must stop a moment. It is midnight, and everything is silent. The breeze blows fairly, and the watchmen on deck barely move. Again there is a sound like a human voice, but more hoarse, coming from the cabin where Frankenstein's remains still lie. I must rise and investigate. Good night, my sister.

Great God! What a scene has just taken place! I am still dizzy with the memory of it. I hardly know whether I even have the strength to tell it, but my record of Frankenstein's tale would be incomplete without this final and astonishing catastrophe. I entered the cabin where Frankenstein's remains lay. Over him hung a form I cannot find words to describe—gigantic, yet crude and distorted in its proportions. As he hung over the coffin, his face was concealed by long locks of ragged hair. One enormous hand was extended. In color and texture it looked like the hand of a mummy. He was moaning, low mournful sounds escaping his throat. When he heard the sound of my approach, his exclamations of grief and horror stopped, and he sprang toward the window. Never have I seen anything so horrible as his face—loathsome, appalling, and hideous. I shut my eyes involuntarily and tried to recollect what were my duties with regard to this destroyer. I called on him to stay.

He paused, looking at me with wonder, and again turning toward the lifeless form of his creator, he seemed to forget my presence, and every feature and gesture seemed

In 1798, Napolean Bonaparte conducted an "expedition" into Egypt. The wonders of ancient Egypt—the pyramids, sphinx, mummies—were thus "rediscovered" by the Europeans.

caused by the wild rage of an uncontrollable passion.

"That is also my victim!" he exclaimed. "In his murder my crimes are completed. My miserable life is complete! Oh, Frankenstein! Generous and self-devoted being! What use can it be to ask your forgiveness? I, who forever destroyed you by destroying everyone you loved. Alas! He is cold, he cannot answer me." His voice seemed suffocated, and my first impulse, to destroy the creature and honor the request of my dead friend, was now suspended by curiosity and compassion. I approached this tremendous being, afraid to raise my eyes to his face—so frightening and unearthly was his ugliness. I tried to speak, but the words died away on my lips. The monster continued to utter wild and incoherent self-reproaches. Finally, I found the strength to address him.

"Your repentance is now unnecessary," I said. "If you had listened to the voice of conscience and felt remorse before taking your vengeance to this extreme, Frankenstein would be alive."

"And do you dream?" said the demon. "Do you think that I didn't feel agony and remorse?" He pointed to the corpse. "My deeds did not cause him even a *fraction* of the agony they cause me! A frightful selfishness hurried me on, while my heart was poisoned with remorse. Do you think the groans of Clerval were music to my ears? My heart was formed for love and sympathy, and when misery forced me to turn to vice and hatred, it was torture such as you cannot even imagine.

"After the murder of Clerval I returned to Switzerland, heart-broken. I pitied Frankenstein, and my pity amounted to horror. I hated myself. But when I realized that he—who was responsible for both my existence and its unspeakable torments—*dared* to hope for happiness; that while he allowed me to suffer, *he* sought the same joy that he denied to me, I was filled with an unquenchable thirst for vengeance. I remembered my threat and decided to fulfill it. I knew this would be torture for me—but my impulse controlled me, I was its slave, not its master. I detested it, but I could not disobey it. But when she died—*then* I was not miserable. I had cast off all feeling, quieted all conscience, to revel in my excessive despair. Evil from then on became my good. Having gone this far,

❷ *How has the Creature murdered Victor?*

I had no choice but to continue. Fulfilling my evil design became an insatiable passion. And now it is ended. There is my last victim!"

I was at first touched by his story, but when I remembered what Frankenstein had said of his powers of eloquence and persuasion, and when I again looked at the lifeless form of my friend, rage burned anew within me. "Wretch!" I said. "It is well that you come here to whine over the desolation that you have made. You throw a torch into a row of buildings, and when they burn down, you sit among the ruins and lament the fall. Hypocritical fiend! If he whom you mourn still lived, you would yet seek vengeance against him. It is not pity that you feel. You lament only because your victim is released from your power."

"Oh, that is not true—not true," the being interrupted. "But I do see how that must be your impression judging from my actions. I do not expect to find anyone who feels my misery. I will find no sympathy. Once I had the love of virtue, and wanted to share the feelings of happiness and affection with which my whole being overflowed. But now that virtue is a shadow to me, and that happiness and affection are turned into bitter and loathing despair, how should I seek sympathy? I am content to suffer alone for the rest of my existence. I have accepted that, when I die, I will be remembered with hatred and loathing. Once I dreamed of virtue, of fame, and of pleasure. Once I falsely hoped to meet with beings that—ignoring my physical appearance—would *love me* for my inner virtues. I was sustained by lofty thoughts of honor and devotion. But now crime has degraded me beneath the lowest animal. No guilt, no mischief, no offense, no misery, can compare to mine. When I run over the frightful inventory of my sins, I cannot believe that I am the same creature whose thoughts were once filled with visions of the beauty and the majesty of goodness. But that is the way of the world. The fallen angel becomes a malignant devil. Yet even that enemy of God and man had friends and associates in his desolation. I am alone.

"You, who call Frankenstein your friend, seem to know my crimes and his misfortunes. But in his description he could not sum up the hours and months of misery

Again, we return to the theme of friendship and companionship.

The final Paradise Lost *allusion.*

that I endured wasting in useless obsession. Although I destroyed his hopes, I did not satisfy my own desires. They were forever intense, gnawing at me like a hunger. I still desired love and fellowship, and I was still spurned. Wasn't that unjust? Am I the only criminal, when *all humankind* sinned against me? Why do you not hate Felix, who drove me—who had been nothing but a help and a friend to him—from his door? Why do you not condemn the peasant who sought to destroy the being who saved his child from drowning? No, these are virtuous and flawless beings! I—the miserable and the abandoned—am an abortion, to be spurned at, and kicked, and trampled on. Even now my blood boils when I recall this injustice.

"But it is true that I am a wretch. I have murdered the lovely and the helpless. I have strangled the innocent while they slept, guilty of no injury toward me or any other living thing. I have condemned my creator—worthy of love and admiration among men—to misery. I have pursued him even to irreversible ruin.

"There he lies, white and cold in death. You hate me, but your hatred cannot equal what I feel for myself. I look on the hands that executed the deed. I think about the heart that thought of it, and I long for the moment when these hands will meet my eyes, when that imagination will haunt my thoughts no more.

"Do not fear that I shall commit any future mischief. My work is nearly complete. No death but my own is needed to fulfill my purpose and finish this story. I will not hesitate to perform this sacrifice. I shall leave your vessel on the ice raft that brought me here and proceed to the North Pole. I shall build my funeral pyre and this miserable body burn to ashes, so that its remains will leave no clue to anyone who would create another like me. I shall die. I shall no longer feel the agonies that now consume me or be tormented by frustrated longings. He who created me is dead, and when I no longer exist, the memory of us both will soon vanish. I shall no longer see the sun or stars or feel the wind on my cheeks.

"Light, feeling, and sense will all pass away, and this is how I must find my happiness. Some years ago, when I first saw the world, when I felt the cheering warmth of summer and heard the rustling of the leaves and the warbling of the birds, and these were everything to me, death would have made me weep. Now it is my only consolation. Polluted by crimes and torn by remorse, where can I find rest but in death?

"Farewell! I leave you, and take my last look at humankind. Farewell, Frankenstein! If you lived and still wanted revenge, you would cause me more pain by forcing me to stay alive than by causing my death. But instead you sought my extinction, to keep me from causing greater misery. If you hadn't abandoned all thought and emotion, you would not wish for a vengeance greater than the misery I felt. Devastated as you were, my agony was still greater, for the bitter sting of remorse will not cease to rankle in my wounds until death shall close them forever.

"But soon," he cried with sad and solemn enthusiasm, "I shall die, and what I now feel will end. Soon these burning miseries will be extinct. I shall ascend my funeral pile triumphantly and exult in the agony of the torturing flames. The light of that blaze will fade away; my ashes will be swept into the sea by the wind. My spirit will sleep in peace, or if it thinks, it will not surely think thus. Farewell."

He sprang from the cabin window as he said this, upon the ice raft that lay close to the vessel. He was soon carried away by the waves and lost in darkness and distance.

Discussion and Writing Opportunity:

What scientific and/or technological advancements have the most potential danger to humanity or life on earth? Do these potential dangers require that research in these fields be stopped or simply regulated and watched?

Writing Opportunity:

Respond to the following review of Frankenstein: *"In* Frankenstein or The Modern Prometheus, *Mary Shelley asserts that knowledge and its effects can be dangerous to both the individual and all of the human race. The novel is an allegory for the problems technology was causing in her day—and even still today. As Victor tells Walton, 'Learn from me—if not from what I say, at least by my example—the danger of knowledge and how much happier that man is who believes his native town to be the entire world, than he who aspires to become greater than human nature will allow.'"*

Insightful and Reader-Friendly, Yet Affordable

Prestwick House Literary Touchstone Classic Editions–
The Editions By Which All Others May Be Judged

Every *Prestwick House Literary Touchstone Classic* is enhanced with Reading Pointers for Sharper Insight to improve comprehension and provide insights that will help students recognize key themes, symbols, and plot complexities. In addition, each title includes a Glossary of the more difficult words and concepts.

For the Shakespeare titles, along with the Reading Pointers and Glossary, we include margin notes and various strategies to understanding the language of Shakespeare.

New titles are constantly being added; call or visit our website for current listing.

Special Introductory Educator's Discount – At Least 50% Off